ALSO BY AMANDA FLOWER

Crime
—and—
CHERRY PITS

A FARM *to* TABLE MYSTERY

AMANDA FLOWER

Poisoned Pen
PRESS

Published by Poisoned Pen Press, an imprint of Sourcebooks
P.O. Box 4410, Naperville, Illinois 60567-4410
(630) 961-3900
sourcebooks.com

Printed and bound in the United States of America.
KP 10 9 8 7 6 5 4 3 2 1

For my nephew Sergio Flecha Flower

And, like the baseless fabric of this vision,
The cloud-capp'd towers, the gorgeous palaces,
The solemn temples, the great globe itself,
Ye all which it inherit, shall dissolve;
And, like this insubstantial pageant faded,
Leave not a rack behind. We are such stuff
As dreams are made on, and our little life
Is rounded with a sleep…

William Shakespeare, *The Tempest*

Chapter One

If Penelope Lee Odders clicked her pen one more time, I might have jumped into the Grand Traverse Bay. Penny Lee, as she preferred to be called, was a woman about sixty years old who fancied herself a hard-hitting reporter covering the annual National Cherry Festival in Traverse City for a newsletter called the *Sweet Cherry News*.

"Now," Penny Lee said as she looked down at her notes and her gray curls fell over her eyes. "What happened in Los Angeles that made you want to come back to Michigan in the first place? Man trouble? Lawsuit? Tell us all." She brushed her hair aside.

I ground my teeth; Penny Lee had asked me the same question about my life in Hollywood a myriad of ways in the last hour. Maybe I was slow on the uptake, but it seemed to me that she was much more interested in my past than my present as owner and organic farmer at Bellamy Farm in Cherry Glen, a small town thirty minutes east of Traverse City.

Penny and I sat on folding chairs on a dock overlooking the gorgeous blue of the bay. Against the dock, the bay began as sky blue and deepened into a vibrant navy blue as it emptied into the deep waters of Lake Michigan. The July morning sunlight, which beat down on our heads, reflected off on the water like crystals and shone on the countless sailboats that made their way out on the lake for the day. My little pug, Huckleberry, sat under my chair in the shade. Huckleberry had been born and raised in LA, and although we had lived in Michigan for just short of a year, he still looked continually confused about how he ended up in the middle of the north woods.

The edge of the dock would have been the perfect spot to sit and reflect on the fact that I had made the right decision to leave my job as a television producer to move back home to save the family farm, but glancing at the woman with frizzy gray hair and pointy nose across from me, I had a brief moment of doubt.

I stood up. "Penny Lee, I'm really grateful to you for this interview. The National Cherry Festival is the biggest event in Michigan, and I know that you must have so many people to talk to and so much to cover, so we should probably stop now as the festival opens"—I consulted my smartwatch— "oh, in ten minutes!" I squeaked. If I want to be at Bellamy Farm's booth at opening time, I had to go now.

Penny Lee stood up and smoothed the wrinkles in her prairie skirt. "I suppose you're right. I'm sorry we had to end before we were able to get to the meat of the matter."

The meat of the matter? What on earth was she talking about? When I agreed to this interview, it was to talk about my farm, our cherries, and the organic baked goods and products that I sold. After many months, the farm was no longer just getting by but making a modest profit as a working farm.

"Thank you for your time," I said. I couldn't believe that I was thanking her, but good manners were so ingrained in me by my grandma Bellamy, it was impossible to not say thank you even in the most uncomfortable situations. Tugging lightly on Huckleberry's leash, I stepped around her to walk up the dock.

"One last question," she called to me.

I closed my eyes for a second and, against my better judgment, said, "Yes, what is it?"

"How long have you and your cousin Stacey Bellamy been fighting over your late grandmother's money?"

"No comment." I stomped away, and my little pug galloped after me to keep up.

I was fuming as I hurried through the festival to reach the Cherry Farm Market, where Bellamy Farm had a booth for the very first time in its over seventy-year history. As a Michigan cherry grower, to have a booth at the Cherry Farm Market at *the* National Cherry Festival was a major feather in our cap. It was something that we could use to promote the farm on social media and in advertisements. To be at the market, your cherries have to meet the highest level of excellence, and my farm director, Chesney Stevens, and I worked tirelessly to bring the farm's half-dead orchard back to life.

Even though we were accepted into the festival by the slimmest possible margin, I knew that each year the farm would improve dramatically, and in a few years, I could see Bellamy Farm being one of the most popular organic cherry booths at the Cherry Farm Market. Or at least that was the dream.

As Huckleberry and I walked through Open Space Park, where the majority of the festival was held on the edge of the Grand Traverse Bay, I glanced at the smaller of the two stages on the lookout for my cousin. She had been avoiding me in town, but I hoped that during the festival, we would have a chance to talk about what to do with our grandmother's stocks. I had to make Stacey understand that I didn't want to keep the money from her. However, for her to receive any money at all, she had to give her consent to the distribution of the inheritance as a legal heir. Just thinking about it gave me a headache. The argument had been going on for months.

There was no sign of Stacey on the stage as I walked by, but I saw Whit Stevens, Chesney's younger sister, next to a silver and red university trailer parked to the right of the stage. From what Whit had said, the trailer was used a green room of sorts when actors were between scenes.

Whit was dressed all in black and had a headset around her neck that was almost hidden by her streaked, bumblebee-bright yellow and black hair. Whit was a college student and worked as the stage manager at the Michigan Street Theater. It was no surprise to me that she had this job at such a young age. She was just as hardworking as her older sister.

Whit folded her arms across her chest as she spoke to a young man about her age. He had longish brown hair that he continually flipped out of his face with a flick of his head.

Whatever he was saying to Whit, she didn't appear too happy about it. My curiosity was piqued, but I knew it was none of my business, nor did I have the time to snoop.

A man bellowed at me, shaking me from my thoughts. "Out of the way!"

I glanced over my shoulder to see a short plump man carrying a giant cherry-headed mannequin on his shoulder. The man's face was as red as the cherry man he carried. I scooted to the side of the park trail, scooping up my ever-faithful pug, Huckleberry, in the process.

The two of us stood there for a long moment watching the bobbing cherry head disappear in the sea of cherry red around us. The color literally was everywhere.

The festival was spread across the entire downtown area, with the carnival rides along East Grandview Parkway, the large music performances at the Bayside Music Stage, and the small acts, the Shakespeare performance, and Cherry Farm Market in Open Space Park.

There were so many things going on that I didn't even notice twelve-year-old Hazel Killian running toward me until she called my name. Her long ponytail flew behind her head like a flag, and her knobby knees moved like pistons on a locomotive. "Shiloh! Shiloh!"

I waved at her.

She pulled up short when she reached Huckleberry and me. She bent over and gulped for air like she had just finished a marathon.

I rubbed her hand. "Hazel, what's wrong? Are you sick? Are you breathing?"

She was still bent over and held one finger in the air in the universal sign for *hold on*. I waited for her to collect herself.

She stood up straight. "Where have you been? Chesney is freaking out. The festival is about to open, but you're not at the booth."

I studied her face, looking for the truth in her statement. It wasn't that I thought she was lying, but she did have a tendency to exaggerate. I highly doubted that Chesney Stevens freaked out about anything. My young farm director was just about the coolest customer there was, and there wasn't anything at the booth that she needed me for. She could do everything I could and twice as well.

Not wanting to make a big issue out of it, especially after my less than pleasant conversation with Penny Lee, I said, "I'm heading that way now."

She tugged my arm. "You have to hurry."

I brushed my blond curls out of my face in time to see another man carrying a second mannequin with a giant cartoon cherry head on the top of it, coming straight for us.

I grabbed Hazel by the arm and pulled her out of the way. She cleared the cherry head just in time.

Hazel pulled herself out of my grasp. "You nearly took my arm off."

I shaded my eyes from the sun. "Sorry. That giant cherry looked dangerous. I don't want to have to tell your father that you got run over by a giant fiberglass cherry." I stepped back on the path but continued to carry Huckleberry rather than walk him on his leash. There just were too many obstacles between where we were and the booth.

"Dad would know it wasn't your fault," she said cheerfully as she walked beside me. "He's always reminding me to watch where I'm going. He says I need to pay more attention and put my head on a swivel, whatever that means."

"I don't think your grandmother would feel the same way," I said. "She'd definitely blame me."

"Yeah, you're right. She really doesn't like you," she said with a shrug.

That was an understatement. Hazel's grandmother, Doreen Killian, had no love lost for me, and I didn't see that changing any time soon.

Hazel looked around. "Besides, if someone was going to kick the bucket here, I think it would be a cherry-related death for sure. Look at this place. All you see are cherries!"

She was right; there were cherries everywhere. This was the first time I had been to the festival in sixteen years, and the very first time as a farmer representing my family farm. It was a major honor to be selected for the market. There was a strenuous application process and a hefty application fee to boot—a fee that was forfeited if you weren't selected. Even though my family had been growing high-quality cherries on our farm for generations, my father never wanted to take the risk of the entry fee. He said it was like gambling and he wasn't a gambler. He was a collector, a collector of obscure Michigan historical artifacts, and he had an entire room in his farmhouse to prove it.

Now that I was making decisions for the farm and my father had more or less retired, I was willing to take risks, so I applied this year.

I was so happy that I did, because Bellamy Farm was chosen to participate, and since Traverse City was a mere thirty minutes from my farm, I would be able to care for the farm and run the booth at the same time. Most of the cherry growers came from farther away and didn't have that good fortune.

The moment I saw the competition, I realized the little makeshift booth I always used at the much smaller Cherry Glen Farmers Market wasn't going to cut it here at the big show. No folding tables and beach umbrellas here, that's for sure.

I spent a considerable amount of money to have a custom booth made at breakneck speed by a local carpenter, and then Chesney did all the trim work and painting. I was happy with the result. The booth was shaped like a giant berry basket overflowing with cherries. A beach ball-size cherry hung from a limb made of green spray-painted PVC pipe. The carpenter made the basket, but Chesney came up with clever ways to make the paper-mache cherries as well as stems and leaves. There really was nothing she couldn't do.

The gamble on the booth put me that much deeper in debt; debt I would have no trouble paying off if my cousin Stacey would just listen to reason.

At the booth, Chesney set three jars of cherry jam into a paper sack and handed it to a customer. "Enjoy the festival! And remember to tell your friends to come to the Bellamy Farm cherry basket. It's the only place that you can buy organic cherry blossom honey, maple syrup, cherry preserves, and baked goods at the festival. It's a one-stop shop that is not to be missed."

The woman smiled in return. "I will, and thank you for selling these to me before you officially opened. There is so much to see, and I only have a couple of free hours to do it. Also, I have to say that your booth is just delightful. I came over to see what you had just to take a better look at it. It's my favorite booth at the market. You should be proud."

Chesney beamed. "We are more than proud, and thank you kindly!"

The woman left, and Chesney grinned at me from ear to ear. "Shi, did you hear that? The booth worked. I told you that it was an excellent idea. It's going to pay for itself!"

Hazel slid behind the booth. She and her father, Quinn, were two of my closest neighbors. They had a small non-working farm about a half mile from me. Quinn was a single dad and a fireman and EMT for the town of Cherry Glenn and worked twenty-four-hour shifts. When he was working, Hazel either spent the time with her grandparents, Chief Randy and Doreen Killian, or me. Hazel loved her grandparents, but they were much stricter than I was, so she always preferred my place over their house in town.

That was fine with me because Hazel was actually doing farm chores, which is how I spent the majority of my days. Having her along made the long days much more fun too.

"How did the interview go?" Chesney asked.

I made a face.

"Bad publicity is better than no publicity," she said in her cheerful way.

"I don't know about that." I sighed. "Penny Lee really just wants to know about my past in LA, not the farm."

She wrinkled her brow. "Why?"

"No idea," I said. "And I don't plan to find out because I am going to do my best to hide from her the rest of the festival."

"Good luck with that. You kind of stand out in a cherry basket," Chesney said.

I made another face.

Hazel was with Huckleberry in the grass under the booth. Huckleberry was in her lap while she read a book and had her earbuds in listening to music. I was glad the two were occupied so that I could talk to Chesney without Hazel overhearing me. "Hazel said that you needed me. She gave me the impression it was an emergency."

"Oh, I wouldn't say it was an emergency. Stacey was here in full hair and makeup for the play." She paused. "And boy was she steamed."

That's what I was afraid that she would say.

Chapter Two

I didn't like the sound of that at all. Stacey and I were currently at odds over my grandmother's stocks, which I had found hidden on the farm. My grandmother had hidden the stocks before her death more than fifteen years ago in the hopes I would find them, cash them in, and use them to save the farm. That was how I intended to use the money, but a disagreement between my father and Stacey, both of whom were valid heirs to my grandmother, had brought everything to a screeching halt. The stocks were valuable, and I didn't disagree with Stacey's claim that she was entitled to a portion of the money, if not half. My father, as my grandmother's last living child, disagreed.

I couldn't help but worry over why Stacey would be looking for me at the National Cherry Festival. She had hardly spoken to me the last four months. She was on speaking terms with my father because he was an actor in the Shakespeare play she was directing at the festival, but things were tense between them as well. My father was the one digging his heels in that Stacey wasn't entitled to any of my grandmother's stocks because she sold her half of the farm. As usual, I was getting the blame for the dispute.

Why was Stacey coming to my booth? How did she have time to pester me at the festival when she had so much to do for the play?

Before I could ask Chesney if Stacey had said what she wanted, a man in a long blue flowing robe and fake gray wig and beard appeared in front of the booth. Leather sandals protected his feet. I blinked to make sure what I was seeing. He looked like Moses come down from Mount Sinai with the Ten Commandments—or at least the Charlton Heston version of Moses.

Hazel stood up and took a good look at him. "Why is he dressed like Gandalf?" Because she still had her earbuds in, she said it so loudly that everyone around our booth could hear her comment. Even the newcomer.

He chuckled good-naturedly. "I will take that as a compliment." He held his arms out wide, blocking the path, and a disgruntled shopper asked him to move out of the way. It seemed a lot of tourists at the National Cherry Festival didn't like it when someone got in their way.

"You have quite a booth here," the Moses doppelganger said. "It's difficult to make anything cherry related stand out at the National Cherry Festival, and you have done it." He fluffed his robe and beamed. "As a creative soul myself, I appreciate ingenuity of any kind."

"You're in the play?" I guessed.

"Why yes," he said and bowed his head slightly. "I'm

playing Prospero in *The Tempest*. The first performance begins in thirty minutes. I'm so thrilled to be part of it."

Hazel removed her headphones. "Why are you walking around dressed like that?"

He gave her what I was sure he thought was a charming smile. "A great actor commits to his character, and part of that is dressing the part."

Hazel cocked her head. "Isn't talking to us breaking character?"

He let out a howl of laughter that caused several people walking by to turn their heads. If he wasn't already being stared at for his fake beard, the laugh did it.

"You must know my cousin Stacey. She's the director," I said.

"Stacey is your cousin?" He looked at our sign. "Bellamy Farm. You're one of *those* Bellamys?"

I wasn't sure how to take his question that I was one of "those Bellamys." I didn't know of any other Bellamys in Grand Traverse County.

"You must be Sullivan's daughter," he went on. "He told me you would be here selling cherries from your little farm. I should have put two and two together when I came to your booth."

Sullivan? No one called my dad Sullivan. He much preferred to go by Sully. I knew from this very comment that my dad must not like this Prospero actor.

"I can't believe Stacey is making you wear that awful wig," Hazel said. "It's really bad. What kind of costume budget do you have?"

"Hazel," I whispered.

She shrugged. "I'm curious."

The actor chuckled. "Curiosity will serve you well through your long life. Prospero is a man quite a few years older that than I am. I have to look the part, as they say."

"Stacey could have gotten you a better wig," Hazel said.

He laughed even harder. "I think she gave me this wig as punishment. Maybe she thought I would leave the play if I had to wear it. However, the joke's on her because I was born for this role. She can try, but she will never be rid of me."

I wrinkled my brow. That sounded a little bit too dramatic. Yes, the National Cherry Festival was a big deal in Michigan, but this wasn't exactly Broadway. He was in an outdoor production under a Ferris wheel.

This conversation was making me more uncomfortable by the second. "Can we interest you in a cherry scone or perhaps some cherry and white chocolate cookies? They are all organic. The cherries were grown on my farm, and I only use organic ingredients in my recipes."

Before the man could answer, a shrill voice cried, "What are you doing with my cousin? Do you plan to cheat on me with her as well?"

Stacey stomped in our direction. Like the man standing in front of the booth, she was dressed in costume, as she would be playing the female lead in the play. Her outfit was a long gauzy lavender dress and she wore full stage makeup, which looked aggressive and too dark in the sunlight.

"I can't have five minutes to myself?" the Moses looka-like asked.

"You're supposed to be backstage with the rest of the cast. The fact I have to look for you this close to curtain time is unacceptable. This is my production and I won't let you ruin it."

"Oh," he said. "Don't worry. You've made that abundantly clear." He waved at her outfit. "What about you? What are you doing right now? Are those your everyday clothes? I think not."

"Looking for you! Whit told me that you left, and I knew I had to go find you to ensure that you made it back in time for curtain. I didn't know you would be fraternizing with my cousin." Her voice rose in volume as she spoke, and a small crowd was beginning to gather around my booth. They weren't there for the scones.

Chesney stepped close to me and whispered, "Is this some kind of skit to build interest in the play?"

"I don't think so," I whispered back and then cleared my throat. "Please, can the two of you take this somewhere else?" I asked. "I'm trying to run a business here."

"Running a business with our grandmother's money." Stacey pointed at the elaborate booth. "How did you pay for this anyway? Everyone knows that the farm isn't even breaking even."

I felt my cheeks grow hot.

She narrowed her eyes at me. "And now you've tossed aside Quinn Killian for that sheriff, only to move on to Dane, a second-rate actor? Grandma Bellamy would be horrified."

I opened my mouth to reply, but Moses, I mean Dane, got the words out first. "Second-rate actor?" he shouted. "You said I was the perfect person to play Prospero!"

"That's because we were together then, and it was before I knew you were married! Do you really think I would have given you the part if we weren't in a relationship?"

An audible gasp rose from the crowd. There was a good chance the show that Stacey and Dane were putting on now would surpass their performance on the Cherry Blast Stage.

"As of right now, you are finished," Stacey spat. "Your understudy will take over for the rest of the festival. I expect you to return your costume immediately." She shook her finger at him.

"You will kick me out of this play over my dead body," he snapped.

She narrowed her eyes into tiny slits. "I can arrange that."

While this argument was going on, Chesney and Hazel swung their heads back and forth with each insult as if they were watching a tennis match. I, on the other hand, was horrified that this was happening right in front of my booth, a booth that Stacey was right about—I really didn't have the money to pay for it. So I needed to sell as many cherry-flavored pastries and concoctions as I could.

"You can't replace me like that," Dane said. "I'm not any actor; I'm the star. Everyone knows that Prospero is the mastermind behind the play. He's the one who is pulling the strings. None of the other actors can do that. Your understudy is a joke. He can barely walk."

I had a sick feeling in my stomach that I knew who the understudy was.

"We will just have to take that risk," she snapped.

He pointed a finger at her. "I made it possible for you to

have a play at the National Cherry Festival in the first place. You wouldn't even be here if it wasn't for my connections."

"Hand over that costume, or you will be sorry." With that, Stacey marched away.

Dane's face was bright red, and he ripped the long gray wig off his head and threw it after her before he strode off in the other direction.

"Wow!" Chesney said.

"Yeah," I murmured.

"What just happened?" Chesney rubbed the back of her neck.

"I don't think want to know."

"I knew that Stacey had a temper, but that was a real blowup."

"She was definitely giving off Lady Macbeth vibes," I said.

"Wrong play, but I do appreciate the Shakespeare cross reference," Chesney said with an approving smile.

Chapter Three

After Stacey and Dane left, it took us a few minutes to entice the crowd to buy scones, muffins, jams, and jellies. However, when they focused on what we had to sell and not the volatile argument between Dane and Stacey, business picked up.

In the end, their argument drew a crowd of shoppers to the booth, and we sold out of the scones and cookies before lunchtime. We were low on jam too. I sent Chesney back to the farm to grab more baked goods and jars of preserves. I would be up late baking that night. I was grateful for that, but my mind wandered back to the fight between Dane and Stacey. Could Stacey have had an affair with a married man? It certainly *sounded* like that was what happened. It also sounded like she didn't know about his spouse until very recently.

It shocked me that Stacey hadn't completely vetted Dane before getting involved with him. She was always so cautious when it came to relationships. She was drop-dead gorgeous with a perfect body, hair, and skin; she could have any man she wanted. However, she had always put her career before everything else. What made her take the risk with Dane? And dating someone in one of her plays? That didn't sound like my cousin at all. She would want to avoid intermingling her personal and professional life.

I worried about it for the entire time Chesney was gone. When she returned, I pulled her to the side. "Can you hold down the booth for a little while? I want to see how Stacey is. That was quite a blowup."

"I was wondering if you were going to go try to find out what was going on with her."

"Why do you say that?" I asked.

She cocked her head. "Shiloh, you're just about the nosiest person that I know."

"Should I take that as a compliment?" I knit my brows together.

"Sure." She laughed. "I can stay at the booth with Hazel. Tell Whit I said hi."

That reminded me that Stacey had said Whit had been the one who told her when Dane left the stage. If there was any drama going on with the cast, she would know about it.

"I want to go with Shi," Hazel said. "I've been stuck in this booth all day too. I'm so bored, and I haven't even seen any of the festival."

"Hazel, I need to talk to Stacey alone," I said. "This isn't a conversation to have in front of twelve-year-old."

"About her married boyfriend?"

I grimaced.

"I'm not a kid anymore. I know what is going on. I watch HBO. Kids grow up faster now than they did back in your day." She flicked her long ponytail over her shoulder as if to punctuate her point.

I raise my brow. "Back in my day?"

She rolled her eyes. "You're as old as my dad."

Which in middle school speak meant I was prehistoric. I decided not to take offense. Instead, I sighed. "Fine, you can come with me, but when I speak to Stacey, can you step aside or something? Maybe go on one of the rides."

"Or I'll subtly eavesdrop like you do."

I groaned. "I've created a monster."

She grinned. "I learned from the best."

"Ches, we'll be back as quick as we can," I told her.

Chesney waved at me. "Take your time. I got this."

The Cherry Farm Market crowd did look a little thinner at the moment. Although there were still dozens of people milling about and shopping, but the lines weren't nearly as long as they had been earlier in the afternoon. Even so, I knew people would be shopping for dessert after they went to one of the food vendors or one of the many restaurants on Front Street. I was grateful that Chesney had run back to the farm for the cookies. I knew we would need them. The market closed at 10:00 pm, and I would go straight home after to bake up a storm. I wasn't looking forward to the long night ahead of me, but there was no doubt the festival had been a boon for my farm and helped get the word out about my fledgling organic baking business.

Huckleberry walked on his leash with his flat nose in the air, taking in all the smells. I wondered if it was confusing for the pug to smell the farm and the city at the same time.

Ahead of us was Grand Traverse Bay and the stage where Stacey's play was held. The stage stood empty. The performance ran from 3:00 to 5:00, and now it was close to 6:00. Even so, I assumed my cousin was still somewhere in the vicinity because she had to collect the costumes from the actors and set up for the next day's performance. Stacey was a professional when it came to her productions and was as good as any seasoned producer that I had worked with in Hollywood.

"Oh! Can we go watch?" Hazel pulled my arm in the opposite direction.

I turned to see what she was so excited about, and then I saw the huge banner that said, Cherry Pit Spitting Contest.

I wrinkled my nose. To me the cherry pit spitting contest had an ick factor. I could be a bit of a germaphobe, which wasn't the most common farmer trait, but during my fifteen years in LA, I had been lathering on hand sanitizer every chance I got.

The cherry pit spitting contest was a tradition in northwest Michigan, and there were whole families that competed, generation after generation. I had never tried it, and I didn't plan to.

"Come on!" Hazel cried.

Normally, I would have just let Hazel go by herself. She was twelve, after all, but with such a large crowd, I was afraid I wouldn't be able to find her afterward. I knew my nervousness of having a child around a lot of strangers came from my life in LA. Most of my work in TV production had been in true crime and that genre gave you a complex about your personal safety and the safety of those you cared about.

I glanced back at the stage. There was no sign of Stacey. Maybe she had already left for the day. Her play was over and she had to be in a terrible mood after her very public argument with her ex-boyfriend or whoever Dane was to her.

"All right, but we can only stay a few minutes," I relented.

She pumped her fist in the air. "Yes! I wanted to watch and learn the technique. I want to enter next year."

I grimaced at this idea but didn't share with her what I really thought about the cherry pit spitting competition.

An emcee stood on a platform with a wireless microphone in his hand. "Folks, that was a riveting matchup in the senior women's competition! So many good spitters."

I *knew* coming over here was a really bad idea.

"But we can only have one winner. Congratulations to Lucy Millhum!"

A redheaded woman that I guessed was about seventy went up to the emcee and accepted her small trophy.

"Congratulations, Lucy." His voice took a dramatic turn. "Now, my friends, it is time for the main event! The men's competition."

Hazel folded her arms. "Why is the men's competition considered the main event? That is so sexist."

I patted her shoulder. "I have taught you well."

She nodded.

The emcee announced the first competitor. He was a tall man in glasses. We watched as he placed a cherry in his mouth, chewed, and moved the pit to the tip of his tongue.

He rolled his tongue around it, then leaned back and catapulted the upper half of his body forward like he was a sling-
shot and the cherry pit was a pebble. The cherry pit flew
through the air and landed yards away on the sandy course.

A judge went out to the spot and called out numbers to
the emcee.

"Sixty-eight feet!" the emcee said. "That's perfectly
respectable, but I have a feeling that that distance won't
hold up."

The next competitor went through the same motions of
putting the cherry in his mouth and spitting out the pit. It
was obvious that his cherry pit went much farther than the
first contestant's.

"Seventy-four feet!" the emcee crowed. "Now the competition is really heating up!"

I had to admit that the distance was impressive. I didn't
even know if I could throw a football that far.

"Amazing job, Ruddy! Our next competitor hails from
our great city of Traverse City. He is a drama professor at the
university, and you might have seen him this afternoon in
The Tempest. Please welcome Dr. Dane Fullbright!"

"Hey, isn't that the guy Stacey was yelling at?" Hazel said.

It was, in fact, the guy. I almost didn't recognize him in his
street clothes: skinny jeans and a gray T-shirt that was just
tight enough to show off his body. His brown curly hair was
perfectly styled and his trimmed beard looked like it had just
gotten a fresh coat of beard oil. He waved at the crowd as if
he was soaking it all in. It was clear to me that this was a man
who loved an audience.

"Dane, do you have any inspiring words before you spit?" the emcee asked.

He smiled and showed off straight white teeth that looked even whiter next to his dark beard. "My students dared me to take part in this competition, and I am never one to back down from a dare. Because what are we if we do not push ourselves?" He paused. "'And, like the baseless fabric of this vision, the cloud-capp'd towers, the gorgeous palaces, the solemn temples, the great globe itself, yea, all which it inherit, shall dissolve; and, like this insubstantial pageant faded, leave not a rack behind. We are such stuff as dreams are made on, and our little life is rounded with a sleep.'"

"Well, okay," the emcee said, looking slightly confused at Dane's soliloquy. "Let's see what you've got then."

Dane bowed and walked to the starting line with a cherry in his hand.

"What was he talking about?" Hazel asked. "That made zero sense."

"He was reciting a speech from *The Tempest*," I said. "A speech he would have memorized in the role of Prospero."

She wrinkled her nose. "What does it have to do with cherry pit spitting?"

I didn't have an answer for that.

Like all the other contestants, Dane ate the cherry and balanced the cherry pit on his tongue and wrapped his tongue around it. He leaned back to spit it out, but instead of letting the pit fly, he grabbed his throat and doubled over.

"Whoa, is he acting out Shakespeare?" Hazel said. "Like a death scene?"

Everyone was completely still for a moment because maybe we were all wondering the same thing. Was the actor putting on an act?

But that wasn't possible. Not with the unpleasant shade of blue his face was changing to.

"No, he's choking," I cried.

No one moved so I rushed forward and grabbed Dane around the waist. I pressed his body against mine and tried my very best to administer the Heimlich maneuver, but he was twice my size and I barely had the strength to pump his body.

Finally, the crowd realized that this wasn't part of the performance, and I heard shouts for a medic.

I squeezed Dane against me a fourth time and saw the small cherry pit hit the sand just two feet in front of us. However, instead of taking in a deep breath, Dane seemed to have even more trouble breathing. He sunk to his knees, and since I was still holding him, I went to the ground with him. His lips were bright red and blistering. The rash spread to his cheeks and nose.

I slid away from him and helped him lie in the soft sand.

"Medic! Medic!" a sharp voice cried.

I felt myself being pushed to the side, and for the briefest of seconds, my eyes locked with Quinn, Hazel's father, who was one of the volunteer EMTs at the festival. He and another EMT began CPR.

I struggled to my feet and felt myself being pulled away. All the while his last speech rang in my head. *We are such stuff as dreams are made on, and our little life is rounded with a sleep.*

Chapter Four

E veryone, please step back and give the medics space to work," the emcee shouted into the microphone.

A short man with a belly that hung over his belt joined him on the platform and whispered in his ear.

The emcee nodded. "Folks, the remainder of the cherry pit spitting contest will be postponed until further notice. There's still a lot to do here at the National Cherry Festival. We will update you all when the program is rescheduled. Please enjoy one of the other events."

"Is Dane okay?" someone shouted from the crowd.

"He looked dead to me," another voice answered.

The emcee held up his free hand. "Please let the very capable medics do their job. If you're concerned for Dane Fullbright, I suggest that you bow your head in prayer."

Somewhat reluctantly, the crowd began to disperse. Hazel and I stood to the side.

Hazel held on to Huckleberry like he was her favorite teddy bear. "Shi, you're like a hero. You tried to save his life."

I had tried, but just like the person in the crowd, I was

afraid he might be dead. I prayed with all my heart that I was wrong, but when he hit the ground his face was as blue as the lake and he wasn't breathing.

As if to answer my question, I watched as the EMTs stopped CPR and shook their heads at each other. Dane Fullbright was gone.

Had I been too slow to offer help? If I had moved a little bit faster, would he still be alive?

I took Hazel by the shoulder and turned her away from the scene. "You shouldn't be seeing this."

She looked up at me. "I know he's dead. Dad is an EMT. Death is something that we talk about all the time."

"Even so, it's hard to absorb so close up," I said. "Let's go back to the booth."

Hazel agreed and we started to walk away when a thin woman with short black hair ran onto the beach. "Where is he? Where is my husband?"

I was the first person within her reach.

She grabbed me by both of my arms. "Where is he?"

"Who?" I asked as I tried to wriggle out of her grasp, but she held on fast.

"Dane! My husband Dane!"

My heart sank.

A police officer in a Traverse City Police Department uniform walked up to us. "Ma'am, am I hearing it right that you are Dane Fullbright's wife?"

"Yes, I'm Lily Fullbright. One of my husband's students came running to my art booth to tell me that Dane had fallen ill. I came as quickly as I could."

"I'm Chief Sterling." On his chest was a badge that said "Chief of Police."

"Mrs. Fullbright, will you please come with me?" the chief asked.

"Why should I come with you? Just tell me here and now what has happened to my husband. I can't stand another second of suspense."

"Ma'am—"

"Tell me!" she bellowed.

The chief cleared his throat and nodded at another officer. The officer took Lily by the arm and led her away.

The police chief turned to me. "Are you a friend of hers?"

I blinked at him. A friend of hers? Of this woman who I had seen for the very first time? I shook my head. "I—we," I said nodding at Hazel, "were leaving the beach and she ran at me screaming about her husband. I've never seen her before in my life."

"Then I believe you should go," the chief said.

I hesitated. "How did he die? Did he choke on the cherry pit?"

He studied me.

"I—I was the one who tried to save him. I'm worried that I wasn't fast enough in giving him the Heimlich."

Compassion creased his wrinkled face. "There was nothing that you could have done. He wasn't choking on the cherry pit. We believe he was having an allergic reaction. Toxicology will tell us for sure. In any case, the Heimlich wasn't going to fix that."

"He's allergic to cherries?"

"We don't know that."

"Could it be murder?" I asked.

The compassionate look on his face dissolved.

I grabbed Hazel's hand and pulled her away from the beach.

"Ms. Bellamy! Ms. Bellamy!" a high-pitched voice called behind us.

I glanced over my shoulder to see Penny Lee coming at us at a fast trot. She waved her notepad in the air.

I pulled Hazel along. "Walk faster."

"Why? What's wrong?"

"I don't want to talk to that woman right now," I said. "Or ever."

Hazel stopped in the middle of the path and looked back. "Which one?"

Her delay gave Penny Lee just enough time to catch up with us. I had to give it to her; she moved fast when she wanted to.

The newsletter editor stood in front of us and gasped for breath, and I felt a twinge of sympathy for her. When she caught her breath, she said, "Ms. Bellamy, I'm so glad you stopped. You might want to get your hearing checked. I was shouting as loud as I could."

Some of my sympathy for her began to fade.

"Penny Lee, I can't finish my interview right now."

She waved her hand. "I wasn't chasing you down for that. I wanted to talk to you about your act of heroism!" Her eyes were huge behind her glasses.

"My act of heroism?"

"My yes! You were the only one to jump into the fray when Dane Fullbright was choking. I would love to get a quote from you for the story I plan to write about it."

"Dane passed away. What I did doesn't make me a hero."

"Yes, it does! You acted when everyone else was in shock."

Hazel nodded vigorously. "She's right, Shi! You're a hero, or almost-hero."

My cheeks grew hot. "I'm flattered, but really, Penny Lee, I would be far happier if you kept me out of the article all together."

"I can't do that!" She set her pen to paper. "But I can use that as your quote."

"Please don't!" I said, but I was too late. She had already jotted down what I'd said and scurried away.

"I feel like that's going to come back to haunt me," I muttered.

"Probably," Hazel said knowingly. "Things come back to haunt you all the time."

She wasn't wrong.

Chapter Five

When we got back to the booth, as I didn't have the wherewithal to chase down Stacey after what we had just witnessed, Chesney took one look at our faces and knew something was terribly wrong. I didn't have the strength to tell her the story, but Hazel was more than ready to share. She let Huckleberry squirm out of her arms and disappear behind the booth, leash dragging jauntily behind him as the whole tale spilled out of the twelve-year-old's mouth in a rush. I only interjected every so often when I needed to clarify or correct something she said.

"Whoa, Shi, you found another dead body." Chesney was incredulous.

"I didn't find another dead body. I happened to be there when a man died. It's very different. Furthermore, there were hundreds of other people there too. We all saw the same thing."

"Was Stacey there?" Chesney asked.

Her question gave me pause. I didn't see Stacey, but the crowd that was cheering on the spitters was huge. She could have been there. Why did that make me feel uneasy?

Chesney's next question made me feel even worse.

"Was it murder?" she asked.

"The police chief didn't say it was murder."

"Sure, but he didn't say it *wasn't* murder either, did he?" She began to refill containers of washed sweet cherries for people to buy and snack on while they walked through the festival. No surprise, cherries were a popular snack in Traverse City. Also, it was no surprise that there were cherry pits littered all over the grass.

I sighed. "Whether it is murder or isn't should not matter to us. We don't know him. The police are handling it."

She cocked her head to the side. "But don't we kind of know him because of Stacey, right? She screeched at him right in front of our booth. The cops are going to hear about it. They had a *very* public fight. They will come and ask about it eventually."

I didn't need that reminder.

And then there was the wife, Lily Fullbright. She would be a suspect. What if she found out that her husband was having an affair with Stacey? How did Stacey find out Dane was married? Was it through Lily? I placed my hands over my ears as if I could squeeze these ideas and questions out of my mind. This was not my problem. This was not my case to solve.

"What are you doing?" Hazel asked.

"I'm trying to stop thinking," I said with my hands still against my ears.

"Oh," she said as if that made perfect sense.

"You had better drop your hands and start thinking again

because trouble is coming your way," Chesney said just above a whisper.

"What are you talking…?" But before I could even complete my question, I saw what she meant. Stacey was marching in a beeline toward me.

This was bad. This was very bad. I knew it in my bones.

She was no longer wearing the gauzy lavender dress and stage makeup. Her face was freshly washed, and she wore khaki shorts and a checkered blouse. She looked like just about every other soccer mom at the festival, although she wasn't a mom and I was certain that she would have zero interest in soccer.

"Shiloh, I need to talk to you." Her declaration wasn't a request. It was an order.

"Right now?" I asked.

She glared at me. "Yes, right now. You think I walked over here for my health?"

"Can you two watch the booth for a while?" I asked. I knew it was best to get this conversation with my cousin over with, and I did want to talk to her about our grandmother's stocks. Though this probably wasn't the best time to bring it up, seeing how her ex-boyfriend had just been killed by a cherry pit.

Chesney nodded, but Hazel wasn't so quick to agree. "I should go with you. Stacey looks super mad. You might need backup."

"I don't need backup to speak to my own cousin," I said.

She gave me a look of disbelief. Hazel was exceptionally astute for a twelve-year-old.

"I'll be fine," I reassured her. "You stay here with Chesney. I think you have seen enough for the day. If your grandmother knew you watched a man die, she'd never let me see you again."

"It doesn't matter what my grandmother wants. It's up to Dad. He trusts you."

"That might be true, but he wasn't happy to see us at the cherry pit spitting competition when Dane went down. And your dad wouldn't want you to overhear our conversation. Stay here."

"Because Stacey had an affair with the dead guy." She rolled her eyes. "I know what that means, and I can help sort it out. I can bring a fresh point of view."

The tween years were a struggle, not just for the tweens but for the adults around them. It did not bode well for the future.

I stepped out of the booth with Huckleberry on his leash. Without saying a word, Stacey marched away from me. Clearly, she wanted me to follow her. I sighed.

Stacey and I left the Cherry Farm Market behind, and before long, we left Open Space Park all together. I had to step double time to keep up with here. Even though I had longer legs, her apparent anger egged her on. Huckleberry couldn't even hope to walk as fast as she was going, so I scooped up the pug and held him like a football under my arm. I really should have left him back at the booth while I spoke with Stacey, but Chesney already had her hands full keeping an eye on the booth and Hazel. I couldn't ask her to add Huckleberry to the mix.

"Where are we going?" I asked when I finally met her stride for stride.

She glanced at me without missing a step. "Do you always have to ask questions?"

"Yes," I replied.

"It's not too far."

We'd been walking for a good ten minutes. Finally, she stopped at a small square brick building that looked like it had been a gas station at one time. Today, it was an art gallery. The name "Lily Fullbright Art" was emblazoned across the front of it, and the door was black with golden flecks embedded in the paint.

She pointed at the door. "I want you to go in there and find out why she killed her husband."

I blinked at her. "What?"

"Lily Fullbright is Dane's wife. She must be the killer. Go find the evidence. It's what you do, isn't it? Other than pretending to be a farmer."

If Stacey was trying to butter me up to do her bidding, she was doing a terrible job of it. Knowing my cousin, she might not even be aware of how rude she sounded. However, even if she were to be kind to me, there was no way that I was breaking and entering into a building that might be even remotely related to a man's death.

"Stacey, I'm not doing that," I said in my most forceful voice.

She glared at me. "Yes, you are. Do you want your father's heart to break because his favorite niece is arrested and spends the rest of her life in prison?"

"First of all, you're Dad's only niece."

"So what? I get along with Uncle Sully better than you do. Do you really think that he wants to be left behind with you?"

Her words stung. My father always had a soft spot for Stacey, and he would be upset if anything bad happened to her. Even when she sold her half of the farm, he wasn't angry at her. If I'd done that, he would have never forgiven me. I reminded myself that she had spent more time with him over the last sixteen years than I had. They, of course, would be closer, but I also knew that a lot of it had to do with the fact I reminded my father of my mother. It pained me to admit it, but I was sure he kept me at arm's length most of my life because of that resemblance.

"Time is wasting. Get in there."

"This is ridiculous. The door is surely locked," I said. "I couldn't get in there if I wanted to, which I don't!"

"Don't you have lockpicks or something? All detectives carry them, right?"

"First of all, I'm not a detective. I may have helped the police from time to time, but that doesn't make me a detective."

"Call yourself whatever you want," she said. "You poke your nose in where it doesn't belong. You've done it since you were a little kid. You used to drive me crazy and follow me around the farm like a lost puppy asking so many questions. It was enough to give me chronic migraines. Did you know that?"

I gritted my teeth. "You know what, Stacey? I'm very sorry about what happened to Dane. From what I overheard, you cared about him at one time and maybe still do. And I'm very sorry that you are in this situation, but it's your problem, not mine. I'm going back to my booth to sell those make believe organic items you talked about." I started to walk away.

"If you don't do it for me," she called behind me, "do it for Hazel?"

If I knew what was good for me I would have kept walking. Turning around was just playing into her trap, but when Hazel's name came up, what choice did I have but to find out what she meant? "What about Hazel?"

"Find the killer so that her father, your *close* friend Quinn Killian, doesn't go to prison too. Because he's just as much as a suspect as I am."

Chapter Six

I glared at her. "You had better tell me what you mean by that."
She opened her mouth to speak but then snapped it closed. Her eyes went wide. I turned and saw a woman about my age in a long flower-printed sundress stumbling toward us in tears. It was none other than Lily Fullbright. She was so upset that she didn't see us standing in the middle of the sidewalk as she struggled to pull a set of keys out of her tiny clutch.

I glanced at Stacey, but she was gone. She left me. Wasn't that just like her? And she took with her the reason that Quinn would be a suspect in Dane's death with her.

If Stacey thought that I would help her now, she had another coming. A knot grew in my stomach. Knowing that Quinn might be in trouble made me ill at ease. He was my friend, and at one time I thought he could have been more than that. But even more than a friendship with Quinn, I cared about Hazel. She had become like a niece or little sister to me over the last year. I wouldn't want anything to disrupt her life. She had already lost her mom; she couldn't lose her dad too.

Black mascara ran down Lily's tan cheeks as she tried to

fit the key in the door lock. She swore. "How many times did I ask Dane to fix this?" she asked herself.

She was so engrossed with the stuck lock that I wasn't certain she knew I was standing just a few feet away.

"Are you all right?" I asked. Even as I said it I knew it was a stupid question. Her husband had just died. He was having an affair. What more could she take?

"Do I know you?" She wiped her face with a crumpled tissue. "What are you doing outside of my gallery? We're closed today." She pointed at the sign in the window that said the gallery was indeed closed during the National Cherry Festival, and if someone wanted to see or purchase one of Lily's pieces, they should come to her booth on Artist's Row.

"We've never officially met." I cleared my throat. "We ran into each other down on the beach." I paused. "Near the cherry spitting competition…"

She scowled at me. "What's your name?"

"Shiloh," I said.

She folded her arms. "What is your full name? I hate it when people just say, 'I'm Brittany,'" she mocked in a high-pitched voice. "It's so annoying."

It was one of those times I had the choice to lie or tell the truth. The thought of lying to her made me sick to my stomach, and I was certain Lily Fullbright had been lied to enough.

"I'm Shiloh Bellamy." I did my very best not to wince when I said my last name. I wasn't ashamed, but it was also Stacey's last name. Under the circumstances that wasn't good.

"Bellamy! Are you the one who was cheating with my

husband?" She looked me up and down. "I don't believe it. You're not his type at all. What was he thinking?"

I shifted my feet. *She didn't have to say it like that.*

I knew that I wasn't looking my very best after a busy day at the festival. I spent over a decade in LA transforming my outward appearance to fit into the Hollywood mold. Now that I was back in Michigan, I had traded my designer dresses and bags for jeans and T-shirts, but I still highlighted my hair and tried to look put together when I wasn't mucking sheep stalls or gathering eggs.

"I'm not that Bellamy," I said.

"I wouldn't think so. Dane was looking for a starlet not a roadie."

Now she was just being mean. I took a breath and mentally gave her a pass. The woman had been through a lot in the last couple of hours. If she needed to lash out at me, I could take it.

However, Huckleberry made a snuffling sound in my arms as if he took issue with her comment. Huck always had my back.

"What are you doing outside of my studio?"

It was a very good question, and one I couldn't tell her the full answer to. I didn't think that she would look on it kindly if I said the Bellamy who *was* having an affair with her husband asked me to break into her gallery.

I cleared my throat and prayed she couldn't tell how nervous I was. "I was on a walk. I didn't know you had a studio along the bay until I got here. I'm not from Traverse City. I'm just here for the festival this week."

Her tears dried up. "You saw what happened on the beach?" She turned back to the door and finally managed to unlock it.

I nodded.

"You were there when began to choke?"

I nodded a second time.

She grabbed my hand and jostled Huckleberry in my arms in the process. "You have to tell me everything. From the beginning. I have to know it all. It's the only way that I can prove that my husband was murdered!"

I blinked at her as she continued to grip my hand. "You believe he was murdered?"

"I don't believe it, I *know*. Dane was murdered and it was for his job! He's a full professor with tenure. The other faculty in his department had wanted to get rid of him for years, but since Dane always threatened to sue when they made noise about it, the university backed off. They finally found a way to get rid of him forever."

"Why did they want to get rid of him?"

"He was trying to move the department ahead into the future. The rest of the faculty was stuck in the past."

"And you think the university killed him for *that*?"

"Not the university as a whole," she said irritably. "But his old department chair. He was jealous of Dane." Her voice choked up. "He wanted to get rid of Dane the since moment he took the position. He's old and bitter if you ask me."

I furrowed my brow. "Who was the department chair?"

"Theo Cassen." She spat out the name like it put a bad taste in her mouth.

I couldn't believe it. Dr. Cassen had been on the faculty when I was a student in the film and theater department at the university. He had seemed like he was a hundred years old then. I just assumed that he was dead, as awful as that sounded.

"If you want to talk," she said, "let's go inside. It's too hot out here."

I pointed at myself. "You're inviting me into your gallery?"

She opened the door and looked over her shoulder. "Are you coming?" She went inside, leaving the door slightly ajar so I could follow.

I stepped into the building after her and looked back just long enough to see Stacey's head peek around the corner with a wide smile on her face. She gave me a thumbs-up. If I hadn't known better, I would have thought she'd planned this.

Lily turned on the lights, and I was momentarily blinded in a flash of white. Huckleberry whimpered and squeezed his eyes shut. I wished I could do the same. Not only were the lights bright, but the entire room, from the floors to the walls to the ceiling, was stark white. The only colors in the room were found in the vibrant paintings on the walls that I could only assume had been painted by Lily herself.

And it was freezing, like Michigan in the middle of January freezing. But instead of snow pants and a thick parka to fight off the chill, I was wearing a Bellamy Farm T-shirt and denim capris. My bare arms felt like icicles, and I held Huckleberry close.

Lily didn't appear to be affected by the severe change in temperature as she paced around the gallery. "Tell me everything. I want to know everything you saw at the cherry pit spitting competition, and who was there. She was there right? His girlfriend, Stacey." She narrowed her small eyes into tiny slits. "I know she was there. She would want to make a scene again."

Again? Did she mean about Stacey's fight with Dane at the Cherry Farm Market or something else?

Lily paced the room. "Start talking."

"For the record, I didn't see Stacey there."

"That doesn't mean that she is innocent. She knew he was allergic to penicillin. She could have put the drug on the cherry pit and then left."

"Wait, he was killed by penicillin?"

She narrowed her eyes. "I thought you knew that."

I shook my head. "All I knew was he didn't choke and had a reaction to something. I didn't know what that something was. The chief said it wouldn't be known until the toxicology report was done."

"I don't need a toxicology report," she said. "I'm his wife and penicillin is the only thing that he was deathly allergic to. It has to be it."

If it was the antibiotic that killed him, how could his death be accidental? Who carried around penicillin? And who other than Lily, and apparently Stacey, knew that he was allergic to it?

I didn't want to think about this. I didn't want to get involved. That's what I tried to tell myself.

I glanced at the door. I could run out of there at any moment. I stood on the balls of my feet, ready to flee, but I

couldn't make myself do it. I wanted to help Stacey, not just
for her sake but for my father's sake too. He really loved my
cousin. There was also the possibility that Quinn was a suspect. But honestly, I would have stayed even if Stacey and
Quinn weren't involved, because I watched a man die.

"I don't have much to tell you," I said. "I was walking
through the festival and stopped to watch the cherry pit
spitting contest. Dane was the third contestant to go. He
seemed fine before he put the cherry pit into his mouth. It
was shortly after that he began to choke or appear to choke.
I don't believe anyone suspected at that moment it was an
allergic reaction."

"Did anyone try to do anything? Did you all stand there
and just watch him die?" Her voice was raw with emotion.

I understood how she must feel, but even so, I felt myself
blush. "I—I tried to give him the Heimlich maneuver."

"What you should have given him was his EpiPen," she
accused.

"I didn't know that. He held his throat. Then, his face
turned red and he began to blister." I knew I sounded defen-
sive, but I couldn't help it. I was the only person that sprang
into action on that beach. I made the best choice I could
have with the information that I had.

Huckleberry buried his head in my shoulder. He apparently still hadn't acclimated to the studio's aggressive
brightness.

She held up her hand. "I shouldn't have snapped at you
like that. How could you have known he would have an
EpiPen on him?"

"If he did, why didn't he use it?" I asked. "Or make some gesture to tell me about it?"

She frowned. "I—I don't know. I still can't believe he's dead. Our divorce was to be final at the end of this month. He died before we were divorced, so this changes everything. I'm a widow now, not a divorcée like I expected to be this summer."

I pressed my lips together. Lily was offering herself up as prime suspect. Did that mean that all of Dane's money and assets were now hers as legal next of kin? Did he *have* any money or assets?

Did she need them? Lily Fullbright was an artist, and by the size and design of her gallery, she gave off the impression she did very well for herself, but it was impossible for me to know how she paid the rent or how involved Dane might have been in her gallery. That was something the police would dive into as soon as possible. As long as the financials were clear and honest, those were questions that would be answered quickly.

The questions that would take longer to answer were the emotional pieces. How long had she known about Dane's affair with Stacey? And could it even be considered an affair if Dane and Lily were on the verge of divorce? Poisoning was a premeditated crime. The killer had to have put some thought into it. Did Lily have access to the cherries at the contest? To penicillin?

I wanted to ask all these questions, but it didn't seem like the right time. The woman was grieving and still in shock. I was nosey by nature, but even I had limits to how far I was willing to push someone.

"Do you think he was killed over the cherry pit spitting competition?" she asked. "There are people I know who would kill to win, and Dane had a very good chance of winning. He had been competing for years."

I blinked. Dane's expertise in the area of spitting cherry pits hadn't been readily apparent to me. He said that he entered the competition on a dare from his drama students.

She dabbed at her eyes. "I can tell that you don't believe me, but it's true. Both Dane and I grew up in Eau Claire. That's where the International Cherry Pit Spitting Championship happens every year. This pseudo competition here at the festival isn't nearly as competitive as that. My father was a world-record holder for spitting pits for ten years straight and taught Dane everything that he knew about it. Dad called himself 'the Great Spitter.'"

I grimaced at the name.

"Dad took it very seriously and practiced in our backyard for hours. It was my job to measure the distance of his pits." Her voice caught. "It was the only thing that he and Dane really connected over. My father didn't understand Dane, his acting, or his need to teach. He told Dane that was all women's work."

Her dad sounded like a super nice guy. Not.

"Dane said that his students dared him to enter," I said. "I got the impression this was the first time he entered such a contest."

"Oh no, he was acting when he said that, probably to put the competition off guard. He's been doing it for years."

I wrinkled my brow. Did that mean he lied? But why

would he lie about such a thing? Or was he playing a joke on his students? Making them think he was about to make a fool of himself when he was in fact an accomplished cherry pit spitter? I had to admit that was odd to say.

I thought back to the competition and tried to remember if I saw a group of college students there. I'm sure there were. Traverse City was a college town, after all. It was constantly crawling with college-aged kids, even in the summer. It was a major summer vacation spot in the state, and there were endless opportunities for summer jobs, so many students stayed all year.

It would be especially easy to find employment during the festival when there was an abundance of short-term jobs to be had. But I couldn't remember anyone paying special attention to Dane.

"Is there anything else you can remember from the competition?" Lily asked.

"I'm sorry," I stammered. "I'm racking my brain, but honestly, everything happened so fast. I met your husband that morning. It was the first time I had ever seen him."

"You met him today? You spoke to him?"

"Yes, like I told you, he told me that his students dared him to enter the competition."

She narrowed her eyes as if I was holding something back. I was dying to ask her what Quinn's tie was to Dane, but for fear that would cause her to suspect Quinn, I kept my mouth shut. I would ask him himself when I dropped Hazel off at home. Knowing Quinn, the conversation would go just as well as the one I was presently in.

I turned to leave and was stopped by a forceful knock on the gallery door.

"Who could that be?" Lily asked. "The gallery is closed. No one takes time to read anymore."

Chief Sterling stepped into the gallery. In his wake followed Antrim County Sheriff Milan Penbrook. He didn't look pleased to see me.

Chapter Seven

Sheriff Milan Penbrook cleared his throat. He was a handsome and tall Black man with glasses and hair that was just beginning to gray at his temples. "Shiloh, we didn't expect to find you here."

"Neither did I. I mean, I didn't expect to be here either." I stumbled over my words. If I had been sitting at a desk, I would have banged my forehead on it. Milan always made me tongue-tied. He was smart, good-looking, and kind, and he'd asked me on a date, which, just like this meeting, caught me completely off guard. I had yet to answer him, and that was months ago. I figured so much time had passed that he rescinded his invitation. Who wanted to date someone who was as indecisive as I was?

Chief Sterling looked from Milan to me and back again. "Sheriff, I didn't know you knew Miss Bellamy."

"She was involved in one of my cases over the winter, the murder on Lake Skegemog."

The chief nodded. "Ahh, I remember now. Why don't I speak to Mrs. Fullbright here, and you talk to Miss Bellamy outside?" He smiled at Lily and me. "The interviews should not take long at all."

I followed Milan out of the gallery, and I was grateful for the blast of hot air. It was bad enough to be half-frozen all winter long in northern Michigan. I didn't need to freeze in summer too.

Outside, even though we were a good half mile down the bay from the festival, I could hear the festivities and a marching band belting out "My Country, 'Tis of Thee." It was an appropriate tune, as the Fourth of July was just days away.

I was certain the city dignitaries were thrilled that the festival had coincided with the holiday this year. That meant even more tourists and locals would be downtown for the fireworks. Business was booming in Traverse City.

But for me, all the music and revelry was just a stark reminder of how life pressed on. A man had died—presumably by murder—and as busy and festive as the fair was currently, it didn't seem that anyone cared. That saddened me. It made me want to find out the truth about Dane's murder. Not just for Hazel or Quinn or Stacey or even Lily. But for Dane.

For me.

Because even though he was a stranger, his life mattered.

I rubbed my arms. "Thanks for getting me out of there. I was freezing to death."

He smiled. "I think living in California all those years thinned your blood."

"That's entirely possible. I'm already dreading another winter here."

He laughed. "At least you plan to stay."

I wrinkled my brow. "I was never considering leaving. I'm all in with the farm."

"That's good to know." His face was blank.

Was I reading too much into this conversation? I set Huckleberry on the ground, and the pug immediately flopped over on his side in front of Milan, awaiting a belly rub.

Milan bent down and gave the dog a pat and a scratch. Huckleberry closed his eyes in bliss.

"Chief Sterling is a nice guy. Did you tell him who I am to you?"

He could no longer hold the blank stare in place, and the right side of his mouth turned up in the corner. He stood. "He is a nice guy and a very old friend of my family's. Traverse City Council could not have picked a better man for police chief." He smiled broadly now. "And who are you to me?"

I wanted to punch him in the arm, but I held back. I didn't know who might be walking by, and I didn't want to be pinned for being a little too friendly with the sheriff in the middle of a murder investigation. "I'm your friend. At least that's what I thought I was."

"You are." He smiled in full now. "But you are in a middle of a bit of a mess, and from what I hear, so is Stacey."

I grimaced.

"What were you doing at the gallery, Shiloh?" Milan's tone turned serious.

"Before I answer that, I want to know what you're doing here. Why are you helping Chief Sterling? This isn't even your county."

"Fair enough," he said. "I was at the festival planning to stop by your booth and see how you were faring, but when I got here, I ran into Chuck, Chief Sterling, and he asked me if I could assist with the questioning the witnesses. Traverse City has a decent-sized police force for a small city, but during the festival, the population around here grows by fifty thousand plus. There are not enough officers to handle security, traffic, and just general public safety for an event of this magnitude, much less the number of officers necessary to thoroughly question every person who witnessed Dane Fullbright's death."

I nodded. "Sounds like the chief could use some help. I'm glad you agreed."

"Chuck Sterling is an old fishing buddy of my dad's. When I said I wanted to go into law enforcement, my father was against it, but Sterling talked to him about it. Eventually Dad came around. I have Chief Sterling to thank for that."

I didn't say it, but this was a far cry from his relationship with the police chief of Cherry Glen, Chief Randy Killian, who just so happened to be Quinn's father. Chief Randy, as he liked to be called, hated any other law enforcement entity working or even asking questions about his cases. I knew for a fact that he would never ask for help in a situation like this, and he would refuse help when it was offered.

"Why are you here?" Milan asked. "And what are you doing with Lily Fullbright?"

Okay, we were getting down to business. I reminded myself to be careful. Milan was my friend, but he was also a cop. I had to do my best not to implicate Stacey or Quinn, both of whom were now on my suspect list and both of whom I prayed were innocent.

I couldn't believe either one of them would do it. Sure,

Stacey had a hot temper, but she wouldn't kill anyone, because it would put her theater at risk. That was more important to her than anything or anyone. Quinn I had known since I was a kid. He was the best friend of my late high school sweetheart and fiancé, Logan, who had died in a car accident when he was twenty-three, and he was Hazel's father. Quinn was a fireman and EMT. He vowed to protect and serve. He just couldn't do this…

"Earth to Shiloh." Milan waved his hand in front of my face.

I blinked at him. "Oh, sorry, it's been a crazy day."

He folded his arms. "Are you here because of Stacey?"

I scrunched up my nose like I did when I was elementary school and I didn't want to admit to my teacher that I had been the one to let the classroom's pet rat out of his cage. The rat wanted to be free. At seven, I thought it was the thing to do. The incident forced the school janitor into early retirement. He really hated rats, so when Chuckles the rat fell on his head from an air duct, he was finished. Chuckles survived the adventure and had tales to tell his other rat friends. I got detention for a week.

Huckleberry sat on my feet. The little pug always knew when I needed his support.

"It is about Stacey, isn't it? You do know she's a suspect, and you have decided to poke your nose into the case. Do you think you can clear her name?"

I bristled at his tone but reminded myself to remain calm. Milan was only doing his job.

"Was he murdered?" I asked. "I overheard something

about an allergic reaction, and Lily Fullbright said that it must have been penicillin on his cherry because it was all the only thing he was allergic to. That doesn't sound like something that would just happen accidentally. She's convinced her husband was killed."

Milan sighed, as if he was annoyed with himself for letting that little nugget of truth out. "There has been no official ruling from toxicology yet."

I took that to mean yes. This was bad news for my cousin.

"Why are you here?" he asked again.

I didn't want to lie to Milan. But he didn't need the whole truth either. "Stacey wanted to talk to me away from the National Cherry Festival," I said. "We went for a walk and ended up here."

I didn't see any reason to share Stacey's breaking and entering scheme.

"And what did Stacey want to talk to you about?" He eyed me.

I didn't say anything.

"Let me take a stab at it. She asked you for help to clear her name because she knows very well she's a main suspect because of the argument she and Dane had in front of your booth earlier today."

I sighed. "Yeah." I couldn't see any reason to deny it. Before he could tell me what a stupid idea this was, I said, "She's my cousin. I have to help her. And…"

"And what?"

"She may stop fighting with me over Grandma Bellamy's stocks if I help her."

"Did she say she'd do that?" he asked.

"We didn't get to that part yet," I admitted. "We were interrupted."

Milan frowned.

"Don't look at me like that. It's my chance to save the farm." And Stacey. And Hazel. And Quinn. But I couldn't reveal my real reason without incriminating all the people I wanted to help.

"And put yourself in terrible risk in the process. It's looking very much like Dane Fullbright was murdered by someone he knew. This was a premeditated attack. Do you think the killer would think twice about getting rid of you too?"

I swallowed hard.

He adjusted his glasses on his nose. "How were you interrupted?"

I stuck my foot in it there. "By Lily," I said. "Stacey saw her coming and left before I could bring up the stocks. Honestly, Milan, even if Stacey doesn't agree about my grandmother's money—I don't really know if she will—I still have to help her. I can't see an innocent person go to jail. Stacey is a lot of things, but I know she's not a killer."

"Your loyalty to your cousin is impressive after everything she's put you through these last few months." His face softened. "You can trust Chief Sterling. Chuck is a good man and excellent cop. I don't think I would have been elected sheriff without his endorsement. I owe him. He'll do this right. Just get out of his way so he can do his job."

"He's a fair guy then?" I asked.

"Very fair. He won't accuse or arrest Stacey unless he's certain, unlike other police chiefs that we know."

He meant Chief Randy.

I rocked back on my heels. "I'm glad to hear that. I don't want anyone to get railroaded."

He laughed. "Railroaded? What is it, 1900?" Then his tone changed. "As for Stacey, you don't have to keep her affair with the deceased a secret from the chief or from me. We heard about it from more than one person. That was what their argument was about, wasn't it?"

I nodded.

"Someone said they could hear her yelling all the way on Front Street."

"Stacey's a stage actress," I said with a shrug. "She was trained to project her voice."

"Apparently." He nodded.

"Don't you think her doing that put her in the clear?" I bent down and picked up Huckleberry, holding his warm body to my chest. I didn't mind the warmth; I was still a bit chilled from being inside of the gallery.

He arched his brow at me. "Where do you get that idea?"

"Well, she publicly yelled at him for not telling her he was married—and I think it's a very important point that Stacey didn't know she was having a relationship with a married man—then he dies a few hours later. If she really wanted to kill him, wouldn't it be wiser to just keep quiet?"

"Not if it was a crime of passion."

"But I thought you said he died of an allergic reaction. How could that be a crime of passion? It would have to be premeditated. No one carries around antibiotics just because, not even a doctor."

Huckleberry made a snuffling sound as if he was in complete agreement with me.

Milan frowned and gestured to the gallery. "You make a good point, but what I would like to know is, when you and Stacey went on your walk, how did you end up here in front of the deceased's wife's gallery?"

I glanced back at the nondescript brick building. You would never know from the outside how many beautiful paintings it held. Maybe Lily liked it that way. Perhaps she wanted customers stepping into the building to expect one thing and find another. If that was true, did it apply to her as well? Was her interest in finding her husband's killer just a screen to keep suspicion off herself? And if that was true for Lily, could it also be true for Stacey?

"I didn't know that it was Lily's gallery until I saw the sign. I didn't even know that she had a gallery. Honestly, I know next nothing about her or Dane. Today was the first time I met either one of them. I didn't even know Stacey had a boyfriend. We aren't close like that."

He nodded. He knew my relationship with Stacey was strained.

"Where's Stacey now?" he asked.

I shrugged. "I don't know. Like I told you, she left when Lily showed up."

"Why were you in the gallery with Lily?"

Huckleberry squinted in the bright sunlight, and I shaded his eyes. It would have been a perfect day if it hadn't been for the murder.

"She invited me in," I said. "After I told her I was on the

scene when her husband died, she wanted to talk to me. I agreed because she is a grieving widow, and I thought she had the right to know. Today was the first time I met her. Truly."

"And did Stacey know her before today?"

I frowned. "You will have to ask Stacey that. I can't speak for her."

"Oh, I intend to, just as soon as we can find her."

"I'm sure you can track her down," I said.

He arched his brow. "Where would you start looking?"

I swallowed. He wanted me to help him find Stacey. I shifted back and forth on my feet.

He leaned forward in anticipation. "Shiloh."

I couldn't lie to him. "She lives and breathes her theater. She's either at the Michigan Street Theater in Cherry Glen or here at the National Cherry Festival resetting the stage for tomorrow's performance of *The Tempest*. She's directing the play. I think they have five or so performances over the week, mostly on the weekends, with a Thursday matinee."

He nodded. "We will be sure to check both of those places. You have been a big help, Shiloh."

I wrinkled my brow. "I have?"

"You confirmed some things. Confirmation is gold to the district attorney."

I didn't like the sound of that because I didn't actually know what I had confirmed. Stacey was in serious trouble, and I had to find her before she learned I had spoken to the police. She would not look kindly on that.

The door to the gallery opened, and Chief Chuck

Sterling and Lily Fullbright came out of the building. The chief walked toward us, but Lily hung back and locked the gallery door.

"Mrs. Fullbright needs to return to her booth at the festival."

I tried not to look as surprised as I felt. Her husband had just died, and she still wanted to sell paintings to tourists?

"Sheriff Penbrook, will you come back with me to the office?" the chief asked. "I want to go over the interviews. There are so many; a second set of expert eyes will be a great help."

Milan nodded and then his gaze slid in my direction. He raised his brow. I knew he was asking what I planned to do without saying it.

"I'll walk back with Lily to the festival. I should return to my booth too."

The chief nodded as if that was a perfectly reasonable idea, but Milan frowned. I suspected he knew I had a long list of questions for Lily Fullbright when we were alone.

Lily watched Milan and Chief Sterling leave. "This is so awful. So many people say that divorce is like a death, and I thought that too. But it's not. This is the real thing. Before Dane was my husband, he was my best friend. We had so much in common. We both loved the arts. We were both from the same tiny town and had dreams of getting out." She snorted. "We only got as far away as Traverse City. It wasn't like we catapulted ourselves to Hollywood like some people do."

I didn't say anything because I was one of those people

who had left rural Michigan for Hollywood…and eventually came back.

She shook her head. "When Dane was offered the professor position at the university, we had to take it. Drama professor jobs are hard to come by, so we stayed. Sometimes I think staying was the demise of our marriage."

I wanted to ask her what she meant by that, but then she said, "I just need to check on things at the booth and go home. My assistant will handle it the rest of the day." She placed a hand on her forehead. "I think I need to lie down."

"Do you have anyone who can stay with you?" I asked.

She shook her head. "I have friends in town, of course, and many of them are in the art community here, but I'd rather be alone right now. This is a lot to digest."

"Of course, you do," I said. "You have had a long day. Can't you just text your assistant and go home from here?"

She shook her head. "She lost her phone. The girl is always losing her phone. The only reason I hired Slade was because Dane said I should hire a student from the college. He's been a poor excuse for a husband, but he really cared about his students. There were times he had a student or two living with us through the summer because they couldn't find off-campus housing during that time. I wasn't thrilled with it. Who wants a twenty-year-old in their house for three months? But I always went along with it because I knew it was Dane's way of showing kindness to these kids."

I nodded. This was the first redeeming bit of news I had heard about Dane Fullbright.

"I had planned to let Slade go after the festival. It's too

late to find a replacement for this important week, but she is really awful at her job. She doesn't understand art, and I watched as she talked a person *out* of buying one of my paintings because she agreed with the customer that it was too expensive. I wanted to fire her on the spot, but Dane talked me out of it. He said I should give her a chance. He's not here to talk me out of anything anymore…"

"Why don't you go home, and I will return to the festival and tell your assistant?"

She started to say no, but then her face relaxed. "Could you do that?" she asked. "I don't think I want to go back to the festival at all. There will be so many people talking about Dane and me. Maybe I'm being a coward, but I'm just not ready to face it."

"You're not being a coward. You've had a terrible shock," I said.

"That's kind of you to say. Please tell Slade to finish out the weekend and close up the booth tomorrow night."

"I'll deliver the message," I said.

"Thank you." She looked at my hand. "You're not wearing a wedding ring."

I looked down at my bare left hand. "I'm not married."

"Divorce?" she asked.

I shook my head. "I've never been married."

"You're lucky," she said. "And you should keep it that way. Avoid it at all costs. One thing I know for certain is I will never get married again."

Chapter Eight

I walked back to the festival worried for Lily Fullbright. If I were the police, I would be looking at her as my primary suspect. After all, she knew about Dane's relationship with Stacey. I was hesitant to call it an affair because Stacey had said that she hadn't known he was married, and Lily and Dane were in the middle of a divorce at the time. It was definitely a gray area, and I didn't like Dane any better for not telling Stacey. He should have been up front about that. Also, why didn't Stacey find out on her own? Anyone dating anyone these days would at least internet search for the person, check all their social media, and check their marital records. Or maybe that was just me…

Perhaps producing all those true crime documentaries in LA for over a decade taught me to never take anything someone says at face value. It was better to be safe than sorry, and Stacey had to be sorry now that she ever got involved with Dane.

But was she? Had they been together long enough that she knew he was allergic to penicillin? I'm not sure I could see that coming up in casual conversation, but maybe I was wrong. He could—and did—die from it, after all.

Artist Row was a bright and colorful section of the festival. The moment I stepped into it, I was transported back to the street fairs that would pop up in LA. I had taken very little time off when I was producer, and when I felt burnout creeping in, I would go to one of the many art fairs or galleries in the area. I rarely bought anything more than a small trinket or piece of jewelry, but I loved to look. It might be because I personally didn't have any artistic talent. Yes, I had an eye for film, but I couldn't paint, draw, or even take a decent photograph. The people who could, like Lily, amazed me.

As I walked down the row, I saw so many booths I wanted to visit. There were painters, potters, engravers, and candlemakers, just to name a few. However, I wasn't there to shop. I needed to find Lily Fullbright's booth and then hurry back to my own. After I did that, maybe I could put all this murder business behind me.

I knew I had come upon Lily's booth when I saw one of her paintings. Her style was distinctive, with swooping strokes and vibrant colors. If you looked at her paintings, you would have thought she was one of the most optimistic people in the world. Everything was bright and cheerful and could make even the most hardened curmudgeon want to smile. It was a far cry from the tearstained Lily Fullbright who pulled me into her gallery.

I had expected to find a college-aged young woman minding the booth, but there was no one there. "Hello?" I asked. I circled the booth a couple of times.

"Hey, if you're looking for the painter, she left," a blacksmith in the next booth over said. Despite the heat, he was dressed head to toe in black and had a heavy leather apron tied around his waist. "Her husband was the guy who choked on the cherry pit," he said. "You heard about that, didn't you?"

I nodded as if I didn't have a first person account of the incident. "What about her assistant? Do you know where she's gone?"

He pointed with mallet toward the bay. "She went that way. She was a real mess too, crying and wailing like it was *her* husband who choked."

I thanked the blacksmith, tugged on Huckleberry's leash, and walked down toward the bay. If I wanted to get away from people, walking to the edge of the Grand Traverse Bay on a Saturday in the middle of the National Cherry Festival would not be my first choice. The docks were covered with adults laughing and drinking and children screaming and running. The least Zen place I could imagine.

I didn't know how I would find Lily's assistant amidst all the activity, but the sound of crying led in me the right direction.

There was a young brunette woman sitting on the end of the dock heaving and leaning over the water. Warning bells went off in my head. If she leaned over any farther, she might fall in.

I came up on her right side with the hopes of not startling her. "Are you okay?"

She looked up at me with a dazed expression. She was very pretty, or at least she would be if her hazel eyes weren't red and swollen from crying.

"I'm fine. Leave me alone." She buried her face in her hands.

Normally, I would have done just that if I'd stumbled upon a crying stranger in the street, but I knew this had to be Lily's assistant. "Do you work for Lily Fullbright?"

She pulled her very short shorts under her legs the best that she could, but they didn't cover much but the essentials. I could imagine her bare legs on the splintery dock weren't all that comfortable. She looked up at me with a squint. "Who are you and why do you want to know?"

Both were fair questions, and I wished I had used my time more wisely coming up for answers for her. I decided to answer as honestly I could. "I'm Shiloh. I was in Lily's gallery just now. She's leaving the festival for the day and asked me to tell you close up the booth after the festival is over for the day, and to open and close it tomorrow. The booth will be closed for the rest of the week."

"Isn't that just like her?" She snorted and then patted at her nose with the edge of her T-shirt sleeve. "She didn't even care about Dane, but she gets to leave as the grieving widow while I'm left here to clean up the mess. He was right about her."

"Oh? Right how?" I winced at how eager I sounded. Luckily the reflection off the water was too bright for her to see my face.

"It doesn't matter," she snapped at me. "Nothing matters anymore. My life is totally over, and there is nothing you can do about it. You can leave."

I didn't move. I was too afraid that if I left she would do something drastic and jump in the water.

I stared out into the bay. Fighter planes flew overhead as they practiced for the air show that would happen on the Fourth of July. I knew Milan and Chief Sterling would want to speak to her, but how forthcoming would she be? Would she answer their questions—like what Dane had to say about his wife?

Did I really want to know? I had liked Lily in the brief time I spoke to her, but I knew when it came to murder investigations, the more information I had the better.

"I'm Shiloh. You're Slade, right?" I asked. It seemed like a simple question, but she had no reason to answer it. If I were her, I would have gotten up and walked away by now. However, she looked too depleted by her tears to stand, much less leave.

"Yeah," she said. "My mother hates my name."

I cocked my head. "Why's that?"

"Because she named me Saldona. That name doesn't fit me at all. When I was fourteen, I asked everyone to call me Slade, and it thankfully stuck. The only one who still calls me Saldona is my mother."

"I like both names, but I do think Slade suits you better." Cautiously, I sat on the end of the dock next to her. I didn't think there was much risk that she would push me in. Even so, I sat a good two feet from her, both to avoid a dip in the bay and to avoid encroaching on her personal space. Huckleberry lay on the dock between us. She didn't seem to mind him being there. It was hard not to like the little pug.

"I can relate to that. I didn't like the name Shiloh when I was young. It was too different from all the other names of the kids in my school. I never thought to change it though. If I had, I'm sure my father would have ignored my request."

"What do you think about it now?" she asked.

"I like it," I said. "It's grown on me over the years."

"I still hate Saldona. Every time my mother says it, I cringe. Honestly, I think that she's held on to it just to spite me."

I guessed her mother felt that Slade changed her name to spite her too, but I didn't offer up that opinion.

"I would never stick my kid with an awful name. In fact, I plan to let my kids name themselves. When they can talk, they can pick their own names."

"I used to live in California," I said. "Letting kids name themselves was a bit of trend for a time. I knew someone whose kid was named Glue. The child picked it when he was four."

She wrinkled her brow as if she were rethinking this whole let the kid name themselves thing.

It was time to steer the conversation back to the issue of Dane Fullbright's death. "I'm sorry about Dr. Fullbright. Lily said that he was your teacher."

She looked me in the eye for the first time. "He was more than some teacher to me. He was my whole world." Her face crumbled. "I can't believe that he's dead. I don't know what I am going to do now."

I stiffened. "What do you mean your whole world?"

"I was in love with him." She began to sob again. "What am I going to do now? I can't go on without him!"

"How old are you?" I asked. The question came out more bluntly than I intended it to. I was just so shocked by her revelation.

"Twenty," she said in a muffled voice.

At least she was a legal adult. Even so, it didn't make me

feel at all better about her situation. What I didn't know was if Dane reciprocated her feelings at all. I prayed that he hadn't, because it would make this case just that much messier.

"Why would you agree to work for his wife?" I thought it was a fair question. "Wasn't that difficult?"

"He said it was the best way for us to stay connected through the summer. I'm not taking summer classes, and working for Lily gave me a reason to stay in Traverse City instead of going home to Ann Arbor for the summer. I applied for several jobs at the university but didn't get any of them." She rubbed her eyes.

"Where are you living?"

"In an apartment with three other roommates. Well, two in the summer. I'm making just enough to pay my rent."

"Did Dane care about you too?" I asked.

"Of course he did! Why do you think he was getting a divorce? He said when that was over, we could be together. Now, it's all over." She wiped her eyes. "I had better get back to the booth. I can't afford to lose my job, even if it's for that horrible woman."

I bit my lip because I knew that Lily planned to let Slade go as soon as the festival was over.

"Is there someone who you can talk to? One of you roommates maybe?"

"No. I don't even really know any of them. I met them on Craigslist when I needed somewhere to live last year. All three of them work late at night and sleep most of the day. It's really like having my own apartment." She stood up and dusted off her backend.

Huckleberry and I jumped to our feet too. "Here. Let me give you my phone number. You can call me if you need anything."

I recited the number to her, and she typed it into her phone. "Thanks. I'll take it, but I'm not going to call you."

I wrung my hands as she walked away. So much for not getting involved.

Chapter Nine

Hazel was slumped over, asleep in the front seat of my new-to-me pickup. I had finally traded in my convertible for something more sensible at the beginning of the summer. Huckleberry slept between us on his side. His belly faced me. Every so often he would kick his legs like he was running in his doggie dreams. As my eyelids grew heavy, I envied them both. I sipped the tepid coffee that had been in the cup holder since that morning, gagging slightly at the taste. Even Jessa's coffee couldn't stand ten hours in a hot truck.

I was relieved when Hazel's house came into view. Quinn and Hazel lived on a small hobby farm just half a mile from my property. Unlike Bellamy Farm, where the farmhouse was nearly half a mile from the road, the Killians' small home was just a few yards from their mailbox.

Quinn's truck was in the driveway, and the house lights were on. I parked by his truck and touched Hazel's shoulder. "It's time to get up, Sleepy Head."

With her eyes still closed, she waved me away. "I don't want to go to school."

I chuckled. "You don't have to go to school. It's summer. But you do have to go to bed. We're at your house."

Her eyes opened just a hair. "It's too far to walk."

"I'm sure you will make it."

The front screen door opened, and Quinn came out.

I hopped out of the truck. "She's exhausted and trying to gather the strength to walk inside. Too much excitement today I guess."

He gave me a look. "I'll get her in. Can you stay here while I put her to bed? I want to talk to you a minute."

"Sure," I said, even though it was the last thing I wanted to do.

He walked around to the passenger side of the truck, opened the door, and picked Hazel up in his arms like she was still a baby. Her head rested on his shoulder.

I watched as he carried his sleepy daughter into the house with a lump in my throat.

After they went in, I peeked in the truck to find Huckleberry rolled on his back and passed out. Apparently, neither Hazel nor Huckleberry were night owls.

I leaned on the tailgate. It was a beautiful clear night, and some of my tiredness faded away as I stared up into the stars. I could see the Big and Little Dippers and Orion's Belt. Beyond those markers in the sky, I was at a bit of a loss for naming any of the stars, but I could appreciate their beauty on a midsummer's night.

It seemed that I had Shakespeare on the mind, and thoughts of one play led me to thoughts of *The Tempest*, Stacey, and the murder. With that came Stacey's accusation that Quinn had a good motive to want Dane Fullbright dead.

I had planned to ask him about it, but on the drive home from Traverse City, I thought it was best not to have that conversation tonight. I wasn't up to it, but now that Quinn had asked me to stay to talk, I didn't know if I could avoid bringing it up.

I heard the screen door bang shut and turned to see Quinn walking toward me. I came around the side of the pickup to meet him.

"It's a beautiful night," he said.

I nodded.

He folded his arms. "I know Stacey was involved with the dead guy, but you're not going to be messing around in this case, are you? Dane Fullbright was a crook and bad news. There is probably a list a mile long of people that are happy he's dead."

I arched my brow. "Including you?"

"I save lives. I wouldn't wish anyone dead. I've seen death close up too many times, but I'm not crying over Dane Fullbright, if that's what you mean."

"Did you know him? How did you know he was a crook?"

"He was a scammer. He started countless fundraising endeavors and took the money and ran. Whatever he promised would happen never did."

"What was he raising money for?"

He narrowed his eyes. "I'm hoping you'll drop the whole thing."

That was very unlikely to happen now, but I didn't say that.

"He was raising money for all kinds of things: an art school run by his wife, dance classes for underprivileged tweens, and a theater school for kids in Grand Traverse County."

"Did you invest in any of them?" I asked, sensing this was all tied to motive.

"I did. I gave him a thousand dollars for the theater school. It was right after we moved back to Cherry Glen. Since we moved here in the summer, I thought it would a great way for Hazel to meet some other kids her age before school started. I wanted to give her something to do instead of sitting at my mom's house listening to her and friends play cards and complain about their neighbors while I was at work."

"What happened?" I asked.

"Nothing," Quinn said. "He claimed that he didn't raise enough money, and the project wasn't going to happen."

"And your money?"

"He said since it was a fundraiser, he was under no obligation to give the money back, and he didn't. The thousand dollars I invested went up in a cloud of smoke, and after burying my wife, moving to Cherry Glen, and buying this farm, I wasn't exactly knee-deep in cash."

True. But I didn't think Quinn would harm a soul. And certainly not commit murder over a thousand dollars.

"So I should be looking at a bunch of angry theater parents as suspects."

"You shouldn't be looking for suspects at all. Besides, we don't even know for sure if Dane was murdered."

"Milan said it was most likely murder."

His brow went up. "Oh, you call Sheriff Penbrook *Milan* now. I didn't realize that the two you were that chummy."

My cheeks grew hot. "He's a friend."

"Sure." The sarcasm in his voice hit me like a brick to the chest.

"Is there a reason you should care who my friends are?" I asked.

"Of course there is. My daughter spends more time with you in the summer than she does with me. I don't want her subjected to anything…" He paused as if he were searching for just the right word. "Inappropriate."

"I wouldn't do anything inappropriate, and Milan was there assisting Police Chief Sterling. Unlike your father, Chief Sterling knows when he needs to ask for help."

"Leave my father out of this."

"Gladly," I said and looked down at the tops of my sneakers. It was getting dark now; I could barely see my own feet. "I need to head home." I looked up into his green eyes and saw something that looked a lot like hurt.

"You probably should." Without saying goodbye, he walked back to the house but stood on the porch until I climbed into my truck and drove away. My heart ached the whole way home.

In the driveway, I parked the truck in between the farmhouse and the barn. Esmeralda the cat waited for Huckleberry and me at the farmhouse's back door, and I would have given anything to go straight to bed, but I knew that wasn't an option. First, I had to take care of the farm animals, and then I had many hours of baking ahead of me.

After putting the sheep and chickens to bed for the night, I finally went into the farmhouse with the cat and dog. I would rather work in my own cabin, but the kitchen and oven were far too small for as much as I needed to bake. Besides, my grandmother had a convection oven installed in the farmhouse kitchen when she lived there. The oven had been a godsend for me. I could make more batches of cookies and muffins faster with it than I could with a standard oven.

I washed my hands and rolled up my sleeves to get to work. Esmeralda curled up on a kitchen chair and promptly went to sleep. Huckleberry settled into his dog bed in one corner of the kitchen and did the same.

That night, my goal was to make ten dozen cherry muffins, twelve dozen cherry drop cookies, and seven dozen cherry granola bars. That should be enough to get me through the next day or even the next two days of selling. The muffins were the fastest to make, so I set to work on those first.

With the first batch of muffins in the oven, I began to sift organic white flour for the cookies. All the while, my mind bounced back and forth between thoughts about my grandmother's stock and about the murder. It was not lost on me that my cousin Stacey was at the center of both of those problems. Was I right in thinking that she would drop her claim to the stocks if I cleared her name? There was no guarantee that was true, and to be honest, I didn't even know if that was fair. I believed she deserved half. It was my father who was putting up a fight.

What didn't make sense to me was why Stacey was so angry at *me* over the stocks and not my father. Did she think

I was manipulating him to put up a fight? She knew as well as I did that Dad was opinionated and strong-willed. I would have no more luck talking him into something than I would giving Diva the chicken a hug.

My dad shuffled into the kitchen. "How am supposed to sleep with all this racket?" He gripped the handle of his cane and stood in the kitchen doorway in his blue-and-white-striped pajamas and brown slippers.

"I'm sorry, Dad. I'm trying to be as quiet as I can." In the stand mixer, I creamed butter and cracked eggs from our own hens on the side of the metal bowl, adding them to the butter one at a time. "The festival has been better than expected, and we nearly ran out of my baked goods today. I have to make more to stay open."

"Do you have to do this in the middle of the night? I can't sleep with you banging around in here."

Dad's bedroom was just on the other side of the kitchen wall. The bedroom had once been the dining room, but when it was clear he shouldn't go up and down the stairs any longer, we moved his bedroom downstairs and tucked the dining room table into one corner of the large living room.

"I'm really sorry," I said as I kept working. "I have to be at the festival so early each morning; this is the only time I have."

He sniffed. "At least it smells good."

The timer pinged, telling me that it was time to remove the first trays of muffins from the oven.

I donned oven mitts and set the hot trays on a cooling rack while I popped two more trays in the oven. "Want a cherry muffin, Dad?"

"I might as well since I'm up. A cup of warm milk would be nice too." He sat in the kitchen chair across from where Esmeralda was sleeping.

I warmed milk in the microwave and gave it to him. I then gingerly removed one of the piping hot muffins from the tin and dropped it on a small plate. "It's hot," I warned.

He squinted at me. "I saw you pull it from the oven with my own eyes. I know it's hot."

I sighed and went back to my cookie dough, this time adding organic sugar to the stand mixer's bowl. I cleared my throat. "Dad, I wondered if you have taken any time to think about Grandma's stocks."

He grunted. "Why are you bringing that up again? I told you to let the lawyers sort it out."

I added the freshly sifted flour to the cookie dough and then glanced over my shoulder. "Lawyers are expensive. It would be better to be sorted out between us."

He snorted and sipped his milk. "There is nothing to be sorted out. I'm my mother's only living child, and the stocks should be mine. She even said in that note for you to use them to help the farm. You're my daughter and the money will ultimately go to you."

"But what about Stacey?" I asked.

"If her father, my brother, was alive, he would get half, but he's not."

"But your brother left everything in his will to Stacey," I said. "Doesn't that include half of the stocks?" I asked. "I don't think Grandma Bellamy had any idea that I would find the stocks over fifteen years after she died and after your brother died," I said. "She must have thought I would find them right away."

He stood up. "But you didn't. I'm not talking about this anymore. Let the lawyers settle it. I trust Stacey. She will come around to the right answer. I bet she's doing that right now."

I knew for a fact that Dane's murder was on my cousin's mind, not our grandmother's stocks.

"I'm going back to bed. Keep it down in here." He deposited the muffin in the top pocket of his pajama top, picked up his mug of warm milk, and without another word, disappeared back into his bedroom.

I sighed and promised him that I would.

Chapter Ten

I woke up the next morning after Dane Fullbright's death with a terrible headache. I had barely slept the night before. Not only had baking taken longer than I thought it would, but I had been preoccupied by Slade's story and Stacey's possible involvement in Dane's death too. I also wondered about Quinn's fundraising story. Was the money he lost investing in Dane's theater school really his motive to kill Dane Fullbright? It didn't seem like a strong enough motive to me, and it had happened years ago. Could there have been another motive that Stacey had alluded too?

I thought of Penny Lee and had to wonder what the news coverage would be of the murder. I suspected it was headline news in Traverse City, the very last thing that city officials would want during the National Cherry Festival. I prayed that Stacey would not be mentioned in any of the articles, but if Penny Lee had anything to say, Stacey's name would surely be front and center.

To add to my headache, my cat Esmeralda (who actually was really Hazel's cat, who happened to live on my farm because her grandmother didn't like pets of any kind), had a terrible case of the zoomies and raced around my little cabin all night long. She was so wound up that Huckleberry barricaded himself in my bedroom closet and only came out the next morning when I waved a bowl of kibble in his face.

Huckleberry was a chicken through and through, but he didn't let anything stand in the way of his breakfast.

After the pug and cat were fed, I put my coffee in a travel mug and savored the first sip. The first order of business for me each morning was to herd my little merry band of sheep to the cherry orchard, feed the chickens, and collect the eggs. I was lucky I was so close to Traverse City. I could do my farm chores as normal without hiring extra help and sleep in my own bed each night and still get to the festival in time.

You would think the chickens would be easier to deal with than the sheep, but you'd be wrong. My flock was led by gang leader Diva, who was known to fly and leap from trees onto passerby's heads. Huckleberry was terrified of her. I was a little afraid of her myself.

However, before I dealt with the chickens, I had to care for the sheep. I had a small flock of Olde English Babydoll Southdown yearlings, and they were small not just in numbers but also in stature. The five sheep were all less than twenty inches tall and would not grow higher than two feet. The breeder had told me that they were a stock of sheep native to England from the times before sheep were bred larger and larger to yield more wool and meat.

The wool would be nice to use for organic products for the farm when shearing time came, but I had zero plans to use my little flock for meat. In fact, after acquiring the little band of puffballs, I would never eat lamb again. I didn't feel the same way about Diva and chickens though.

Huckleberry might be terrified of the chickens, but he loved the sheep. They were a bit bigger than him, but I thought, since they were so low to the ground like he was, he felt like he was on a more even playing field with them. Also, the sheep couldn't fly, so Huckleberry gave a point in their favor for that.

I opened the cabin's front door, and Esmeralda and Huckleberry raced out ahead of me on the long dirt road that ran from the farmhouse to the cabin that once had been my grandmother's. It was in that cabin a year ago I found the note my grandmother left me. In the note, she alluded to the fact that she had hidden money somewhere in the "heart of the farm." She assumed I knew what she meant. It took me six months to figure it out, and ultimately I found it accidentally. Had the old porch on the main farmhouse not caved in from rot, I would still be looking for the heart of the farm to this day.

I savored the cool morning air as I headed to the farmhouse. I loved this walk. It gave me time to enjoy my coffee and mull over the plans that I had for the day. On this morning, my plans were set. I had to go to the National Cherry Festival, and I had to catch a killer.

When we reached barn, the four ginger barn cats all stood at attention at the door. They were ready and waiting for their marching orders from General Esmeralda. She walked down the line as if she was inspecting each one in turn. The smallest of the orange cats shook slightly as Esmeralda looked him in the eye.

I set my travel mug on the hood of my truck. "Esmeralda, will you leave those poor barn cats alone? You're terrorizing them."

She squinted at me and swished her plume of a tail across the dirt as if to say, "You're next."

I didn't take this personally. Of course I was always next on Esmeralda's list. I believed the only reason that she put up with me at all was because I was her access to Hazel, who she adored.

I opened the barn door all the way, and the sheep greeted me with high-pitched *baa*s. Their little teddy bear faces looked up at me, and my heart just melted. They were as adorable as advertised. Southdowns could come in a variety of colors from white to black to brown and all the combinations in between. My little herd of four girls and one boy were all teddy bear brown save for the boy, Panda Bear, who was spotted black and white.

I knew I shouldn't pick favorites, but there was something about Panda Bear that made him special. Huckleberry also had a strong affection for him.

Since Panda Bear was the only male, he was in a separate pen from the ladies at night. I let him out first. He sauntered out of his pen and bumped noses with Huckleberry like they were long lost brothers. There *was* a slight resemblance.

Then I let out the girls, and Huckleberry, the little sheepherder, and I walked the short distance to the cherry orchard.

The reason that I walked the sheep to the cherry trees each morning was the main reason I had bought them in the first place. As it was my livelihood, I had to keep my orchard healthy, and since I was an organic farmer, the option to use pesticides and herbicides to keep invasive insects and plants off my cherry trees was off the table. I needed a more creative way to protect my trees.

One way to keep pests from attacking the trees was to make it more difficult for the crawling insects to climb into the cherry trees. The best way to do that was to keep the grass and foliage around the trees trimmed and short.

In the summer the weeds on the farm grew like, well, weeds. It was a constant battle to keep up with them, and I didn't know a single farmer who didn't have a weed problem. The sheep helped with that issue. They would eat anything, and they especially loved weeds like thistle, poison ivy, and dandelions. They kept the grass and plants around the orchard short, and that was good for the trees and ultimately the cherry crop.

Worker bees hummed by the two hives that Chesney had set up fifty feet from the orchard. The bees zipped into the trees and returned to the hive with their hind legs heavy with pollen. As much as I didn't want insects in the trees, bees and other pollinators were welcomed and encouraged.

An electric fence encircled the orchard. I let the sheep inside of it, whistled for Huckleberry to come out, and turned on the fence.

Panda Bear slow-blinked at me like a cat saying, I love you. I found myself smiling. At least I had done one thing right when it came to the farm. The sheep had been an expensive but solid investment. They protected the cherry orchard and were adorable at the same time.

I wished I could stay in the orchard all day and watch Panda Bear and his ladies work, but there were cherry pastries to sell and a murder to solve in Traverse City.

"You seem to be quite pleased with yourself," a man's voice said.

My back tensed as I turned around and saw Tanner Birchwood standing at the edge of my orchard—an orchard he very much wanted to be his.

Chapter Eleven

Tanner flashed his brilliant smile, which stood out more than ever against his tan skin. He was my closest neighbor and when I said *closest neighbor*, I meant it. His two hundred acres butted up against my two-hundred-acre farm, and his land had once been in the Bellamy name.

When my grandmother died, the farm was divided between her two sons, my father and my uncle, Stacey's father. When my uncle died, Stacey inherited the farm, and she had about as much interest in farming as a house cat had in swimming. She sold her land and used the money to buy the Michigan Street Theater.

Ultimately, Tanner became the new owner and spent the money he earned from his apparently very successful business career in Chicago to turn his property into an organic farm called Organic Acres.

I have been a tad unjustly miffed that he would do that at the same time I was trying to turn Bellamy Farm organic.

But the one thing he wanted desperately but couldn't have was the cherry orchard, because it was on my side of the property line.

To be a farmer in Grand Traverse County and not have at least a small cherry orchard was a bit embarrassing. It was what the region was best known for, after all.

Starting a cherry orchard is a laborious undertaking. Even though my family's orchard had been in disarray and half-dead when I returned to Michigan, there was enough life in it to bring it back.

Tanner was a decent guy and a good farmer. He was making a name for himself growing organic hops for local breweries. I had wanted to get into that business too, but I thought it wasn't a smart move to be in direct competition with him. It was bad enough sharing a property line.

He certainly was easy on the eyes with his flowing blond hair and perpetual tan. At one time, I thought he and my cousin would end up together, but apparently Dane Fullbright caught her eye instead.

"Good morning, Tanner," I said as cheerfully as I could muster.

"Shouldn't you be at the festival?" He paused. "But then again, maybe you're not as dedicated to it as I thought you were. It's a shame since it's such an honor to be chosen for the Cherry Farm Market." He didn't even bother to try to keep the envy from his voice.

"What do you mean by that? I was at the festival all day yesterday and will be for the rest of the week." I hated it that he knew what buttons to push to get a rise out of me.

"When I stopped at your booth yesterday, you weren't there. Chesney said that you had other business." He held up his hands as if in surrender. "I didn't ask her what that other business was because it's not *my* business." He chuckled.

"What were you doing at the fair?"

He dropped his arms to his sides. "I was doing what just about everyone else was, having a good time. Also, as I'll have my own orchard going in within the next year, I wanted to size up the other cherry farmers. I must say, I didn't see any real competition. When my orchard is established, I will have no problem getting into the festival. I mean, they let *you* in, right?"

As he said that, I remembered why I didn't like Tanner. He handed out insults like candy at Halloween.

"As you say, I should be off to the festival…" I picked up Huckleberry. The little pug wasn't nearly as fast as I needed him to be when I had to escape a boorish man.

"I see you brought the sheep out again. That really was clever of you to do that," Tanner said. "I would have gone with a different breed though. Larger sheep could eat more weeds, but to each his own."

I didn't say anything and started to back away.

"I'm surprised that you didn't ask me why I was looking for you at the festival." He arched his too-smooth brow. There was a definite sign of Botox in use. They handed it out like gumballs in LA, so I knew what I was looking at.

If I was smarter, I wouldn't have taken the bait when he said something like that, but like always, my curiosity overcame my common sense. I heard myself say, "I just thought you were coming by for a neighborly hello."

"I was," he said. "But I was mostly there to ask why you killed Dane Fullbright."

I stared at him. "You think *I* killed him?"

"I was walking by and it looked like you were trying to throttle the guy."

"I was giving him the Heimlich. I thought he was choking."

"Since he died, I take it you weren't successful."

I made sure one last time that the electrical fence was on and secure. I hated to leave Panda Bear and the ewes alone with Tanner. I didn't trust him one ounce, but I needed to get going. I still had to tend to the chickens and check in on my father before I left for the festival. I couldn't be late today. It was Sunday, and Chesney was attending church that morning, so she couldn't get to the festival until after one.

I stopped. "How do you know his name?"

He stared at me. "What are you talking about?"

"Dane Fullbright. How did you know that was his name?"

His cheeks reddened under his tan skin. "I—I must have heard it. Everyone in the crowd was talking at once when he went down. It was bedlam."

"That's not the reason," I said on a hunch. "You knew it before you saw me with him."

"I didn't." His face turned even redder. "I didn't. I promise you. However, even if I did, what would it matter? He's not a friend or a member of my family. I know a lot of people. I don't know what you're getting at."

To be honest, I didn't know what I was getting at either, but it seemed odd to me that Tanner would know who Dane was.

I reminded myself that Grand Traverse County wasn't LA. People might actually have heard of each other. Even so, I could not shake the uneasy feeling it gave me.

"You should stick to sheep, Shiloh, even if the ones that you bought are way too small for the job." He stalked away.

I'd never trust a man who insulted my sheep.

I carried Huckleberry all the way back to the farmhouse, and by the time we got there, Diva and her gang of chicken assassins were all up in feathers over the fact I was late. I set Huckleberry on a hay bale near the barn door and opened the chicken coop.

Knowing that Diva was going to be one angry bird, I backed away and covered my head. However I wasn't fast enough and Diva charged, hitting me across the face with her wing. It could have been worse. She was known to use her beak or her talons when she was in a very bad mood, which happened regularly.

Her chicken minions followed closely behind her, and before I knew it, all the hens were roosting in the small maple tree by the barn, looking like they were willing to leap onto my head.

The back door to the farmhouse opened, and my father let the screen door slam shut behind him. "What are you doing to those chickens that they are making such a racket? I'm trying to get into character here!"

My father stepped out with his cane in hand. I knew that he hated to use it, but I was glad to see it. He didn't get around as easily as he used to.

"Sorry, Dad," I said. "I'm running a little late. Diva and the chickens weren't happy about that."

"I don't blame them. You're late for my breakfast too. I had to make my own toast."

I bit the inside of my lip. I loved my father, but our relationship was a complicated one. There were times, like when his toast was late, that he treated me more like hired help than like his daughter, and he certainly didn't treat me like an equal partner in the farm, even though I had made all the decisions since the moment I moved home. I admit not all those decisions had been good ones, but they had been mine.

"I'm sorry about your toast, Dad," I said. "It's good to know that you can make it yourself."

He narrowed his eyes. "I had to. Stacey will be here soon to pick me up. She wants to go over some things with me today before the performance."

I wrinkled my brow. "I thought you knew your lines for the boatswain."

He grinned from ear to ear. "I'm boatswain no longer. I am now Prospero, and I can tell you that I have been studying for this role my entire life."

"*You* are replacing Dane Fullbright?" I had expected that Stacey would give Dad the role since he knew the play backward and forward, but it still was a bit of surprise to have my suspicions confirmed. It was a concern too. The play was on a black-painted stage in the hot sun. As the lead, Dad would be onstage more than anyone else, and he certainly had the most lines. He could suffer heatstroke. Even though I knew he wouldn't want to hear, I said, "What about the heat? You could fall ill. I wouldn't want to stand in the sun that long."

Dad scowled at me. "I will sit in the air-conditioned trailer between my scenes. Honestly, Shiloh, you treat me like a child at times. At least Stacey recognizes my abilities."

"I do too, but—"

Dad's pocket began to ring, and he fished in his trousers to find his phone, wobbling on his cane. It took everything that I had not to run over and steady him. However, I knew how insulted he would be if I did. It was a difficult balance to keep my father safe and allow him to retain his pride.

Finally after what seemed like a decade, he removed the small flip phone from his pocket. At this point he was so frustrated that he answered the phone gruffly. "Yeah, what is it? Oh, hello, Stacey," he said in a much kinder voice. "Yes, Shiloh is still here... I'm sure that won't be a problem... All right." He ended the call.

I raised my brow in question.

"That was Stacey. She can't take me to the festival today."

"Why not?" I asked.

"She has something she has to do."

"What's that?"

"How should I know?" He shook his cane at me.

I wanted to say that he could have asked, but I reminded myself that most people weren't as nosey as I was. Also, Dad might not know about Stacey and Dane's relationship, nor that his niece was a murder suspect.

He pointed the cane at me. "You're taking me to the festival instead. I'll go collect my things." He turned and went back into the house.

I looked down at Huckleberry, and he stared back at me with sad pug eyes as if to say it would be a long car ride.

Chapter Twelve

D ad recited his lines to Huckleberry, who sat in between us, the entire drive to Traverse City. Huckleberry looked like he might pass out if he had to hear one more soliloquy.

I hated for the little pug to take the brunt of my dad's acting, but it gave me time to mull over my plans for the day and wonder why Stacey couldn't pick up my father for the festival. What was she up to, and did it have anything to do with Dane Fullbright?

By the time we arrived at the booth, I hadn't come to any conclusions about Stacey's motivation.

Dad examined my cherry basket booth. "You spent six thousand dollars on *this*?"

"Yes," I said as I unpacked the crates of baked goods and fresh cherries I had brought with me that day.

"Was that wise?" He looked up at the paper-mache cherry Chesney had made as if it were an ant at his picnic—not that Dad ever actually went on picnics.

"Dad, I love you, but you really aren't the one who should be giving me any financial advice." As soon as the words came out of my mouth, I regretted them. There was no need to remind my father that he had almost lost the farm.

I expected him to snap back at me for the comment, but instead, his face was solemn. "You're right. You're far better at managing money than I ever was. Without you the farm would be lost."

It was the first time in my life my dad had showed a glimmer of regret over how he managed the farm. I always thought that he didn't care.

I didn't know what to say back, and I was saved from speaking by the arrival of a customer.

The woman was about forty but could pass for a teenager in dim light. She had the largest green eyes I had ever seen. Freckles danced across her nose. The only indication that she wasn't in her teens was the gray running through her red curls. She examined the wares on my table. Today, I had added free samples of my homemade cherry vanilla soap. Adding soap and creams to my offering of organic items was a new venture. I was doing anything that I could think of to diversify and make more money to keep the farm afloat.

She picked up a two-ounce bar of soap.

I smiled at her. "You are welcome to have that. It's a free sample. I'm sorry to tell you that I can't sell anything to you until ten o'clock. The Cherry Farm Market committee is very strict about sales being open during the festival hours."

"I'll take the soap," she said and held it up to her nose. "But I wasn't going to buy anything. I'm another vendor. I have a booth just down the way there. I sell cherry candies. I'm Karla Wiggins." She smiled a little wider and nodded at my father, who was sitting in one of the two folding chairs in the booth, working on the crossword puzzle in the *Northern Express*.

Dad grunted in reply and licked the tip of his pencil.

Karla didn't seem at all daunted my father's less-than-friendly response. "I just wanted to stop by and say it was such a brave thing that you did yesterday."

I frowned. "Brave? What did I do?"

She blinked at me. "What did you do? You jumped into the fray and tried to save a man. You were unsuccessful of course. He's dead."

"I heard that," I said quietly.

"I was there when it happened," Karla said. "And it was a shock."

I couldn't believe my luck. I had an eyewitness standing right in front of me. "You were there?"

"I sure was. My, wasn't it a scene? I felt like I was on episode of a cop show when the police came in. I have never been in the middle of something like that!"

I *had* been in the middle of something like that before, and maybe it made me a little more reluctant to be excited about it.

"Do you care if I keep setting up my booth while we talk?" I asked.

"Of course not," she said with sparkling green eyes. "You go right ahead. I have had my booth ready to go for ages." She examined the cherry basket. "But I don't have something nearly as fancy as this. It must have cost you a pretty penny."

"Six thousand dollars," my father interjected from his folding chair.

I sighed. "It's something I can use again and again," I said, as if that made up for the hefty price tag.

"Yes, you can," Karla agreed. "I'm sure you will be invited

to come back year after year. Oh! I see that you are an organic farm. My husband and I have been thinking of getting into that too. You get a decent price for your crops. That must be how you are able to afford such a unique booth. But the work to go organic! It's just so much easier to spray and go."

Yes, it was easier to spray, for the farmer. Not for the land, or the creatures living on it, and not for people eating the fruit. I kept my opinions to myself on Karla's use of pesticides and made a mental note not to purchase anything from her booth.

"I am sorry that you were there when Dane died," I said.

"I'm not. It was so interesting for me. I spend all day at our farm with my husband and my brothers. If I hear one more conversation about tractors, I just might scream. It was nice to have something else to think about."

"Oh," I said, not knowing how else to reply. "When you were there, did you see anything out of the ordinary?"

"I saw a man die."

I felt my cheeks grow hot. "Yes, I know that, but before Dane started to struggle. Did you see him with anyone?"

"Oh sure. I saw the woman in the play with him just before he went up to the line to spit. They were having a very involved conversation and neither one looked happy about it."

My heart began to race. Stacey? It had to be Stacey.

"Do you know the woman's name?"

She shook her head. "No, but she was in the same costume that she wore on stage. I had just gone to the matinee on that day you see. So what she had been wearing was fresh on my mind."

"Was she wearing a high-waisted lavender dress?"

My father shook his newspaper as if he was tired of this

conversation, but I didn't care. I had to know if the woman she had seen was Stacey. I couldn't see it being anyone else.

She shook her head. "No, she had wings."

"Wings?"

"Yes, and lots of glittery makeup. She was pretty. Honestly, I think she would have looked nicer without all the makeup. She even had glitter on the backs of her hands. I noticed it when she handed Dane his cherry."

"Wait. What?" I yelped. "This woman handed Dane a cherry?"

Karla nodded. "Oh yes, she plucked it out of the container on the table and handed it to him. She said, 'It's a winner.' That might not be her exact wording, but it was something along those lines."

A mystery woman from the play gave Dane the cherry. She had to have been the one to poison it, right? That's not too far a leap, was it?

Karla glanced over her shoulder. "I'd better get back to my booth." She wiggled her fingers at me and left.

"Dad, who is this other woman in the play?"

My father folded his newspaper and laid it across his lap while Huckleberry snoozed in the shade of his chair. "My goodness, Shiloh, I feel like I have failed you as a father if you don't know *The Tempest*."

"I do know it, and Miranda, who is Prospero's daughter, is the only female role."

"There is Ariel," he said. "A sprite. I suppose you could say with gender unknown. The part has been known to be played by both men and women."

I almost smacked myself on the head. "Ariel. That makes so much sense. What's the name of the woman playing it?"

"Can't remember," Dad said.

"What do you mean that you can't remember? You must have been rehearsing with her for weeks."

Dad shrugged "That doesn't mean I know her name. I call her Ariel onstage." Slowly, he stood up, leaning heavily on his cane. "I should head over there now. I want to check the stage for my marks. I didn't hit all of them in my first performance as Prospero. I know the lines by heart. Where I have to sit or stand is a bit harder to remember." He took a step forward and wobbled a bit.

"Do you want me to drive you over to the stage?" I couldn't stop myself from asking.

Dad gave me a withering stare in return. "I can make it the few yards there. I need to work the kinks out of my legs before I go onstage in any case."

"I could walk with you."

He scowled. "What about the booth? You're not even finished setting up."

"I'll get back in time for opening."

His face softened just a touch, but for my father, any sign of tenderness was noteworthy. "All right. I'll let you walk me. I know it's because you want to talk to the woman playing Ariel, not to keep me upright."

I hooked a leash on Huckleberry's collar. "Can't it be both?"

At that, my father actually chuckled.

Chapter Thirteen

The walk from Bellamy Farm's booth to the Cherry Blast Stage was painfully slow, and I felt like I was about to burst. I was on the cusp of solving the case, but there was no way I could get my father to move faster than he already was.

In the back of my mind, a little voice was telling me that I should call Chief Sterling or Milan. If this woman really had poisoned Dane, the police should be involved. However, I wasn't one hundred percent sure that Karla the farmer was a reliable witness. I had an inkling that she was the kind of person who liked to embellish stories just a little too much.

Finally, we reached the stage. Even though the performance that day wasn't until 1:00 p.m., people were already sitting in the folding chairs set in front of the stage.

Dad climbed up the short steps onto the stage. "Yes, yes, there is my mark." He pointed at a blue masking-tape *X* on the stage floor. "Very good. As Prospero, I don't have to move around much, as I send Ariel out to do my bidding."

"You still have a long time before your performance, Dad." I glanced around. From what I could tell, he was the only actor there. "Are you sure you don't want to wait with me at the cherry booth?"

He shook his head and painstakingly climbed down the steps from the stage. He walked to one of the chairs in the front row and sat. "I can sit right here until it's time to get into costume. I can prepare myself." He closed his eyes as if he was visualizing himself onstage.

"I know you will be great. I'll do my best to be here to watch at least part of the show."

He looked up at me. "I don't expect you to do that."

"It's important to you," I said. "I want to see you in your leading role."

It could have been the sunlight, but I could have sworn I saw tears gather in my father's eyes. He looked away quickly.

Dad cleared his throat. "There's Ariel."

"What?" I looked around me, but didn't see anyone with wings.

"There." He pointed with his cane at a mousy-looking young woman who stood alone under a maple tree. It looked like she was talking to herself, but it was just as likely she was talking to someone on speakerphone.

"Why don't you go solve a murder and leave me be?" my father said, shooing me away.

As he said that, I told myself that I had definitely not seen tears in his eyes.

I thought about saying, "Break a leg," but given my dad's recent mobility issues, I didn't think that would be very sensitive. "You'll do great, Dad!"

He nodded and shooed me again.

I left my father to visualize his performance and approached the woman under the tree. As I got closer, I realized she couldn't have been more than nineteen. She had thin dirty-blond hair that hung limply by her face, perfectly round glasses that sat on the tip of her nose, and mouth a bit too wide to be attractive. She was an interesting-looking girl. I could see why Stacey gave her the role as Ariel. There was an ethereal air about her, as if she wasn't totally living in the present.

She held a hand out in front of herself and said, "'All hail, great master! Grave sir, hail! I come to answer thy best pleasure; be't to fly, to swim, to dive into the fire, to ride on the curl'd clouds, to thy strong bidding task Ariel and all his quality.'" She delivered the lines perfectly and I had to stop myself from clapping. Had I been a Hollywood casting director, I would have hired her on the spot.

I took another step forward and a twig snapped under my tennis shoe. The actress's gaze snapped in my direction. "Are you spying on me?"

I blinked. That wasn't the reaction I expected.

"I'm so sorry. You delivered that speech so beautifully. I was captivated."

"Thank you," she said, mollified. "I've been working on it for months. Ariel is a very complicated role. He cares for Prospero in his way but is starved for his freedom. I know what that is like."

I wasn't even sure I wanted to ask her what she meant by that. "Well, I can see why Stacey gave you the part. You act it wonderfully."

"Stacey didn't want to give me the part. I think she wants to play all the parts herself."

"Who did you get the part from, then?" I asked.

"Professor Fullbright made her give it to me. Boy, was she mad at him when he did, too."

I rocked back on my heels. She had given me the perfect opportunity to bring up Dane, and I wasn't going to miss it. "Are you one of Dane's students?"

She cocked her head. "Yeah. How would you know that?"

"I'm Shiloh Bellamy. Stacey is my cousin, and she told me that she contacted the university about hiring students for the play. I didn't catch your name."

"Oh, I'm Paisley." She shrugged. "Stacey is okay. I mean she is a great actress, and even though she didn't want to give me the part, I still admire her. She was on Broadway. That's what I want to do, so there's a lot I can learn from her. I have to be on her good side to do that."

"It can be tricky to stay on Stacey's good side."

"You're telling me. Professor Fullbright sure wasn't. I thought she was going to gouge his eyes out at our dress rehearsal, she was so furious at him."

That was more bad news for Stacey. "What was she mad about?"

She shrugged. "Personal stuff. Everyone knew they were dating. It's *never* a good idea to date inside your company of actors. That's one example of Stacey's that I will not follow."

"That's a smart idea," I agreed. "Was it uncomfortable to know that Stacey and Dane were dating?"

She shrugged. "What do I care? I'm here because I have a job to do. I don't have time for middle-aged drama."

Middle-aged drama. Ouch.

"It's a bummer that Professor Fullbright is dead. I was really counting on a reference letter from him when I applied to an acting program in New York after graduation. He would have been the only teacher willing to do it."

From what Karla said at my booth, I had gotten the feeling that she and Dane might be romantically involved. I wasn't getting that from Paisley. She certainly wasn't brokenhearted like Slade had been over Dane's death, but then again, I knew she was a good actor.

"Someone told me that she saw you at the cherry spitting competition with Dane Fullbright, and you were with him just before he went up to the starting line."

To my surprise, she said, "I was there. I was trying to convince him to come back to the play. That old guy who took his place is okay, but he's not steady on his feet."

I didn't think it was the time to tell her that "that old guy" was my father.

"We needed Professor Fullbright for the play. He wasn't as good an actor as Stacey, but without him, the play was going to bomb." She shook her head. "I need this production to be perfect. You really never know who is in the audience. A talent agent or someone could be here on family vacation. I can't miss an opportunity to do my best."

"A talent agent will be able to pick up on your skill even if the actors around you are struggling," I said.

She narrowed her eyes at me. "How would you know?"

"I was a producer in Hollywood for many years."

She looked me up and down. I was wearing khaki shorts, a cherry-red Bellamy Farm T-shirt, and my blond hair was up in a ponytail. "What are you now?"

"A cherry farmer," I said.

She shook her head sadly. "Did you get caught up in a scandal? Was money involved? I've watched all the Hollywood documentaries."

"No," I struggled to keep the offense out of my voice. "I left by my choosing. I could still be out there if I wanted to."

"Sure. I think everyone who leaves believes that."

"I'm serious. I came home to save the family farm." I didn't know why I was defending myself to this teenager.

"Hey, it's okay, everyone has ups and downs. I'm sure you could get on a public access channel around here with your skill set. Or maybe start up a YouTube channel," she suggested.

I ground my teeth. "What did Dane say when you asked him to come back?"

"He said no and Stacey was making a big mistake that she would regret. He knew a lot about her theater, so she should be careful."

I shivered. All this time I had dismissed my cousin as the primary suspect because I knew she would never do something that would put her beloved Michigan Street Theater at risk, but what if the motive was to protect the theater? Did Dane really have dirt on the theater, or was he just saying that to Paisley to make himself look tough after being fired from the play? In any case, I had to give the possibility of Stacey as a suspect more serious thought, as much as it pained me.

"Is it true you gave Dane the cherry he choked on?"

She shrugged. "Yeah."

"You know that's what killed him, right?"

"Sure. But I didn't have anything to do with that. I just handed it to him."

"It looks bad."

"Not for me. All the cherries were on these little paper dishes and they were labeled with the person's name. I just gave him one with his name on it." She shrugged her shoulders again like it wasn't any big deal.

Thankfully, from the conversation, I was certain that Paisley wasn't romantically involved with Dane Fullbright, which is what I had feared when Karla mentioned there was a girl with him before he died. I couldn't take any more romantic entanglements in this already confusing case.

"Can you describe how the cherries were laid out?"

"I can do better than that; I took a picture of it." She tapped at her phone screen. She held it out for me to see. "I took a picture of it because I thought it was weird. Like, what does it matter which cherry you pick and pit you spit?"

"Who put the cherries out like that?"

She shrugged. "I don't know. I just handed him the one with his name on it."

"How long were they out?"

"I don't know that either."

"Can you text that picture to me?" I asked.

"If you really want it, okay." She shook her head as if she never would understand old people. I was at most twelve years older than her. I did my very best not to roll my eyes.

I gave Paisley my number, and in seconds, I had the photo on my phone. It was a photograph of a folding table covered in a red-checkered tablecloth. On the table were two lines of small paper baskets. On the side of each basket, there was a contestant's first and last name. I didn't recognize any of the names other than Dane's. In each basket was a single cherry. I zoomed in on Dane's basket and examined the cherry. I couldn't tell if it looked different from any of the others. Was this before it was poisoned? But Paisley said that she handed it right to Dane. I knew *he* didn't poison it.

"Did you take any other pictures when you were standing by the cherries?" I asked.

"Yeah."

"Can you send them all to me?"

"Okay," she said. "But I don't know why you want them. They are pretty boring."

"I'm old. I like boring," I joked.

"Makes sense," she said.

I did roll my eyes that time.

"I have to get back to the stage," Paisley said. "Enjoy the pics." She tossed her limp hair over her shoulder and walked away.

I remained under the tree and texted Milan.

"I found something." I sent the picture. "This was right before he died." I went on to tell him about Paisley and my conversation with her.

His text back read, "That means that anyone could have tampered with Dane's cherry if it was labeled and sitting out in the open like that."

"Right. We need to find out who was around the cherries before Paisley got there."

"We don't need to do anything. Chief Sterling and I need to find that out."

I shook my head. *Good luck keeping me out of this now, Sheriff.*

Chapter Fourteen

A s much as I wanted to hang around the stage and wait for Stacey to arrive, I knew I had to return to my booth. The Cherry Farm Market was open, and I was losing money not being there.

Paisley texted me five additional photos from the afternoon that Dane died. I decided to examine them when I got back to the booth.

It was nearly 10:15 a.m. by the time I made it back. There was already a line waiting for my return.

I smiled. I never expected this kind of response to my cherry products with so many other cherry farmers represented from all over the region. However, the smiled died on my face when I saw Penelope Lee Odders at the front of the line.

Penny Lee had her notepad in hand. This wasn't good.

"Hi, Penny Lee," I said brightly as I slipped into the booth and put on my Bellamy Farm apron. "Can I interest you in some of my organic cherry strudel?"

Penny Lee narrowed her eyes at me. "We aren't here for the strudel." Her tone of voice was reminiscent of a sheriff in an old western.

"Okay. Just cherries then."

"We aren't here to buy anything from you at all. We're a group of concerned citizens who want to know what happened to Dane Fullbright," Penny Lee announced.

Behind her were five other people all close to Penny Lee's age. A man who was on the shorter side folded his arms and glared at me.

"I don't know what happened to Dane," I said.

"You were the one who threw him around like he was a rag doll." The man in the back pointed at me.

Visitors to the festival walked by and avoided my booth.

"He was twice my size. I couldn't throw him anywhere," I said. "I have to ask you to leave. I'm trying to run a business."

Penny Lee shook her notepad at me. "I knew when you left our interview unexpectedly yesterday morning that you were up to something."

"I wasn't," I said. "I was late to open the booth."

"It seems you make a habit of being late to open." She checked her watch. "Where were you at ten? We have been waiting for you a full fourteen minutes and thirteen seconds."

I opened and closed my mouth. How was I going to get rid of Penny Lee and her friends?

"Excuse me. Excuse me!" my best friend, Kristy Garcia Brown, called. "Woman with twin toddlers coming through. You don't want to mess with me. I can change two diapers at the same time."

Penny Lee's gang of concerned citizens backed off.

"I need cherry jam for the twins from Bellamy Farm. Get out of my way!" Kristy shoved the stroller in front of the group. "If you're not buying anything, you can move along."

Penny Lee blinked and then she scowled at me. "I will get to the bottom of this, Shiloh Bellamy. I promise you that."

Not if I did first.

Kristy tucked a strand of black hair behind her ear. "What was that all about?"

"I thought you knew by the way you drove them off with the stroller."

She laughed. "I have no idea. I could just tell you were deep in the weeds. The look on your face is always a dead giveaway."

"What look is that?" I asked.

"The look that says you'd rather jump in the bay than be where you are at the moment."

"I must get that look a lot."

She nodded. "You have no idea."

I wiggled my fingers at the twins in greeting, and they looked up at me with their bright eyes and round cheeks. Kristy was Mexican and her husband Kent was white. The twins had their mother's dark hair and complexion, but their father's blue eyes. They could not be more beautiful. Kristy was already stressed over the high school years. She feared there would be boys lined up around the block.

"What brings you to the festival today?"

"Kent is working at the brewery all day and night, so I thought the girls and I would make an outing of coming to the festival, especially the market," she said. "It's always good to check out what the big one is doing and see what I can bring back to Cherry Glen."

Kristy was the manager of the very popular Cherry Glen Farmers Market that ran twice a week through the warmer months in the middle of town.

"The booth turned out great. You're going to use it at our market, aren't you?"

"For sure. I have to get my money's worth out of it."

"What was that all about?" Kristy asked.

I told her as quickly as I could while I got the rest of the booth ready for the day. I had my price list out, all my products, and glossy brochures about the farm with my contact information and the website on it.

"Shi, will you ever learn to sell cherries and not find dead people?"

"Apparently not."

"However, I do like one bit of this story."

"What's that?" I put single cherries in small paper cups for customers to taste test before they bought.

"You saw Sheriff Penbrook." Kristy's dark eyes brightened.

I gave her a withering look.

"Did he ask you on another date?" She hopped from foot to foot in excitement.

"I should have never told you about that."

"What you should have done was say yes and stop thinking Quinn Killian is going to get his act together."

I put my hands on my hips. "First of all, you were the one that was all gung-ho about Quinn, and second of all, that's not the reason I haven't answered Milan yet."

"Oh?" She wiggled her dark brows. "And what is the reason?"

"I—I'm busy," I muttered.

She snorted and picked up a soap sample. "This smells amazing!"

I let out a sigh of relief at the welcome change of subject. "I've been playing with the recipe. The vanilla is from store-bought organic essence, but I grew the cherries and luffa. I just had to think of something to do with the imperfect cherries. You know, the ones not good enough to go to market."

"You're a true entrepreneur, Shi."

I gave a sigh of relief. "Thanks. I'm not ready to sell them yet, but I thought I would hand out samples and see how they go over. This small box is all I have for now." I sighed. "I have to diversify to make the farm viable. I need to try as many things as possible to make money and see what sticks."

"This one will stick; I just know it," she said. "Will all the soaps have cherry in them?"

"I don't know. Since the lavender field came in so well, I could do cherry lavender or just lavender."

"Or lavender vanilla," she said. "Don't box yourself in with just cherry." She waved her hands around. "A lot of Michiganders will need a break from them after this week."

I could see that.

"Handing out samples is a great idea. You know, I will spread the word. I bet they will sell well and you can talk to Norman Perch about putting them in the general store in the Glen too."

"That is a good idea, Kristy. I hadn't thought of that."

She grinned. "I'm full of good ideas." She paused. "What I'm not good at is solving murders, and I wish you weren't either."

Chapter Fifteen

By the time Chesney arrived at the booth that afternoon, sales were back up. I was grateful that Kristy had been able to chase Penny Lee and her not-so-merry band of followers away. Where had she found those people anyway? And who were they?

I shook the questions from my head because I had enough mysteries to solve that week already. While I'd waited for Chesney, I continually checked my phone to see if Milan had texted me back when I asked him three times in a row if he made any progress. Thankfully, common sense prevailed, and I hadn't texted a fourth time.

Chesney dropped her backpack onto the grass behind the booth with a thud. I was surprised it didn't make an indent in the ground.

"What do you have in there? Rocks?" I asked.

She shook her head. "Books. Big ones. And journal articles, my laptop, and notebooks. I hope it's okay if I work on my thesis research while I sit at the booth today when it gets slow. I'm so far behind."

"Of course it's okay. Are you sure you can work today? If you need to go home and study, I understand."

"No way. I really want to be here. It's valuable for my research. I'm doing a paper on public perception of organic foods versus chemically treated foods."

"Don't most people see organic as good?" I asked, hoping that the answer was yes, because I had invested a great deal of money into Bellamy Farm so it could be certified organic. It was an expensive endeavor.

"A lot of people do, but you'd be surprised the number of people who won't buy organic because they believe it's hype or a governmental trick. Also, there are a lot of people who just can't afford it."

I wrinkled my brow. "We can't do much about the conspiracy theorists, but maybe there's some way to get our organic crops and foods to those who might want them but can't afford it. I'm sure that you can come up with some ideas."

"That would be awesome!" Chesney cried. "I'll start making some notes." She bent over and opened her backpack and pulled out a yellow notebook and pen.

"While you're making notes, do you mind if I go to the play on the Cherry Blast Stage? My father is now in the lead role, and I would love to see him."

"Wow, your dad got Dane's part?" She blinked. "Whit told me that Stacey had already filled the role, but she never said it was Sully."

I nodded.

She wrinkled her nose. "That doesn't mean he is a suspect, does it?"

"I hope not. He's not a suspect to me."

"I know that you have already discounted Stacey as a suspect too," she said. "You can't count people out just because they are relatives of yours. You have to look at all of this objectively."

"You're right," I said, but I held back what I had learned about Stacey from Paisley: the fact that Dane apparently knew something about Stacey or the theater that could ruin her business. If she heard that, Chesney would be convinced Stacey was a primary suspect. It was no secret how much Stacey cared about her business. However, it did give me the idea to ask Whit about it. If anyone else in Stacey's theater would know about something amiss, it would be the stage manager.

"I'll keep an open mind," I said and glanced down at Huckleberry, who was snoring in his bed under the booth. "Can Huck stay with you?"

He snuffled in his sleep and kicked his right rear leg. It must have been quite a doggie dream.

"Of course." She nodded. "He's an excellent study buddy."

As I made my way to the stage, I remembered the other photographs that Paisley had texted me. Finding Penny Lee at my booth had made them slip my mind.

I stepped off the path between the Cherry Farm Market and the Cherry Blast Stage and pulled out my phone. Under the shade of a tree, I flipped through the photos.

Three of the pictures were blurry, and I couldn't make out any of the faces of the people in them. Good thing Paisley was a better actor than she was a photographer. However, one of the pictures did come out clearly. Paisley had captured the paper basket with Dane's name on it. I zoomed in and looked for any evidence of powder or liquid that could have been the remnants of penicillin. I couldn't tell. To me, it didn't look any different from the billions of other cherries I had seen in my life.

In the next clear picture, I saw an arm close to Dane's paper basket. The arm was covered by a bright yellow sleeve. Who would wear long sleeves like that in this heat? I bit my lower lip. It could be a tourist from a warmer climate, but it had been eighty-five degrees with high humidity during the afternoon of the cherry spitting competition. I would have roasted in that outfit.

I looked closer at the picture. I only saw a bit of the upper arm and shoulder in the upper corner of the photo. I couldn't tell if it was a man or woman's arm. There was just the edge of a bright red patch on the person's shoulder.

"You seem to be absorbed in your phone. Are you texting a boyfriend?"

I looked up to see Quinn standing in front of me. He was wearing a Traverse City EMT T-shirt and cargo pants. His hair was brushed back from his face and it shone in the sunlight.

I tucked my phone in the back pocket of my shorts. "Is Hazel here?"

He chuckled. "No hello for me? Just looking for Hazel?"

I blushed. "Sorry. She just mentioned yesterday that you'd be home today and she'd be hanging out with you."

"Things changed," he said. "I am off from work today, but I knew the crew here could use the help, especially after yesterday. I volunteered." He sighed. "Hazel is at her grand-parents'. She wasn't happy about going, but my mother was complaining that she hadn't seen Hazel all summer. That's a bit of an exaggeration, but my daughter has been spending most of her summer at your farm."

"I don't mind," I said.

"I know." He offered me a smile. "And Hazel loves it there, but my mother doesn't love her being there, as you well know."

I did know. If Doreen Killian had her way, Hazel would never come to my farm again.

"I'm glad she's spending time with your parents. I know how much they care about her."

"That's gracious of you, considering." He smiled. "And the phone?"

"Phone?"

"Why did you look like you were solving world hunger while you were looking at it?"

My blush became even worse. "I was looking something up," I said.

He raised his brow as if to ask what I had been look-ing up, but I pretended I didn't notice. "I won't keep you," I said. "I'm sure you have somewhere you need to be." I started to leave.

"I heard that you turned Sheriff Penbrook down," he called after me.

I spun around. "What are you talking about?"

"I know he asked you out and you said no." His hands were at his sides, and for a moment, he looked like the unsure high school boy I'd known when we were young, when Logan had been the glue that held us together.

I pushed the memory to the back of my mind. Our combined memories of Logan were the biggest reason we could never be anything more than friends.

"I don't know why it's any of your business."

He shoved his hands in his pockets. "I was just curious. As your friend."

Yeah, right.

"If you really need to know, I didn't turn him down; I just haven't given him an answer yet."

The smiled dropped off his face.

Chapter Sixteen

P aisley stood in the middle of the stage next to my father, transformed. Her limp hair glistened and was full and fluffed with bright pieces of ribbon woven through it. She wore glittery eye makeup and bright blue eyelashes. Her dress was pieces of gauze sewn together in a haphazard away, but it worked.

She billowed her wings and danced around my father. "The King's son, Ferdinand, with hair up-staring—then like reeds, not hair was the first man that leaped; cried, 'Hell is empty, and all the devils are here.'"

My father wore the same long robe Dane had worn when I met him. It was almost impossible to believe that was just yesterday morning.

Dad did a decent job, but Paisley shone onstage.

"She's amazing," I heard someone whisper behind me. "Seeing her now, I know there was no part in the play for me."

The voice sounded vaguely familiar. I was sitting in the back row. When I glanced over my shoulder I saw Slade, Lily's assistant, standing with a young man in a bright yellow flight suit. There was a red cherry patch sewn on the right shoulder. It was the same patch I had seen in one of Paisley's pictures.

"Let's go," the young man said. "This is boring."

Slade nodded, even though she looked pained to leave the performance.

She took his hand and let him walk her away.

I had taken the last empty seat at the stage. It was in the middle of the last row. "Excuse me! Sorry! Excuse me!" I said as I tried to get out of the aisle as quickly and quietly as I could. By the glares I was getting from the play goers in my row, I wasn't doing a great job at either.

By the time I escaped, Slade and her young man were nowhere to be seen. When I glanced back at the play, I found Milan standing right behind me. I yelped.

Two people in the back row turned around and shushed me.

"You nearly knocked that last guy into the grass. What's the rush?" Milan asked.

"You too?" I asked as I was thinking about Quinn just sneaking up on me. Now, Sheriff Milan Penbrook was doing it too.

"Me too?" he asked.

"Never mind."

"What was the rush?"

"I saw someone, a young woman—Slade."

"Lily Fullbright's assistant."

I nodded. "Right."

"The only reason I can see that you would want to follow Slade would be because of the case," he said.

When I didn't say anything back, he sighed. "I had hoped

that you would stay out of it. Chief Sterling is a nice man and a careful cop. He would not want you involved."

"Noted," I said. "Now, do you want to know why I was following her?"

"Sure. I might not want you involved, but you do have a knack for getting people to talk."

"Sheriff, that is one of the nicest things you've ever said to me. You're going to make me blush."

"Great," he said.

I removed my phone from my pocket. "I wanted to talk to her about this photo."

He looked down at the picture. "What about it? It's the picture that you sent me already." He paused. "No wait, it's a different shot."

"Right," I said. "Do you see the sleeve?"

He removed his glasses for a closer look. "Don't tell anyone I'm at an age that I should probably be looking into readers."

I ran my fingers across my lips like I was zipping them closed and threw away the imaginary key.

"There is someone wearing a yellow jacket."

"It's a flight suit," I said. "During the play, Slade, Lily's assistant, was standing with a young man in a yellow flight suit."

"You think the individual in a flight suit had something to do with Dane's death?"

"I don't know about that, but it could be him."

"Where did they go?" Milan asked.

I shook my head. "I don't know. I lost sight of them."

"I have a hunch where we can find someone in a yellow

flight suit." He started to walk away and then glanced over his shoulder. "Are you coming?"

I hurried after him, not about to ask him why he had changed his tune and now wanted my help.

He told me anyway. "You're going to look for flight suit guy no matter what I do," he said, "so I might as well have you close so I can keep an eye on you."

I scowled at him. "I don't need a babysitter."

"Trust me, you do," he said with a teasing sound in his voice.

We walked through the park and into neighboring Clinch Park. Up ahead of us, I saw a large group of people standing in the middle of an open green.

I increased my pace. "What is this?"

"The Grand Traverse Aviation Club. They're sponsoring the air show on the Fourth of July. I remembered when you mentioned the flight suit. Any of these guys look familiar?"

Every last one of them was wearing a yellow flight suit with bright red cherry on the right shoulder. How could I possibly pick out the right person? I shook my head.

In the middle of the group of twenty or so men in yellow flight suits was an old-looking silver plane with a Captain America white star with red outline painted on the side of it. Beyond the men, a trailer was parked in the grass with the words "The Grand Traverse Aviation Club" emblazoned on the side of it.

Milan answered my unasked question. "It's a Wildcat from World War II. That one doesn't fly any longer. They just brought it in for display, but I do think they will have one flying on the Fourth." He paused. "You sure you don't recognize any of these men?"

I shook my head again. "I'm not sure I could pick out the guy Slade was with in this group if I tried. He was dressed exactly like them from the flight suit to the shoes. He was young, at most in his early twenties, so I could rule out half of them from age. However, with the ones left, I just don't know. I was more focused on his outfit than his face."

He nodded. "Let's see what we can find out."

I followed him.

A man with white hair and a drawn face stood by the plane's left wing and spoke to the group. "This is our opportunity to expand our reach. People need to know about these old planes to save them for future generations. I'm expecting all hands on deck to hand out flyers and talk to visitors about the club."

"Sam, the flight suits are kind of hot. Do we have to wear them the entire festival?" a large man to the right of the airplane asked. As if to prove his point as to how hot he was, he wiped at his sweaty forehead with a crumpled paper towel.

"I don't care if they are hot. This is how we will stand out in the crowd. You're working for something bigger than yourself. Remember that," Sam said.

"We should have gotten T-shirts made," another member of the group complained.

"T-shirts! Do you think the man in the cockpit of this plane flying over the Pacific wasn't hot?" Sam bellowed. "He was boiling and protecting our country. The least we can do is withstand a little bit of discomfort for the honor and remembrance of him and all the others like him." He cleared his throat as if he was pushing the emotions he felt back down. "Now, come forward to get your stack of flyers. Do not lose them between now and the Fourth. We don't have the funds to make more copies."

The men grumbled to themselves and got in a single file line to collect their stack of flyers from Sam. As each man stepped forward, I took a close look at him. What struck me most was there were no women in the group. I didn't know if that was by design or coincidence.

I scrutinized each face.

"I don't think he's here," I whispered to Milan. "I really don't recognize any of the faces."

"You're sure?" he whispered back.

I shook my head. "I'm not sure. Not one hundred percent."

"Remember," Sam called to the men as they were about to disperse. "Keep those flight suits on. We have to represent the club."

Low grumbles ran through the men as the meeting broke up.

Sam spotted Milan and I standing on the outskirts of the meeting and walked over to us. "Can I help you?"

"Just admiring the Wildcat. Is that F4F or F-M2?" Milan asked.

Sam's eyes lit up. "F4F. You know your planes."

"My grandfather was a Navy pilot in the fifties and sixties."

"What did he fly?"

"F4U Corsairs in Korea and then moved on to jets later."

"Oh, I have only seen one of those in action once in my life. Gorgeous plane."

"My grandfather would love what you're doing here. I wish he were still alive to see this. He knew everything there was to know about the Wildcat."

"Do you serve, too?" Sam asked.

"Army reserves," Milan answered. "Pops was disappointed that I wasn't a career navy man."

I raised my brow. I hadn't known Milan served in the armed forces. With that, I realized that there was a lot I didn't know about him… and a lot more that I wanted to know.

Sam held out his hand to Milan for a shake. "Sam Jennings."

Milan shook his hand. "Milan Penbrook." He nodded at me. "This is Shiloh."

Sam gave me the slightest nod and went back to his conversation with Milan. "I can understand your grandfather's wish for you to serve in the navy. I was a mechanic on the aircraft carriers."

"I did one tour in Afghanistan, and I went to the police academy. I was called to serve at home."

Sam raised his bushy eyebrows. "Are you a police officer now? You're out of uniform."

Milan chuckled. "It's my day off. I'm just spending some time at the festival." He winked at me, and I felt my cheeks grow hot.

"God rest his soul," Sam said. "We are grateful for your grandfather's service. We would love to have a young man like you in our group even if you're an army man." He handed Milan a flyer.

I peeked at the glossy piece of paper in the sheriff's hand. The headline read: "Join us in preserving the history of the skies!"

Sam smiled at me. "Is this your wife?"

"Oh no," Milan and I said at exactly the same time, and then we stared at each other as if we were both surprised by the other's strong reaction.

I cleared my throat. "We're just friends enjoying the festival together."

"That's a shame," Sam said. "You make a handsome couple."

I refused to look at Milan.

"Were you at the festival yesterday?" Milan asked. "I don't remember seeing this Wildcat here."

"You're right. The plane came in this morning." He frowned. "We were having some issues with the organizers. They thought the Thunderbirds Air Show on the Fourth would be enough. They just don't understand. We can't just entertain people. We have to educate the public too, or the meaning of the air show is lost. The U.S. Air Force isn't the only arm of the services with planes. The Navy also needed to be represented."

"My grandfather would have appreciated that." Milan cleared his throat. "So you all were around in your flight suits yesterday too?"

Sam scowled. "Yes, most of them were wearing their flight suits yesterday and mingling with the crowds."

This meant the bright yellow sleeve in Paisley's photograph could have been any one of the men in the aviation club.

"Someone in one of your flight suits was seen at the cherry pit spitting competition yesterday."

Sam nodded. "I'm not surprised. It's a popular event. I have no interest in it, but it would be a good place to spread the word about the club."

"You weren't there?" I asked.

He shook his head. "It could have been any of our members."

That's what I was afraid of.

"Did you hear about the man who died?" Milan asked.

Sam bristled, and his friendly demeanor shifted just a little. "I did." He cleared his throat. "It has been very nice talking to you both, but I must get back to work."

"Did you know him? Dane Fullbright?" I blurted out.

He stared at me. "I have never heard that name in my life." His eyes darted back and forth, and I knew he was lying.

I wanted to say more, but Milan grabbed my hand and squeezed it, signaling me to stop.

"It was nice talking to you," Milan said, still holding onto me. Our fingers weren't intertwined, but I still felt like my hands were burning hot and it wasn't from the outside temperature.

"You too." He walked over to another man in a yellow flight suit. "Jack, where is Cayden?" Sam asked.

Jack pulled at his gray beard. "Don't know, sir."

"Was he at the meeting?"

Jack shook his head. "Not that I saw."

The man sighed. "That kid will be the death of me." He pointed at Milan and me. "Don't have children if you can avoid it. You think they will feed you soup while you're in the nursing home, but that only happens if they don't kill you from stress before you're sixty."

I couldn't help but wonder if Cayden was the mystery guy in the flight suit with Slade.

And I couldn't stop myself from asking one more question. "Is your son wearing a flight suit too?"

He scowled. "He'd better be. I told him he had to wear one. It's good for us to be represented by the younger generations. Too many young kids want to forget the past. They don't think about the future either. Always living in the present leads to mistakes." His face clouded over.

"Would he be hanging out with a girl?"

"What girl?" Sam snapped.

"Slade?"

"Is that homewrecker here?" he bellowed. "Keep her away from my son!"

Chapter Seventeen

"H omewrecker?" I asked.

"She broke my son's heart and ruined his future. He was accepted to go to the Naval Academy right out of high school and instead he opted to stay in Michigan because of her. He stays and gets a job in Traverse City to be close to her, and then she dumps him after a year."

"Can't he go to the academy now?" I asked.

"He could, but he refuses. He insists that she will come around and wants to be here when she does. He tells me he's in love with her. What do young people know about love?"

I assumed that last bit was a rhetorical question, so I asked, "Did he say why she broke up with him?"

"He wouldn't tell me why." Again his eyes bounced back and forth. I hoped that Sam was never in a position to be a spy; he would be horrible at it.

"We're sorry to hear that," Milan said.

"Me too." Sam removed his phone from his pocket. "It was nice meeting you." He walked away.

I took a step to follow him, but Milan, who was still holding onto my hand, pulled me gently back. "We will talk to him again," he promised. "We should get you back to the festival."

I opened my mouth.

"Let's get well out of earshot," Milan whispered. "Before we speak."

Milan was silent all the way back to Open Space Park, and I was close to bursting with everything I had to say.

He stopped by the edge of the docks. "Are you breathing? Your face is all red."

"I'm trying not to talk. It's hard for me."

He chuckled. "I bet it is." He rubbed the back of his neck. "I'm helping Chief Sterling any way that I can. However, it's one thing to ask witnesses what they saw right after the incident; it's quite another to be talking to possible suspects without at least one of Sterling's officers on hand. It could ruin any chances we have if there was a court case."

"Do you think Sam Jennings is a suspect then?" I asked.

"I can't say that, but I do believe he was lying to us that he didn't know Dane or why his son and Slade broke up."

"I thought the same!" I cried.

"I thought you might, which was why I had to pull you out of there before you did something rash like accuse a man of murder with no evidence."

I folded my arms. "I wouldn't do that. That's Chief Randy's territory."

"Fair enough." He nodded. "I'll tell Chief Sterling what we learned. I'm sure there was at least one witness who noticed a man in a bright yellow flight suit hanging around the cherry pit table. When we find out who that person is, we might close in."

"Or it's another dead end," I said.

"Or that. Dead ends are the backbone of police work. You eliminate different possibilities until you come to the right conclusion. Sadly, sometimes a clear conclusion is never found."

I nodded and hoped that wouldn't be the result of this case. If it was, Stacey would be viewed with suspicion for the rest of her life. I knew what that was like. For fifteen years, I had been blamed for Logan's death. It was finally proven false, but the stress and lost sleep I suffered from the suspicion while I was still very much grieving my dead fiancé was immense.

I shook the memories away. Stacey and I might not always get along, but I wasn't going to let that happen to her. "I missed too much of the play, and I don't want to make a scene trying to find another seat. I'll have to catch one of Dad's next performances. They have two more, a matinee and one at the end of the festival to close it out."

He nodded. "That sounds like a good idea to me. Stick to cherry selling."

"This doesn't mean I'm out of the investigation," I said.

"I don't think I could keep you out, as much as I'd like to try," he replied.

Chesney and I worked through the rest of the afternoon at a good pace. Business was brisk, and all the visitors seemed to be in high spirits. It was almost possible to believe there hadn't been a murder committed here just the day before.

Chesney's younger sister, Whit, stumbled into our booth.

There were dark circles under her eyes, and she fell into one of the folding chairs. "Ches, can I use your car?" Whit asked.

Today she was in all black, from her tank top to her cargo pants. She even had on black combat boots.

"Why?" Chesney asked her sister. "We drove here separately."

"I know," the younger girl said. "But I need your SUV. Stacey wants me to take some of the extra props we aren't using back to the university. Why I have to do it today after stage-managing a full show, I have no idea. But that's Stacey."

"What is she having you take back?" I asked.

"Some crates and random stuff. I don't even know why it was all brought here. We had always planned to have a slimmed down set." She kicked a tuft of grass. "It's a lot to move. Will you help me take it over?" She gave her sister her sweetest smile.

"Whit, I have to work here and research my thesis. I can't just pick up and leave. Don't you have stagehands to help you?"

"Do you think Stacey hired extra help for me?" Whit snorted. "Come on. It's going to take me twice as long to do it alone, and I'm exhausted."

"And I'm not?" her older sister shot back.

"I have an idea," I interjected. "If it's okay with you, Chesney, I can go with Whit to the university and unload the set stuff. It will be fun to see my old stomping grounds. I attended the same university and was a film major too. I studied in the same building."

Whit stared at me. "When was that?"

"Oh, close to fifteen or so years ago."

Whit's eyes went wide. "I wasn't even in kindergarten yet." I sighed.

"That's fine with me," Chesney said. "That's really nice of you, Shiloh." She gave me a look.

"What?" I asked.

She rolled her eyes.

"Can Huckleberry stay with you?" I asked.

The little pug, who was curled up in his dog bed under the booth, lifted his head when he heard his name.

"Of course. Huck and I will be fine," Chesney said.

"Let's go," Whit said and headed for the parking lot.

When I caught up with her, I said, "We can take my truck. It will be easier than loading stuff into the SUV."

"Great. I was afraid I would have to make multiple trips even with Ches's car."

The Cherry Blast Stage was quiet. According to the program, the next performance would be a jazz band starting at eight.

"What is it we are moving?" I asked.

She pointed at a huge pile of crates, barrels, and plastic totes.

"All of that?"

"Stacey said she didn't know what direction she wanted to go with on props and costumes until she was in the setting, so she brought everything. As the stage manager, that should have been my decision, and I would have never brought so much stuff." She ran her hand through her black and yellow hair. "If I wasn't a student at the university, I would just drop it at the campus entrance and run, but I have to keep the drama department on my good side at least until graduation."

"Hey, do you all need help?" a tall young man with long brown hair called.

"Oh, wow. Yes, I didn't know that you were still here. I thought you left when everyone else did," Whit said.

"I did, but I came back to meet up with some friends."

I knew I had seen the young man before, but I couldn't place him. "I'm Shiloh Bellamy, Stacey's cousin," I said before he could make a comment about my last name.

"Oh hey," the young man said. "Is Sully your dad?"

I nodded.

He grinned. "That old guy is a hoot."

I smiled.

"I'm Eliot Cassen."

"Eliot plays Ferdinand in the play," Whit explained.

He gave a theatrical bow. "That is true."

I must have seen Eliot around the stage at one point, I thought.

"Have you come to one of the shows?" Eliot asked.

"One, but I had to leave early."

He shrugged. "Maybe you will get to come to one the other performances."

"That's what I'm hoping."

He changed the subject. "What are the two of you are doing?"

Whit explained our mission.

"My dad worked at the university," Eliot said, "so I know maintenance will help you unload there. I can help you load up here. It shouldn't take long."

I frowned. "You said your dad used to work at the university. Are you Theo Cassen's son?"

"Yeah, that's my dad. You know him?"

"I had him when I was a student there." What I didn't add was his father was close to retirement when I was a student. It was clear that Dr. Cassen waited until much later in life to have a child.

He nodded. "He was a great teacher. He loved his job."

"Are you studying drama too?" I asked.

"Here and there," he said vaguely. "I like it but haven't declared my major yet. I'm not sure being a theater major will get me a good-paying job. I don't want to teach it like my dad did. It's just too political."

I wrinkled my brow.

Whit shifted back and forth on her feet impatiently. "Let's get this over with."

"I'll grab my truck and pull it as close to the stage as I can."

A few minutes later, I was able to park my pickup under a tree ten yards from the stage. With Eliot's help, we had the back of it loaded and ready to go within twenty minutes.

I slammed the tailgate shut. "We'll have to drive slowly to make sure nothing falls out, but we should make it. It's only a few miles." I glanced at Eliot. "Where did you learn to pack like that?"

"Like I said, my dad worked at the university. I got a job there in high school with the maintenance department. Most of my time was spent moving professor and staff offices around."

"Sounds like fun," Whit said.

"It wasn't."

His blunt reply made both Whit and I laugh.

Eliot checked his watch. "I'd go with you, but my friends have already texted me asking where I was."

"It's totally okay," Whit said. "We appreciate your help. I already called maintenance and someone should be waiting for us at the loading door behind the theater."

"Cool." He waved and jogged away.

Whit shook her head. "He has way too much energy for me."

I cocked my eyebrow at her. "He's your age."

"I know. He's like a robot."

As I drove the truck at five miles per hour—because I really was scared one of the crates would roll over the side—I asked Whit, "How do you like being the stage manager at the theater?"

"I love it. It's hard work, but I'm learning a lot. Way more than I would ever learn in class. I just have one year left for my degree. If it was more than that, I might have quit. It's just not as valuable as my work for Stacey."

"I'm glad to hear you plan to finish your degree."

She slumped in her seat. "You sound like my sister. The super nerd. She's going to be in school forever. Who in the world spends that much time studying crop rotations? It's weird."

I shrugged. "Everyone has their own passions," I said.

"I guess," she replied, sounding unconvinced.

"Everything at the theater going well?"

She looked at me. "You just asked me that."

"No, I didn't." I drummed my fingers on the steering wheel. "I asked you how you liked working there."

"It's kind of the same thing."

"Not really," I argued. "I wondered if the theater was having any issues, that's all."

"Is this about the money?"

"What money?" I glanced at her and then returned my eyes to the road.

"The money that you and Stacey are fighting about. It was your grandmother's or something. She said you were keeping her from her fair share."

I took a deep breath. "I'm not keeping it from her. My father believes it should all go to him."

"She told me that her uncle would never do that to her. She says you're the one behind it."

"That's not true."

She folded her arms and leaned back in her chair. "It's what she said, and she sounded pretty sure of it. I can't see her putting her uncle in the lead role of her play if she thought he was cheating her out of her inheritance, do you?"

Now it made sense to me why Stacey was angry at me but not my father over the stocks. She thought I put him up to it. That wasn't true at all. I wanted him to agree to give her half of the money. Half was better than what we had now, which was nothing at all.

As we rolled into campus, Whit told me where to turn to drive behind the campus theater. I had been there before, but it was a long time ago.

Two men in maintenance uniforms chatted by the loading doors.

Whit hopped out of truck's cab, putting an end to our conversation, and I never did get to ask her what kind of trouble the Michigan Street Theater was in.

Chapter Eighteen

After we unloaded my truck, Whit said that she wanted to visit some friends who were on campus and would grab a ride back to her car later. As a result, I left campus with no more answers about the case but a bit more clarity as to why Stacey had been so put out with me these last few months. What I needed to do was to trap my father, Stacey, and myself all in a room together and talk it out. I never had much luck making that happen, but it was worth a shot.

I returned to the booth, and the rest of the day was happily uneventful. I didn't make any headway in the case, but Chesney and I sold so many cherries and cherry treats that it raised my spirits.

People were there to buy, and we received countless compliments on the soap samples. That made me excited to launch the new personal care side of my business. My brain was already buzzing with other things I could make, like lip balm, hand lotion, and foot scrub. As much as I wanted that all to happen, I had to focus on the job at hand, as well as my pastries and baked goods—or what was left of them. It seemed to me that I would have another long night baking in the farmhouse kitchen.

Night fell, and we were packing up the booth for the night. "Good work, Chesney. I don't know how I could do this without you."

She laughed. "I don't know how you could either."

I laughed too and picked up the empty pop bottles and food containers that we had eaten out of that day. There was a recycling can at the end of our row that faced the bay. "I'm just going to toss these and then we can load the truck."

She gave me a thumbs-up as she finished packing up our display.

I carried the trash to the end of the row, waving and smiling at other vendors as I went. This was what the National Cherry Festival was supposed to be: everyone having a good time and celebrating the region's number one crop—not murder.

Thinking of the murder brought thoughts of Stacey to mind. I shot Chesney a quick text that I would be back in a few minutes and hurried over to the Cherry Blast Stage. I just wanted to see if my cousin was still around. My father thankfully had gotten a ride home right after the play. Stacey hadn't been there when Whit and I loaded the truck a few hours before, but I wouldn't have been the least bit surprised if she came back after the jazz concert just to make sure the musicians hadn't scuffed up any of her marks on the stage.

The festival had ended at 10:00, and now it was close to 11:00 and pitch-dark out. I could still see a handful of people in the park. Everyone was moving fast on their way home. The first weekend might be over, but the festival was not. It had six more days to run, plus the Fourth of July right in the middle of the week. I just hoped I would be able to survive it.

The lampposts near the stage shone, but the stage itself was dark. I glanced around. There was no one nearby. Beyond it, a few people strolled along the beach, but they were too far away and it was too dark to make out any of their features.

There was no way Stacey would stand around here in the dark, even to double-check what mistakes someone else might have made. I turned to leave when I heard a creak like someone taking a step on the weathered platform. I spun around. The creak came again.

"Hello?" I called and put my foot on the first step leading up to the stage.

Pounding feet ran behind the curtain. Without taking a second to think, I ran up the stairs. I threw the curtain aside just in time to see someone jump off the back of the stage and run through the park.

"Hey, wait!" I called.

The figure kept running until they were out of sight. My heart was beating out of my chest as I looked around. There was an old steamer trunk on one side of the stage. I turned the flashlight on my phone to see better. Sitting on its side in the middle of the trunk was a medicine bottle. I walked over and picked up the bottle.

Behind me, the curtain was thrown aside and footsteps thundered up the stage. "Police! Freeze!"

The lights blinded me and caught me crouched over the trunk, holding a penicillin bottle with my cousin's name on it.

Chapter Nineteen

Milan came to see me at the police station. I sat in Chief Sterling's office, examining all the photographs on his walls. Most of them were of him fishing with what looked like his sons and grandsons. Everyone in the pictures looked happy and quite pleased with their catch of the day. Maybe I should tell the chief that my father was a big fisherman too. It could earn me some points.

The chief had excused himself for a moment to kindly fetch me a bottle of water just before Milan walked in. I felt like I had been talking for days.

He sat in the chair next to me. "Want to talk about it?"

"I haven't been arrested." The words came out a little shorter than I intended them to.

He waved his hand. "Oh, I know. When Chuck called me, he told me you were only here for a statement. He knows we're friends." He paused. "What happened?"

"You probably heard it from the chief."

"I did, but I want to hear your version." His voice was calm, but the hand resting on his thigh twitched ever so slightly.

I told him about the end of my day at the festival. "I didn't see the person's face as they were running away from the Cherry Blast Stage."

"That seems to be a pattern with you. You didn't see the face of the person who was in the flight suit with Slade either."

"It was dark," I said. "And I did see the face of the person in the flight suit, just not very well. Would it be better if I lied about it?"

"No," he said, placated. "Honesty is always appreciated." He adjusted his glasses on the bridge of his nose. "How are you getting home?"

I shrugged. "Chesney closed up shop. She has the extra set of keys and took my truck and Huckleberry home," I said.

I loved the fact that Chesney had been nonplussed by my revelation that I was being taken to the police station. She'd said she would leave her car in the parking lot and take my truck and Huckleberry back to Cherry Glen. She'd pick me up in my truck the next morning, and we would return to the festival. That was assuming I ever got out of this police station.

"Chesney offered to come back for me," I went on to say. "I told her not to since I didn't know how long this will take. I know she's working on her thesis at night. I don't want to keep her from her studies. Worst case scenario, I'll call an Uber to take me home."

"You're going to have an Uber drive you all the way out to your farm?"

"Sure," I said. "I used them all the time in LA."

He shook his head. "I'm taking you home." His tone left no room for argument.

Chief Sterling came back into the room with my bottle of water. He handed it to me. "Sorry it's not cold."

"It's fine. Thank you." I opened the bottle and took a gulp. "I feel better already."

"Well, I wouldn't be surprised if you weren't a little dehydrated," the chief said. "From what I have heard, you have been running all around the festival butting your nose in where it doesn't belong. You must be exhausted. It's a wonder you've sold any cherries at all with all the poking around you've been doing."

I wanted to say that I hadn't been doing that poking around on my own. Milan had been with me some of the time, but I didn't know how much the chief knew about that.

I sipped my water. "How did the police arrive right when I was onstage? I didn't call them."

"We got an anonymous tip that there was someone creeping around the Cherry Blast Stage. I took it seriously, of course. We can't take any chances after what happened to Dane Fullbright. The mayor and the National Cherry Festival folks are all up in my business telling me that the festival must continue without any more issues. I sent two of my officers there, and they found you." He walked around his desk and sat down.

"I wasn't the one creeping around," I said.

"They said you were crouching like you were hiding. That sounds creepy to me."

"I was bent over because I was looking at something."

"This?" He set the medicine bottle in a plastic evidence bag on the desk. It was the same one that I had found on the steamer trunk, the same one that had my cousin's name on it.

The chief studied my face. "You were holding it when my officers found you."

"I was." There was no point in denying it. "I found it on the steamer trunk." I squeezed the water bottle so tight in my hand it made a crackling sound. "Am I in trouble for that?"

"It does look suspicious, but Sheriff Penbrook has vouched for you. You're not under arrest, but this does shine an unflattering light on your cousin."

I knew that all too well. I glanced at Milan with questions in my eyes. What had he said to the police chief?

The chief nodded at the bottle. "It seems to me that we have to pick Stacey Bellamy up and bring her in again for another chat. Maybe she can shed some light on why this bottle was backstage."

"Maybe she was sick and was keeping it secret to avoid having to cancel the show," I offered. Even to my own ears, my reasoning sounded like a stretch.

"The date on the bottle is February," the police chief said. "And there are only two pills inside."

"You think Stacey used it to kill Dane?" I looked from Milan to Chief Sterling and back. "That's ridiculous."

"The evidence is irrefutable. Her name is literally on the bottle," Chief Sterling said. "I would be a fool to disregard it."

I cleared my throat. I had finished my water at this point, and my throat was still terribly dry. "She would never do that. Her play would be at too great a risk. It could jeopardize her theater too. You don't understand how much she loves the Michigan Street Theater. It's her whole world."

The chief shook his head. "I admire your family loyalty."

"I'm telling you someone planted that bottle backstage," I said. "Stacey would have never been so dumb as to leave it there. If she were to kill someone—and I can assure you she never would because she has too much to lose—she wouldn't make a mistake like that. She's a planner."

"So you say she premeditates," he said.

"Not murder!"

Milan placed a hand on my arm. I hadn't realized I was raising my voice.

"Shiloh," the chief said. "I really do appreciate your perspective, but I do wonder something."

I knit my brow together. "What's that?"

"Why are you so dead set on protecting your cousin when she is determined to run your family farm into the ground?"

I had no way to respond to that.

"What do you mean, Chief?" Milan asked.

Chief Sterling leaned back in his chair. "From our investigation into Stacey Bellamy, we have learned that she is having a dispute with Shiloh over their grandmother's money. From what I understand, your grandmother died over fifteen years ago. That's a long time to be fighting over money."

I managed to speak. "It's recently discovered money, and I'm not fighting with her over it. It's a misunderstanding."

"Not from what I hear," Chief Sterling said and leaned forward, placing his elbows on his desk. "Are you sure you want to go to all this trouble for someone who treats you so badly? Because I can assure you when I interviewed her, she had nothing kind to say about you."

My chest ached, and I had nothing more to say.

A few minutes later, I signed my statement about what I had seen that night on the Cherry Blast Stage and left the police station with Milan.

We walked into the parking lot, and I could see just the edge of the park that surrounded Boardman Lake. It was a large recreational lake and park with great trails. When I was a college student and Logan came up to visit me, we walked those trails often. I hadn't been back since he died.

Milan unlocked his truck and opened the passenger side door for me. I thanked him and climbed in.

As soon as he closed his door, I said, "Tell me the truth. Do you think Stacey did this?"

He glanced at me as he started the truck. "I don't know."

He might as well have said yes.

Chapter Twenty

M ilan parked his truck next to the farmhouse, and I opened my door. "Thanks for showing up at the police department for me," I said. "I'm sure you have work piling up in your own county."

"Some," he said with a shrug. "But most of that has to do with boats speeding on Torch Lake and expired fishing licenses. It's nothing my deputies can't handle for a few hours without me."

I was about to hop out when the farmhouse's back screen door slammed open. My father shuffled out on his walker. He must have been in a rush to get outside if he was willing to use the walker. He hated it even more than his cane.

I jumped out of the truck and ran over to help him down the two steps to the grass.

As I reached out my hand to him, he brushed me away. "I got it. I got it. You treat me like a child sometimes, Shiloh."

I bit the inside of my lower lip.

A car door slammed, and Milan walked over to us. "Good evening, Sully."

Dad eyed Milan. "Sheriff Penbrook," he said. "What did Shiloh do this time to get a ride home from the police?"

"She's not in trouble," Milan replied.

My father snorted. He turned back to me. "I, for one, am glad to see that you're finally home. I would have been nice to know where you were. I called Quinn to ask him if he knew anything. He's been out looking for you."

"Looking for me? Why didn't he just call or text me? Why didn't you, for that matter?"

"We tried," Dad said. "But you didn't pick up."

My face grew hot as I recalled I'd turned the sound off on my phone when I went into the police station. "I'm sorry, Dad. Chesney knew where I was. I should have asked her to let you know."

"Where's the pug?" Dad looked at my feet as if he expected Huckleberry to be right there.

"He must still be at Chesney's. Since she didn't know what time I'd be back, I'm sure she took him home. I'll text her to make sure."

Huckleberry stayed with my assistant during the few times a year that I had to travel and couldn't take him with me. He always came back from her house a tad bit heavier and a whole lot lazier. Chesney and Whit didn't expect much of the pug when he was there.

I sent Chesney a message and received a text immediately telling me that Huckleberry was with her and they were enjoying a frozen pizza together, just as a truck's headlights came bouncing down the drive. The truck screeched to a stop next to Milan's pickup.

Quinn jumped out of his truck. "What is going on?" He addressed the question to me. "Shiloh, where have you been?

Why didn't you answer your phone?" He pointed at Milan. "Was it because you were with him?"

"Do you want me to run to Chesney's and get Huckleberry?" Milan asked. His voice was mild, but I noticed how his eyes narrowed when Quinn arrived.

I shook my head. "No, he will be fine for the night. He's living his best life."

"In that case, I should head home. It was nice to see you, Mr. Bellamy." He nodded at Quinn. "Killian."

Quinn scowled at him. "Penbrook."

Dad shuffled back to the steps on his walker. "Well, if that's done, I'm going back into the house. I have a historical society meeting tomorrow. Since no one in this town knows a lick of history, I have to go in there ready to fight. I'm glad to have a few days off from the play. It's rough on these old bones. Shiloh, do you know where my Epsom salts are?"

"They're on your bathroom counter, Dad."

"Good. I'll give my feet a good soak in the morning." He went back into the house and the let the screen door bang shut behind him.

Quinn stood two yards from me, his chest heaving.

"Where is Hazel?"

"She's spending the night at my parents' house." He glared at me.

"Are you okay?" I asked.

"Am I okay? No one knew where you were. I thought for sure you had been attacked."

I cocked my head to one side. "Because I didn't answer my phone?"

"Do you not understand that someone has been murdered? And you asking questions about it makes you a
target?"

"I do understand that," I said. "But this isn't my first
investigation. Why are you acting so overprotective now?
Hazel wasn't with me today, and I can very well take care
of myself."

"Or Penbrook can take care of you," he muttered.

I glared at him. Quinn was my friend, but as far as I was
concerned, he already had his shot to be anything beyond
that. He passed on the chance, so he was not in the position to tell me who I should be friends with...or date. I
stopped myself from saying any of this to him. Taking a deep
breath, I said, "If you have to know where I was, I was at
the Traverse City Police Station giving a statement, which
is why I couldn't answer my phone. Sheriff Penbrook was
kind enough to give me a ride home since Chesney left in
my truck with Huckleberry. I didn't know how long I would
be, so I didn't want them to have to wait for me."

Quinn seemed to consider this.

When he didn't say anything, I went on, "If that's all, I'm
going to bring in the sheep and go to my cabin for the night.
It's been a very long day."

"I'll go with you to bring in the sheep."

"You don't have to," I said.

"Please let me. I don't like the idea of you walking around
the farm in the dark by yourself."

His comment was laughable. Half of the time, I was walking around the farm after dark by myself; this was especially

true on shorter winter days. The chores had to be done whether the sun was shining or not.

"All right," I agreed and turned toward the orchard.

In two paces he was walking next to me. I stayed quiet. The truth was even though I was annoyed with him, I was glad that he was there. I was shaken up about what I had found onstage and worried for Stacey, even if she said what Chief Sterling said she did

The sheep were waiting by the edge of the electric fence. By the looks of it, they had been ready to go back to the barn a while ago.

Panda Bear was at the forefront of the little flock and baaed at me like he was encapsulating the frustration of himself and all his ladies.

"I'm sorry, Panda Bear and girls. I really thought I would have been home sooner."

Panda Bear baaed at this too, as if to tell me that was exactly what I should have done.

I turned off the fence, opened the gate, and let the sheep out. "All right. To the barn with all of you."

They baaed as one and started walking toward the path that led to the barn by the farmhouse.

As I closed the fence up for the night, a flash of light at the far end of the orchard gave off a soft glow. It was as if someone was in the orchard and was looking at their cell phone.

"Hello?" I called into the orchard. "Who's there?"

The light went out. I shivered. Had it been real?

"Shi, what's wrong? Did you see something?" Quinn's voice was elevated.

I stared again into the orchard. "No, it was just a flicker of light. It might have just been a lightning bug. I'm getting used to seeing them again. I never saw them in LA."

Quinn looked like he didn't quite believe me. I didn't blame him. I didn't quite believe myself either.

Chapter Twenty-One

The next morning, Esmeralda and I led the sheep back to the orchard. It felt odd to be walking around the farm in the morning without Huckleberry. We had just been apart one night, but I really missed my little pug. And I was dead tired. I had stayed up until three in the morning baking more goodies for the booth. Next year, if I got into the Cherry Farm Market again, I would plan ahead a little better.

Esmeralda also seemed to be a little down in the mouth with Huckleberry away too.

As we followed the sheep into the orchard, I said, "You miss Huckleberry too?"

She looked up at me with disdain and flicked her tawny tail back and forth before making a 180 and marching away.

She missed him. I knew it.

While the ewes got right down to business trimming the weeds, Panda Bear waddled over to me for some head scratches.

"You're a sweet boy," I told the bundle of wool.

He closed his eyes in bliss.

Across the orchard, I heard Esmeralda yowl.

"Esmeralda!" I ran to her with Panda Bear and the ewes right behind me. I gasped when I found the little part Siamese cat's tail caught in a snare. "Oh my goodness!" I fell to my knees next to her.

She was tugging hard on her tail, and it only made the snare tighter. I placed my hand on the back of her neck to calm her and, as carefully as I could, I removed her tail from the snare. The lucky thing was she was a long-hair cat and most of her tail was fur. A good amount of fur got caught on the snare, and she had a bald spot on the right side, but the wire hadn't broken the skin. There wasn't even a red mark. Even so, Esmeralda was livid.

She hissed for all she was worth and bolted to the gate. She stopped just on the other side of the electric fence and began licking her tail as if her life depended on it. It worried me that she might actually be hurt.

The sheep watched with dumbfound expressions. I can't say I blamed them. I knew I looked the same way.

There was no way I was leaving the flock in the orchard if there was a chance there were other snares or traps for them to wander into. I clapped my hands at Panda Bear. "Back to the barn."

He stared at me, and after I made some shooing motions, he seemed to understand what I was getting at because he walked out of the orchard. The four ewes followed him.

When I was through the fence, I looked behind me. Nothing seemed to be amiss in the orchard. Ten yards away, I saw the property line for Tanner's farm. He wouldn't hurt my animals, would he? I shivered and felt sad it had gotten to the point that I was suspicious of my neighbor. But I couldn't think of another person who would care in the least what I did in the orchard.

Unless it was related to Dane Fullbright's murder. I frowned as the idea crossed my mind.

What other possibilities did I have? Could a trapper have dropped the snare while moving through my land or even placed it there in hopes of catching a rabbit? But that didn't make any sense at all. The trapper would have to know he was trespassing. It wasn't like the farm was close to any public lands or hunting areas. Furthermore, it wasn't hunting season.

The snare looked new, and I was certain I would have seen it if it had been in the orchard for any long period of time. Chesney and I were both meticulous about checking the orchard several times a week. The cherry trees were the future of the farm. Without them, Bellamy Farm didn't stand a chance.

Esmeralda was still licking her tail as if she was personally insulted by the incident.

I tentatively walked over to the cat. "Hey girl, let's go back to the farmhouse. You can spend the day like a house cat." I bent to pick her up.

She hissed at me with all the rage her little body could muster. I ignored her and scooped her up. I thought she might scratch me, but to my surprise, she stopped struggling.

I carried Esmeralda back to the farmhouse. She lay in my arms as if she was the perfect lap cat. The sheep walked behind me, and we made our way back to the barn. There was a small pen to the left of the barn that Chesney had built. It was a good place for the sheep to be in times of bad weather. They could let themselves back into the barn if necessary.

Panda Bear led his ladies into the pen. Holding Esmeralda in one arm, I closed the gate behind them.

Just as I latched the gate, my truck came up the driveway. Chesney was behind the wheel, and Huckleberry's little snub nose was pressed up against the passenger side window as if he couldn't wait to jump out and greet me.

Esmeralda fought in my arms, and I set her down as gently as she would allow.

Huckleberry leapt over Chesney's lap and galloped to his best cat friend. Esmeralda yowled in his face, and he nuzzled her with his flat nose.

"What happened to her tail?" Chesney asked when she climbed out of the truck.

I held up the snare that still had a bit of the cat's fur attached to it.

"What is that?" Chesney's green eyes were huge behind her glasses.

"A snare. It was in the orchard. Poor Esmeralda walked right into it."

"How did it get there?"

"I have no idea."

"It wasn't there when I did my last walk through the orchard over the weekend. I would have seen it. I'm very thorough," Chesney said.

I dropped the snare to my side. "I know that you are. All I can think is someone put it there to hurt the sheep."

Chesney shivered. "That's awful. Who would do that?"

I was reluctant to share my thoughts on Tanner. It wasn't fair to share his name with anyone, even Chesney, when I had zero proof. I knew he was upset that his side of the old Bellamy Farm didn't have an orchard, but I had never known him to go this far to sabotage anything. A snide comment here and there was the worst I had ever received from him.

"I don't know. Maybe it was a trapper?"

"Way off course," Chesney said. "I mean, the way the trees are lined up, it's clear that it's private property and a working farm. Not to mention the fencing around the orchard."

I thought about the light I saw—or thought I saw—the night before in the orchard. Could that have been someone setting the trap or the moonlight catching the metal wire? I shivered. Now, I wished that I had investigated it more fully, no matter how tired I might have been at the time.

"What if it's related to the murder at the festival?" she asked in a worried voice.

I twisted my mouth. "That crossed my mind, but it just seems like the killer would have to go pretty far out of their way to come to my farm. Also, I don't know how this would be meant to scare me off the case. There would be a very good chance that I would never make the connection between the murder at the National Cherry Festival and my sheep being injured."

She folded her arms. "In any case, I think you should report it to the police."

I shook my head. "Can you imagine what Chief Randy would say? He'd just dismiss it, or worse."

She sighed. "I guess, but I think we both have to keep our eyes out more for a few weeks."

I nodded. "Panda Bear and the ewes have done a good job keeping the weeds and grass down around the cherry trees. I think we should keep them closer to the barn for the next couple of days until we know more."

"Agreed." She gave a curt nod.

The back screen door opened, and my father stood on the stoop. Esmeralda ran over to him and meowed for all she was worth as she rubbed against his legs. She made sure that he saw the bald spot on her tail.

"Shiloh Bellamy, what did you do to that poor cat?"

I sighed.

Chapter Twenty-Two

Even though Chesney was kind enough to drive my truck to the farm, she couldn't ride back with me to the festival as we planned. She had more work on her thesis to do and then a group presentation she had to work on with some of her classmates in the afternoon. Since she worked better at home, she was going to have Whit drive her into Traverse City later in the day.

There were no more play performances at the festival until Thursday, so Whit had the day off.

After dropping Chesney off at home, I decided to pop in at Jessa's Place to see what the latest gossip in town was and how much of it pertained to me. I also had a handful of soaps I made over the last several weeks. I thought Jessa would be the perfect person to give the soap a test since she washed her hands so many times during a day.

The bell over the glass door rang as Huckleberry and I walked inside. Every face in the room turned to see who it was and the whispering began.

Hazel was sitting at a stool at the high counter in the back of the diner. She waved at me.

"What are you doing here?" I asked as I glanced around the room for any signs of Quinn or perhaps his mother.

"Waiting for my grandmother. She's next door at the beauty parlor."

"The beauty parlor is open? It's not even nine yet."

"It's open for my grandmother," Hazel said.

I raised my brow.

"Grandma doesn't want anyone to know that she dyes her hair," Hazel explained. "So the hairdresser opens early for her."

"She's almost seventy. I would be surprised if she didn't dye her hair."

Hazel shrugged.

"Where's your dad?" I asked.

"He just started a new twenty-four-hour shift, so I'll be at my grandparents'. I wish I could be with you at the National Cherry Festival, but my grandparents threw a fit over it, considering the dead bodies and all."

I could imagine. "Dead *body*. There was just one."

"Right. I'm just glad my grandma lets me sit in here while she gets her hair done. The smells in the salon give me a headache, and all Grandma and Mary Jean do is talk about everyone in town. They especially like to talk about you."

"Terrific," I said.

"Shi, what'll you have?" Jessa asked as she buzzed by.

"Just a coffee for the road," I said. "I'm on my way to the festival. I have to say I'll be glad when it's over. It's wearing me out. Selling and smiling all day, and then baking all night to restock what we sold. It's lucrative but draining. I would rather be on the farm with my sweet sheep and terrifying chickens." Huckleberry made a snuffling sound at my feet. "And my loyal pug of course."

"I wish I could go to the festival," Hazel said with a sigh. "We really have to find this killer."

Jessa's eyes went wide. "For land's sakes, don't let your grandfather hear you say that. He'll string Shi up by her toes from the Sherman tank."

I grimaced. The Sherman tank was a retired military tank from World War II. It had been donated to the town decades ago and stood just at the entrance of downtown. I didn't know if its location was chosen as a welcome or deterrent. "That was a very specific visual, Jessa," I said.

She shrugged. "I read a lot." She disappeared into the kitchen. A moment later, she returned with a tray full of eggs, bacon, and French toast. All of it smelled heavenly, and my mouth watered.

Get a hold of yourself, Shi, I told myself. Eating when I was stressed was never a good idea. It would start with one piece of bacon, and the next thing I knew, I would be seated at the counter with the Monday breakfast special.

Huckleberry snuggled next to the pie case and waited patiently for Jessa to notice how hungry he was. He lay on side with his legs splayed out as if he didn't have the will to go on.

Jessa pointed at him without missing a beat while she served her customers. "He might not be much of an attack dog, but he is a smart little devil."

"Especially when it comes to food." I chuckled.

She pointed at the box in my hand. "What do you have there?"

"I wanted to show you something I made and get your opinion," I said.

She waved us over to the counter. Hazel spun on her stool. I smiled. I remembered doing that a thousand times when I was a kid and would come into the diner with my grandmother.

I set the box on the counter and opened it. Reaching inside, I pulled out one of the bars of Luffa cherry vanilla soap wrapped in brown paper. I unwrapped it and handed it to Jessa.

She picked it up and smelled it. "This is nice. You made it?"

I nodded. "I thought it would be a good use for the cherries that I can't sell. The ones that are irregular in size, bruised, or a bit odd looking."

"That's what I like about you, Shiloh. You are always thinking just like me. We lady entrepreneurs need to stick together."

"I agree," I said. "Anyway, I was wondering if you could test it in the diner. See how it holds up through the day from a lot of use."

"I'd be happy to. Sure smells better than the cheap soap I buy at Costco when I go into Traverse City once every six months for supplies. I'll feel downright fancy using it." She turned to Hazel. "What do you want for breakfast, sweetie?"

"Nothing with cherries," Hazel said. "Maybe a breakfast sandwich with bacon."

"Tired of cherry-flavored food?" Jessa asked her with a wink.

"So tired. Do you know what I ate when I was at the festival?" Hazel didn't wait for Jessa to answer. "A cherry scone, cherry barbeque ribs, and a hamburger with cherry ketchup. I don't think I can ever eat cherries again."

"Don't say that," I said. "Cherries are my cash crop."

"I'm happy to help you grow them and sell them; just don't make me eat them."

"Fair enough," I said.

"Jessa, I could use a warm-up." An old farmer held his white coffee mug up in the air.

"Hold onto your hat, Jimbo. Can't you see I am having an important conversation?"

Jimbo lowered his mug and the other old farmers at his table laughed. No one pushed Jessa's buttons if they wanted her coffee, and her coffee was very good. Not to mention the diner was the only place to get coffee this time of day on a Monday aside from a person's own kitchen.

Jessa shook her head and picked up the coffeepot from the counter, handing it to me. "Shiloh, do you mind walking around and warming up their mugs while I make Hazel some pancakes? I'm making a breakfast sandwich for you and sausage for Huckleberry."

"Please don't; coffee is fine."

She gave me a look. "Fine is not good enough when you come to my diner." She walked through the swinging door into the kitchen.

Hazel spun on her stool at the counter, and I could hear

Huckleberry sigh from the other side of the room. He was getting a wee bit impatient waiting for his treat. At the moment, the revolving pie case beside him didn't have any pies in it. Jessa never revealed which flavored pies she made for the day until after the breakfast rush at 10:30 a.m. Many times townsfolk came in the diner just to see what the flavor of pie was. It was a brilliant marketing strategy. "You have to hold them in suspense. That's how you keep them coming back," she would always say.

I supposed that was true, and I wondered how I could apply it to my farm and other businesses. It was tricky as a new business to keep customers in suspense and at the same time deliver what they wanted. That wasn't so much a problem for Jessa because everyone wanted pie.

I checked the time on my cell phone. Huckleberry and I needed to be on the road in ten minutes if we wanted to arrive before the Cherry Farm Market opened for the day. I knew that Jessa would be fast, and I had to admit, just the smell in the diner had made me hungry.

I walked around with the coffeepot, starting with the vocal Jimbo. I warmed up his cup, and the three other old farmers at his table all held up their own mugs. It had always been my opinion that no one could drink coffee like a farmer. I knew there was a very good chance the mugs I was filling were their fifth cups of the day.

I was filling a cup when Jimbo cleared his throat. "I heard that you might have killed a man at the festival. What is this, your fourth dead body?"

I stared at him. "What?" All the while I was still pouring the coffee.

"I heard that you killed a man."

"Jimbo, you old coot," one of his friends said. "It wasn't her. It was the other Bellamy girl who killed the man. You know, the pretty one who owns the theater."

"That's right."

"Miss, miss…" I half heard the old man whose coffee mug I was filling, but I was too startled by this conversation to pay him any mind.

"Where did you hear this?" I asked.

"Oh, well, everyone coming home from the festival is saying so, and the Traverse City police were at the theater yesterday. You can imagine how Chief Randy took that. He sure hates to have any other cops on his turf."

I knew that all too well.

"Miss!" the old man cried, but it was too late. The coffee was spilling over the sides of his mug. It happened just in time for Chief Randy to waltz into the diner and witness another mess I'd made.

Chapter Twenty-Three

Chief Randy hooked his thumbs on his duty belt and took in the scene. He was a tall man and a little on the thicker side, with his belly hanging well over his belt buckle. His ever-present aviator sunglasses sat in the breast pocket of his uniform, and what hair he had left stood in tufts on the top and sides of his head.

Hazel jumped off her stool. "Grandpa!"

While Chief Randy was distracted, I set the coffee carafe on an empty table a few feet away and hurried to the counter to grab a roll of paper towels. I placed the wadded-up paper towels down on the growing puddle. "I'm so sorry. I can't believe that I did that. Did any get on you?"

"No, ma'am," the old fella said. "And don't you worry about it."

I finished cleaning up the mess and threw away the soiled paper towels just in time for Chief Randy to walk over and see what all the commotion was about.

"What do you have going on over here, Shiloh Bellamy? You working at the diner now? Can't make ends meet at the farm?"

His rapid-fire questions set my teeth on edge just like they always did, but I held back any smart retorts because Hazel was still holding on to the chief's arm and smiling up at him.

Hazel may not like going to her grandparents' house because she hated her grandmother's endless list of rules, but she dearly loved both of her grandparents. That was especially true for her grandfather, Chief Randy. I never wanted to say anything that would disparage him in front of her.

Unfortunately, the police chief and his wife didn't feel the same way about me.

"The farm is doing fine," I said. "I stopped by the diner for breakfast on the way to National Cherry Festival."

Chief Randy's bushy eyebrows wove together on his forehead. "You're taking Hazel to the festival?"

"Not today." I swallowed and glanced at the swinging kitchen door. If Jessa could return with our food so Huckleberry and I could get out of there, that would be great.

"Dad said I'm staying with Grandma today, but I'll go to the festival if the two of you are busy." Her voice was hopeful.

The chief looked down at his granddaughter. "I don't know if that's such a great idea. A man was murdered there."

"Oh, I know!" Hazel interjected. "We were there when he died."

"You were what?" His eyes nearly bugged out of his head.

"Yep, and Shiloh gave him the Heimlich. We didn't know he was poisoned. Everyone thought he was choking. She was the only one who did anything about it. Can you believe that? She's a hero."

"I can certainly believe Shiloh jumping in where she doesn't belong. Not so sure about the hero bit." He let go of his granddaughter's arm and scowled. "That city chief didn't tell me you all were involved when he barged into my town to visit the Michigan Street Theater." He locked eyes with me. "To visit your cousin who is the killer."

"See, see, everyone is saying that she's the killer," Jimbo crowed from his seat.

I glanced at the men at the table, and they were all watching our conversation closely. One of them turned up his hearing aid.

Thankfully, Jessa came out of the kitchen with a large brown bag of food and a drink carrier. "What is all the fuss out here? I leave the floor for five minutes and I hear arguments." She eyed Jimbo. "You had better not have started this."

The old man held up his mole-speckled hands. "It wasn't me."

It kind of was Jimbo, but I wasn't going to out him to Jessa. She would cut off his supply of coffee for the rest of the day, and that was just too cruel.

"Hazel is telling me she wants to go to the National Cherry Festival with the cousin of a killer," the chief said.

Jessa frowned at him. "Her name is Shiloh. My word, Chief Randy, can you work on your manners?"

"She's not going. It's too dangerous," the chief said with a pout.

"We already know that," Jessa said. "Now stop getting your drawers all in a bunch and sit down for your breakfast. I have chicken fried steak and gravy this morning."

The chief's face softened. He really loved Jessa's chicken fried steak. "Hazel will have a better time with us. Doreen said she was planning on doing some grocery shopping today." He nodded at his granddaughter. "You could help her clip coupons before she leaves."

Hazel's eyes went wide. "Maybe *we* can go to the festival. You, Grandma, and me."

I did my very best to hide my grimace. That sounded like a terrible idea.

He squished his big eyebrows together again. "That's not a bad idea. It's slow around here today with everyone caught up with the goings-on in Traverse City." He rubbed his chin. "And maybe I should return the favor to that old chief and just show up on his doorstep. I bet he wouldn't like it much either."

"You should," Hazel said confidently.

Jessa handed me the brown paper sack of food that looked like it held a lot more than one breakfast sandwich for me and sausage for Huckleberry. She then gave me a drink carrier with an orange juice and black coffee. "You'd best be on your way." She ushered me toward the front door. "Get out before the chief follows you all the way to the festival," she whispered.

I thanked her and called Huckleberry to come with me.

The little pug could smell the sausage and was already on his feet. I didn't need to ask him twice.

As I drove away, Doreen came out of the beauty parlor. Her curls were tightly set, and she glared at me for all she was worth.

Chapter Twenty-Four

I ate the breakfast sandwich on the drive to Traverse City, and Huckleberry enjoyed his sausage. The pug licked his lips, then stuck his head in the food bag sitting between us just to double check what else might be in there.

I took the bag away from him. "Jessa tucked some of her apple hand pies in there. We are saving them for later."

He whined.

"I like the idea of pie for breakfast too, but we have to do better. After the festival, you and I will have to go on our healthy diet. No diner food for me and no table scraps for you."

He buried his face under his paw as if to say that was the worst possible punishment he could imagine. In Huckleberry's world, it probably was. He rolled on his side like he was too overwhelmed by this news to go on.

"You're spoiled," I said.

He sighed and closed his eyes. He was definitely going to take a nap under the booth when we got there. If he didn't fall asleep before we even reached Traverse City.

I sipped my coffee and realized the encounter at the diner would have been the perfect time to tell Chief Randy about the snare that had trapped Esmeralda in my orchard. I had been too distracted to mention it. Also, I still wasn't sure I wanted to report the incident to the police. I didn't know for a sure if a crime had been committed.

In the back of my mind, I knew that wasn't true. The snare hadn't been there the last time I walked to the back of the orchard two days before.

When I reached the booth, I immediately missed Chesney being there. I was running late as usual, and if my farm director had been available that day, the booth would have already been perfectly put together and ready for business.

Since I was the one responsible for getting the booth up and running, I would be lucky to have everything out for opening time.

It took me several trips to unload my truck, and I was walking back to the booth with the last load when my heart stopped. There was someone inside my booth.

I dropped the cart handle. "Hey!"

A face popped out of the cherry basket. "Hi!"

I blinked. "Kristy? What are you doing here?"

"Chesney called me. She said that you might need some help today, and since she couldn't be here, she asked me if I had the time. It's not a market day in Cherry Glen, so of course I have the time."

I picked up the handle of the cart and rolled it over to the booth. "Where are the twins?"

"At my in-laws," she said as she flicked her black ponytail over her shoulder. "They have been begging to have a day with them all summer, and Mama needs a break."

"Working at the National Cherry Festival is a break?"

"Shi, you have clearly never been a mother. Going to the dentist by yourself is a break. Not being around toddlers for ten minutes is a break. Just be warned, if you ask me for a snack, I might lose it."

"Noted." I stepped into the booth. All my wares, from the cherries themselves to the baked treats, were perfectly displayed.

"You did all this while I went back to the truck?" I blinked. It looked so much better and more lovingly placed than I would have been ever able to do. She even has my handmade soap out on display.

"Those are samples. They aren't for sale," I said.

"You need to sell these soaps. You gave out samples yesterday to get the word out, and now it's time to make money."

"Okay," I said with sigh, but I was quite happy with Kristy taking over. I was still more than a little bit shaken by Esmeralda's entanglement with the snare and my encounter with Chief Randy at Jessa's. I told myself that all I needed to do was take a deep breath and focus on selling and stop worrying about murder. That was easier said than done. However, with Kristy jumping in to help, I felt like the day really had the potential to turn around.

"Thank you so much for coming. Chesney was right. I really could use the help, and everything looks perfect. You really have an eye for product display."

She grinned. "Thanks. I'm pretty happy with it." She peeked into the cart and began unloading more muffins and cookies. "And I'm so proud of you. Having a booth at the

National Cherry Festival just one year after you came back to Michigan is no easy feat. It's proof that you're making it work and that you are saving the farm."

"The festival is intense," I admitted. "But you're right. I know what a big deal it is."

"It's a big deal for Cherry Glen too. It will bring more people to our local farmers' market because you're here. Do you know that Bellamy Farm is the first farm from Cherry Glen to be invited to participate in the festival in over twenty-five years? Many have tried, but until now, no one was up to the festival's standards. It's a real boon to you but also to the community as a whole."

"I hadn't realized that it had been that long since anyone from Cherry Glen was in the festival."

"It's not easy to get in. It seems like every year, the festival has more and more rules. Since your farm has been certified organic, that definitely gave you a leg up. I know Tanner tried too."

The hairs of the back of my neck stood on end. "He tried this year?"

She nodded. "He asked me to write a reference letter for him just like you did."

"And did you?" I asked.

She shrugged. "Sure. The more farmers from Cherry Glen who do well, the better the farmers' market will be."

I nodded and wondered if I should tell her about what happened when I went to my orchard that morning.

"He's been certified organic a few months longer than you, but what it really came down to was he doesn't have enough cherries to sell." She took a breath. "He planted trees, but as you know, it takes years for the young trees to really take hold."

I nodded. "I did have a head start since the orchard was on my father's side of the farm not my uncle's."

She nodded. "Besides, the baked goods you make with the cherries really gave you a leg up. As far as I know, he didn't have anything value-added like that."

I frowned. It seemed more and more likely that Tanner would have a reason to hurt my farm. For the last year, we had been in competition with each other, but I never thought that it would go any farther than some awkward conversation over the property line.

A woman came up to the booth. "Do you have any soap? I stopped by here yesterday to smell it, but you were all out."

Kristy stepped forward. "We are so glad that you came back. The soap is a brand new product. We are thinking of doing a whole line."

The woman held the soap up to her nose. "I love the smell. Oh, you should. This would make a fabulous hand lotion too."

"We love that idea," Kristy said.

"I'll buy two bars," the shopper said. "I know my daughter will love this as much as I do. I wish you had more to buy for my friends too, but I don't want to hog it all."

I smiled. "We hope to have it up on our website by the end of the month. We just have to ramp up production." I handed her one of my business cards. "The website is listed there."

After she left, Kristy said, "Shi, this soap idea is great. A skin care line could be amazing for the farm."

"I wasn't thinking full skin care. I'm not a chemist. I'm not even sure I could pull off a lotion."

"You need to see the big picture, Shi," Kristy said.

"I believe that I should scale modestly until we find our footing. I don't want to make the same mistakes my dad did with the farm."

She sighed. "Fine, but when you get that money from your grandmother, you can scale faster."

That was assuming that Stacey and my father could come to an agreement without continually putting me in the middle. However, I had a more urgent plan for the inheritance than just jumping into a new sales market, and that was paying my debts and my father's debts, both of which were considerable as we struggled to keep the farm in operation. Once I paid off all the debt, it would be tempting to put the rest of the money in the bank under lock and key where I knew it was safe. However, I knew from my years in Hollywood that you had to spend money to make money. I hoped I didn't have to spend all of it and land back where I started.

Business was brisk at the booth, and before too long my stomach was growling, reminding me that it was well after lunchtime. As if she could read my mind, Kristy said, "I'm starved."

"Me too," I admitted. "How about I walk into town and pick up some noncherry food, and you stay here and mind the booth?"

"Fine with me," Kristy said. "I'm having a lot of fun. Working in a farmers' market booth is so much more fun than managing an entire market. I can just sell cherry pastries and don't have to fix anyone else's problems."

I smiled. "I really appreciate the help."

"I know you do, and I know you will return the favor sometime in the future with free babysitting while Kent and I have a night out."

I chuckled. "Sure, I'd be happy to. Huckleberry loves the twins."

At our feet the little pug, who had slept through the morning, snorted. The snack overload from Jessa had really done him in.

I removed my apron and hung it over the back of one of the folding chairs.

"Just promise me one thing before you go," Kristy said.

I didn't like the sound of that. Usually Kristy's request for a promise meant that she had a new idea in her head, and I was the one who would be charged to execute it.

"Don't try to solve this murder."

I blinked at her.

"Why?" I asked. Kristy had never asked me to stay out of a murder investigation before. In fact, there had been several times that she encouraged me to participate.

"Because I'm afraid you will get yourself killed."

Chapter Twenty-Five

K illed?" I yelped.
Kristy folded her arms over her chest. "You have almost been killed before, more than once. You're not a cat with nine lives."

I let out a breath. "So you don't know any particular reason why I could be killed?"

She threw up her arms. "No, other than a killer is on the loose."

"I appreciate the concern, Kristy. I really do, and I know you're coming from a good place. But if I don't clear Stacey's name, she could go to prison. Not to mention, the dispute over my grandmother's stocks will go on forever. What motive would she have to settle it if she's locked up?"

"She might need the money for attorney fees."

I gave her a look.

"You know, I almost didn't even bother saying anything to you about not getting killed because I knew this was how you would respond. You're as stubborn as your father."

I wrinkled my nose, but I didn't refute her claim. As much as I didn't like the comparison, I knew she was right.

"How about I make you a deal?" I asked.

She arched her brow. "Go on."

"I'll clear Stacey's name and then drop it. She's the reason I'm involved in the first place. If the Traverse City chief of police removes her from his list of suspects, then I'm done."

She squinted at me. "Okay." The word was a little drawn out, but I'd take it. She added, "But you had better keep that promise."

I smiled, hoping that I could. What I didn't tell her was how difficult it might be to clear my cousin's name considering the penicillin bottle I found last night.

Kristy stood up to help another customer. Over her shoulder, she said, "Tacos sound good."

I laughed. "Tacos it is." I coaxed Huckleberry out of his bed. "You're coming with me, buddy. We could both use a little exercise."

After rolling over a couple of times, he finally stood up and let me click his leash on. With Huckleberry in tow, I left the booth with one mission in mind. Well, two missions, if I counted tacos for Kristy. I needed to talk to my cousin. The evidence against her was growing.

I didn't even know if she was at the festival since there were no play performances today. I texted Stacey asking if we could meet. A text came immediately back and told me to come to the stage.

The stage where Stacey's actors performed was the same stage where smaller bands, local singers, and even magicians performed throughout the festival.

I knew for a fact that Stacey hated the idea of sharing the space.

People were already grabbing seats in the audience for the big band concert that would be on the stage that afternoon. The festival was doing all that it could to appeal to every person who might come.

Stacey peeked her head through the curtain. "Shiloh, over here." She waved at me.

I bent over, picked up Huckleberry, and hurried onto the stage. Behind the curtain there was a sound system, ropes to raise and lower the curtain, a few props, and little else. I had seen all of this the night before, but everything was clearer in the light of day. The trunk where I had found the pill bottle was still there.

Did Stacey know about the pill bottle? Chief Sterling had to have told her, right? But the real question was, did she know that I was one who found it and turned it over to the police?

"I'm glad to see you, but I will admit I'm surprised you're here today. Dad said the play was done for a bit."

"I'm always here," she said. "I have to keep an eye on things."

I wasn't sure what she meant by that but thought it not wise to press her about it just yet.

"I assume you spoke to Lily at her gallery the other day," Stacey said. "What did you learn? Can you prove she is the killer?"

I blinked. My mind was on the bottle of penicillin not a days-old conversation with Lily Fullbright. "I didn't have much time to talk to her alone because the Traverse City police chief showed up."

She wrinkled her nose. "I met him. Did you know he came to my theater yesterday and wanted to be let inside?"

"Did you let him in?"

She scowled. "Yes, what choice did I have? If I didn't let him in, he said that I would have to go with him down to the station. Can you believe that?"

"So, he didn't question you at the station?"

She glared at me. "Of course not. They only question criminals at the station, and the only thing I'm guilty of is thinking that horrible man really cared about me."

I had been questioned at the station. In fact, I had been questioned at a police station more than once, but I wasn't a criminal. However, I didn't think it was the time to bring that to Stacey's attention. I cleared my throat.

"Can you tell me about your relationship with Dane?"

She folded her arms. "You want all the intimate details?"

I waved my hands in the air. "No, thanks. I just want the basics. How long were you together? How did you meet? How did you not know he was married?"

She narrowed her eyes.

"I can't help you if I don't have the right information," I said.

"We met at the university. I asked for a meeting with the head of the drama department at the end of April because I already knew that we would be performing *The Tempest* at the festival. The university would be the best place to get some student actors who could play most of the roles, and they would be free."

"Free? You didn't pay any of them?"

"No, what Dane and I came up with was they would get one drama credit for being in the play. It would give them experience, and it would give me the cast that I needed." She examined her perfectly shaped, pale-pink nails. "There was a flirtation from the start. I was hesitant though. I don't like to mix business and pleasure. I saw it happen way too much when I was in New York, and it always ended badly for all those involved."

I tried my very best not to make a face. "But you agreed to date him."

"In a moment of weakness, yes, but he didn't ask me out until early June. We hit it off right away. We were together a month. When you're working on something like this, you spend long hours with the other people involved. It's difficult not to become emotionally entangled. I let my guard down. That was my fault, but he's a liar, so I put most of the blame on him."

My heart softened toward Stacey just a little. Everything else aside, she was still my cousin. Other than my father, she was the only living relative I had on this earth. I also knew what she said was true. Although it had never happened to me personally, I knew several coworkers in LA that had similar relationships start that way. Not a single one of them lasted longer the project.

Knowing my cousin, who cared more about the Michigan Street Theater than anything else, I guessed that the same would have been true for her. After the play wrapped, her interest in Dane would have come to an end. She only made a big scene at the Cherry Farm Market because he made a fool of her, and no one made Stacey look like a fool and got away with it.

"How did you find out he was married?"

"His wife told me."

I raised my eyebrows.

"It was that morning, before I saw him with you in the market. We were at intermission during dress rehearsal, which was thirty minutes long. At that time, the cast always scatters, and I'm left behind to set the next act with Whit. Dane was always one of those who left. I should have known then that he was a bad guy. A decent man would have stayed behind and helped us." She shook her head.

The question was, how did Lily Fullbright learn about the affair? Only Lily could tell me that. I would be surprised if she was at the festival today. If I were her, I would stay as far away from it as possible.

"I was furious. I went to look for Dane immediately, and when I saw him in front of your booth, I lost it. Part of me expected him to say it was all a lie, but he admitted it. I felt like such a fool. I will never let a man, or anyone else, make me feel like that again."

I believed her, but I had to push a little bit more. "Did you ever ask him if he was married?"

"He told me he wasn't when we first met."

I pressed my lips together.

"I know what you're thinking. That I was stupid. And maybe I was. Do you know at forty years old I haven't had one serious relationship?" She held out her hands. "And look at me. I want to get married. I want to have children. I woke up after my fortieth birthday and asked myself what I was doing with my life."

This was the most forthcoming that Stacey had ever been with me.

"I poured myself into acting and tried to make it on Broadway. When that didn't work, I came home with my tail between my legs and decided that I could prove myself by saving the Michigan Street Theater. I did that. It's doing better than anyone could have expected, but now what?"

I didn't have an answer for her, and her situation was hitting a little too close to home for me. After Logan died, I poured myself into work too, and I hadn't been in a serious relationship since. It was shocking to see that Stacey and I were so much more alike than I realized.

I wasn't sure how to respond, so I said, "I assume the police talked to you about the pill bottle."

She narrowed her eyes. "How do you know about that?"

I held up my hands. "You're the one who asked me to look into this case. I have to follow up on every lead to do that. Why did you have the medicine? What was it for?"

"If you must know, I had strep throat a few months ago. The urgent care doctor gave me the script. I took it and got better. That's the end of the story."

"Why didn't you finish the bottle? I thought for antibiotics to work, you have to finish the course."

"That's what they tell you, but I've never been a rule follower."

How well I knew that.

She went on. "I was feeling better and back to my old self, so just stopped taking them." She shrugged. "I don't think that's a crime."

"You didn't throw the pills away then?" I asked.

She scowled. "They were in my medicine cabinet. Out of sight and out of mind. There was nothing nefarious about it. This was before I ever started a relationship with Dane. It had nothing to do with him."

"But it does have something to do with him because he was allergic to the medicine in your medicine cabinet, and the bottle somehow ended up at the National Cherry Festival where he died."

"Well, if you say it that way, it does sound bad."

"It is bad, Stacey. I'm surprised the police haven't arrested you already."

"Oh, they tried, but they were stopped."

"Stopped how?"

A smug expression crossed her face. "By Chief Randy."

"What? How can he stop another officer outside of his command from making an arrest?"

She shrugged. "I don't know, but I do know that's what happened."

I pressed my lips together. "How did the medicine bottle get here?"

She folded her arms. "How should I know? All I can think is someone broke into the theater and stole it from my apartment backstage. And that person has to be Lily."

"But how would she have known that you even had it? You said you had strep throat before you and Dane got involved. Also, you didn't know he was married. What did Lily know about the two of you"

"How do I know what she knew and or didn't know? You're the one who is supposed to be finding that out. Did you learn anything from her at all?"

"Not really," I admitted.

She threw up her arms. "You're supposed to be helping me." She pointed her finger at me. "If you don't fix this, you will never see the money from Grandma Bellamy's stocks. Never."

"Stacey, that money is for Dad, you, and me. If you don't sign, none of us will get it."

"That will be better than you getting it all."

"I don't want it all. That's Dad."

She snorted. "I know it's coming from you."

"It's not. We just have to meet with my dad and explain." I changed my tone. "Why can't we split the money from the stocks?" I asked. "That is what Grandma Bellamy would want. I know she wouldn't have left you out."

To my surprise, tears gathered in her eyes. "She did leave me out. She left the note to you. She told you about the hidden money. Not me, who has been back here for years. She always loved you more." She threw the curtain open and stomped onto the stage.

I pushed the curtain aside to see her run down the stage steps and disappear into the crowd of tourists.

I stepped back and let the curtain fall, enclosing myself backstage again, just as I had the night before when I found the pill bottle with Stacey's name on it.

I finally knew why Stacey had hated me all these years. She was jealous because she believed our grandmother, who we had both adored, loved me more.

Chapter Twenty-Six

After leaving the stage, I decided to walk along the lake. Sailboats bobbed in the bay, and further out, I could see people zigging and zagging back and forth on jet skis. What I wouldn't give to be out on the water.

As much as I loved the water, I had to stay on dry land. I'd promised Kristy tacos, after all.

Young couples walked along the shore, and I thought of Stacey's admission that she wanted a husband and family. For whatever reason, I had never seen that for her or frankly for myself. Perhaps it was because we had both witnessed the unfortunate marriages our fathers had been in.

Along the water, young couples smiled brightly at their phones while they took selfies.

There was one couple at the end of the dock not taking photos but arguing. When I got a bit closer, I realized it was Slade and the young man I had seen the day before in the flight suit. He wasn't wearing his bright yellow flight suit now, but it was definitely him.

I felt my heart rate pick up. I pulled my ball cap down further over my face and inched my way closer.

"You have to understand. I was confused. I know I made a mistake," Slade said.

"You made a massive mistake. Do you know what could happen to me if I'm involved in this? It could ruin my whole future."

"I don't want that."

"I would hope you don't, but I feel like I don't know you at all. I leave for two seconds and you take up with a married guy. It's gross."

Tears streamed down Slade face. "We were broken up. I wish you would accept that."

He pointed a finger at her. "No. You thought we were broken up. I never agreed to it. We are meant to be together. Everything I'm doing is for you to build our life together. You threw it all away." He called her a horrible name.

People walked by the couple and sidestepped them. I could understand their hesitation to get involved with what was clearly a domestic dispute, but the man was being awful to her.

"Cayden, please let's just be over and done with," Slade whimpered.

He grabbed her arm. "That will never happen. I came to this air show to prove to you how much I cared, and you threw it back in my face."

"Hey," I called and hurried forward.

Slade and Cayden looked over at me.

He looked down at his hand gripping her arm and dropped it. I could already see the bruise forming there. "This is none of your business," Cayden snapped.

"It is my business. Slade is a friend of mine. Isn't that right Slade?"

"Y-yes, that's right. She's my friend." Her voice wavered just a little.

"I don't know you. How can she have a friend I don't know about?" he said.

Slade winced.

"Is this something else you've hidden from me?" Cayden asked.

"I don't know who you are," I said. "Does that mean you're not her friend either?"

"I'm her fiancé," he snapped.

"I don't see a ring on her finger, so I doubt that."

"I'm saving up for it. Besides, you're too old to be her friend. Get lost."

"Slade never mentioned you," I said with a shrug. "Now, I would suggest that you let go of her arm before I call for help. Believe me, I can scream very loudly."

He narrowed his eyes.

Slade took her chance and came over to stand next to me. "She is my friend."

He pressed his lips together. "You'll be sorry for how you treated me. Just as sorry as your dead professor." He stomped away.

I shivered. Was Cayden being dramatic or was he confessing to murder? In any case, he was someone that Chief Sterling needed to take a look at. Any new suspect would take some of the pressure off Stacey. But would Cayden have known to break into Stacey's bathroom and steal her prescription? It seemed farfetched even to me, and I had a wild imagination when it came to this sort of thing.

Slade watched him go. Her chest heaved. "Thank you," she whispered and glanced at her upper arm.

"Are you okay?"

"I'm fine," she whispered.

"That bruise looks pretty bad."

"I've had worse."

I bit my lip. "I was heading into town for lunch. I need a break from the festival. Want to come with me?"

She gave me a slight nod. "Where were you going?"

"My friend Kristy is helping me out at my booth today, and she wanted tacos. There's a taco stand on Front Street."

"I like their tacos. I go there all the time."

I smiled. "I thought you might. I went there when I was in college too. Honestly, I can't believe it's still there after all these years."

"Everyone goes there," she said, looking the most relaxed she'd been since we met.

I was happy to see it. "Let's go."

The city of Traverse City was built for tourism. Between the cherries, the skiing, and its close proximity to national parks and Lake Michigan, it was a favorite vacation spot for so many people in the Midwest. Before I moved to LA, I had always viewed Traverse City as a big city. One day in California set me straight on that, but no one would argue that it wasn't the biggest town west of Lansing in the Mitten State. It was the one place in a reasonable distance where you could have all the amenities you might need or want. It wasn't unusual for me to travel to the city at least once a week when I craved civilization while working long hours on the farm alone or with only Chesney for company. However, after the National Cherry Festival, I thought I would take a couple of weeks off from those more frequent trips. Total isolation on the farm appealed to me right about now.

I removed a packet of tissues from my small backpack and handed them to Slade as we reached Front Street.

"Thank you," she sniffled. "I don't know why I'm crying."

I could think of about ten reasons this young woman had to cry, but I didn't share any of those with her at her moment. It was clear to me that Slade needed to collect her thoughts before she could tell me what was really going on.

The Taco Joint was one of the oldest restaurants on Front Street. Front Street was the main street in the city and where the best shopping and food was for miles. It was paved in red brick and lined with ornate lampposts and flowerpots. On a summer afternoon, it was always hopping, but in the middle of a summer afternoon during the National Cherry Festival, there was barely enough room to move.

The service at the Taco Joint was fast. The best thing about it was you could put in your order at the outdoor counter and they would text you when it was ready so you didn't have to stand around and block the sidewalk. There were plenty of shops and other businesses nearby to keep you occupied while you waited.

The line to order was long but moved swiftly. The Taco Joint team was a well-oiled machine. When we finally made it up to the counter, I ordered food for Kristy and me and told Slade to get whatever she wanted. It was my treat.

She ordered a vegan burrito and a Coke. For Kristy and me, I ordered six tacos, two burritos, and churros. It had been a rough week.

I gave the cashier my phone number, and we were on our way.

"Do you want to walk while we wait?" I asked.

Slade squinted at me as if she were seeing me for the very first time. "Walk? I don't like walking."

"Okay. Do you want to sit and wait somewhere?"

She looked this way and that. She was looking for something or someone, and if I wasn't mistaken, she was frightened.

"Why don't we wait over there?" I pointed to an empty bench across the street. The back of the bench was up against a brick wall. "We can see everyone coming and going from there."

She nodded and followed me across the street. We sat on the bench in silence for a few minutes. I could tell she had a lot on her mind, and I didn't want to intrude on her thoughts.

"When I first met Cayden, he was really sweet. We were just kids then."

"What made him change?"

She shrugged. "I don't know. He always had a lot of pressure from his dad to succeed. His dad really wanted to fly for the navy and couldn't. There was something wrong with his eyes, and he failed the sight tests. He put all his hopes on Cayden. I guess it just got to Cayden over time."

I knew full well the impact parents' behavior could have

on their children, but it still didn't excuse or really explain why Cayden treated Slade so poorly. A lot of people lived with that kind of pressure and never hurt anyone.

"What's the story with you and Cayden?"

She looked up and down the street. "We grew up in the same town. We have always been together, since we were little kids. He's very possessive. He's always been that way. It wasn't until he went away to flight school and I stayed here that I really saw he wasn't good for me. I just thought my fate was sealed and I always had to be with him." She took a breath. "The next time he came home on leave, I told him how I felt. He was furious and pushed me against the wall."

I shivered.

"I knew I had to end it, but I was afraid. I had started taking acting classes at the university. Acting isn't my major, but I always loved it. I had to take three art courses for my degree, so acting was the perfect choice for me. I'm usually shy, but when I'm playing the role of another person, I come alive. Anyone's life is better than mine."

"So you met Dane through those classes," I said.

"He's the only theater instructor at the university. It's not a big department."

I nodded.

"He was nice to me from the start. He could tell I was shy and went out of his way to make me feel included. After a time, I became more comfortable in class and more comfortable around him. He asked me to stay after class one day because he wanted to go over a part I was playing in a skit. He could tell I needed the extra help."

My stomach clenched as I heard her story.

"Did anything happen romantically that night?"

"No, not at all. We were just talking about our lives. We were both in bad relationships. He said he was filing for divorce from his wife. She was very critical of him. I told him I was dealing with the same situation. I had been with Cayden for as long as I could remember, but I knew he was not good for me. I told Dane everything, and he was so compassionate."

I'll bet, I thought.

"Over the semester we grew closer. He listened to me. I had never had that before. We fell in love." She turned and looked at me. "But I promise you he didn't so much as hold my hand when I was his student. He said that we couldn't see each other until I finished his class, so the next semester I flipped over to painting for my art credits."

"Was that his idea?" I asked. "To choose painting?"

"Yes." She looked at me as if she didn't understand the implication.

His wife was a painter with a studio. Slade taking painting classes would give her the skills or presumed skills to be Lily's assistant. My head spun. Dane had been a master manipulator of all the women in his life. It made me wonder two things. Who else had he manipulated? And who had figured it out and killed him?

"How did it end?" I asked.

She looked at me. "He died."

My eyes went wide. I would bet all the tacos in my order that she didn't know that Dane was dating Stacey at the same time he was seeing Slade. My heart hurt for this poor girl. Her longtime boyfriend was cruel to her, and then the next man she met cheated on her while he was also cheating on his wife. The whole thing made me queasy.

My phone beeped, telling me that our food was ready. The sound woke me up from my disgust and anger at Dane Fullbright.

"Are you okay?" Slade asked.

I blew out a breath. "Yeah, I just now know what it feels like to be angry enough to kill, and I don't like that feeling. Not at all."

Chapter Twenty-Seven

When I got back to my booth, Kristy took the food bag from me. "Where did you go? You were gone for two hours." She peeked in the bag. "Did you get chicken or beef?"

"Both. Sorry it took so long."

She pulled a taco from the bag, unwrapped it, and took a big bite. She closed her eyes for a moment. After she wiped her mouth with a paper napkin, she said, "So good. The Taco Joint is my favorite. They are almost as good as my abuela's tacos. Almost." She stared at me. "Aren't you eating?"

"I lost my appetite."

She took another taco from the bag and sat down. "What happened?"

"I can't tell you, but it doesn't have to do with me directly. It's someone else's secret to tell."

A customer came up to the booth. I jumped out of my seat. "Keep eating."

She nodded. I didn't have to tell her twice.

The booth was busy through the rest of the afternoon, so I didn't have much time to think about Slade and her troubles. However, every time there was a short break, her face came to my mind. I had to find a way to help her.

I could tell Milan, and I planned to. However, I knew it would be very hard to prove abuse if Slade didn't want to press charges. I couldn't see her doing that. She just wanted Cayden out of her life.

Kristy checked her watch. "Ack, it's seven already? This day went by so fast. I hate to leave you here alone, but I have to go pick up the girls."

"Thank you for coming, Kristy. I don't know how I would have survived without your help today."

"You would have been stuck at the booth and had no time to do your little detective work." She wiggled her eyebrows at me.

She was right about that.

"Promise me you will keep a low profile the rest of the night and stay out of trouble." Kristy slung her purse over her shoulder and picked up the bag of cherry treats and jam that I insisted she take home to her family. She had a bar of cherry vanilla soap in her purse as well.

"I'll be fine. The festival closes at ten. If things get slow, I'll start packing up at nine or so and head out. I don't know how much traffic the festival will get on a weeknight."

"Just be careful, okay? You looked really shaken up after you came back with the food. Also, you forced me to eat all six of the tacos because of it. I would have had the burritos and churros too if I had room. I will be sending my trainer bill to you."

I laughed.

Her expression grew serious. "I hate leaving you alone."

"She's not alone," a deep voice said.

Milan was standing in front of the booth. He was so tall that the paper-mache cherry that hung from the booth's basket façade grazed the top of his head. He wore faded jeans and a Michigan State T-shirt. His glasses sat on the tip of his nose, and he pushed them up with his index finger.

"Hello, Chief Penbrook," Kristy said in a high-pitched voice. She looked at me and grinned. "You have the night off?"

He smiled at us, flashing his straight teeth. "I'm officially off duty, but a sheriff is always on call. But with so many people in the city for the festival, my little county is relatively quiet. That will surely change on the Fourth, when the lakes are covered with amateur boat captains. Otherwise law-abiding citizens seem to lose all self-control on Independence Day."

"Don't I know it!" Kristy said. "Kent, the girls, and I will watch fireworks on the TV this year. The girls hate the 'big booms,' as they call it."

At our feet Huckleberry snorted. He felt the same way about the "big booms."

"Well, I had better head out." She held up her shopping bag. "Thanks for the treats, Shi. Nice to see you, Sheriff. I'm glad I don't have to leave Shiloh all on her lonesome."

"Nice to see you too," Milan said with that kind smile of his.

Kristy walked out of the booth and behind the sheriff. She made a heart sign with her hands before disappearing into the crowd.

"Did she give me bunny ears?" Milan asked as he entered the booth.

"Nope."

He pressed his lips together as if he wasn't sure that I was telling the truth, but there was no way I was telling him exactly what Kristy did behind his head. I didn't want him to read anything into it.

Thankfully a group of customers came up just then. I turned to help them, while Milan settled into one of the folding chairs. Huckleberry jumped onto his lap and snuggled in. If my pug loved him, I was in big trouble.

The ladies bought bags of cherries, cherry jam, and white chocolate and cherry cookies. Each bought a small bar of soap to boot. Maybe Kristy was right and I should invest in developing beauty products. However, I reminded myself to scale carefully. I'd worked too hard and too long to pull Bellamy Farm back from the brink. I didn't want to throw all the time and money away with the hopes of expanding even more.

"So business has been good?" the sheriff asked in a casual voice.

I removed a full box of cherries from under my table behind the booth and began refilling containers. "Really good. It was even better with Kristy there. She is a true salesperson. She could convince person allergic to cherries to buy a pound." I winced when I realized the joke I had made was a tad too close for comfort to the way Dane Fullbright actually died.

"Speaking of Kristy, why did she make you promise you'd be careful?"

"I told her about last night."

"Learn anything interesting when you were out snooping today?" he asked.

"I did." I didn't even bother to deny it. "You know about Slade, right?"

"Slade Carra?" He nodded. "She told an officer Dane was dating her."

I didn't know why I was surprised Milan knew this. He was a great cop.

"Right. She has a very jealous ex-boyfriend, who I think you should add to the suspect list."

"I hate to hear about anyone in a relationship like that," Milan said. "So many of our calls to the sheriff's department are domestic situations. Every last one of them breaks my heart. The worst part is so many go back to their abusers."

I nodded. "I'm afraid that Slade might do that now that Dane is gone. I think in a lot of ways, she saw him as the person who was going to rescue her from Cayden."

He sighed. "Too many young women don't realize how strong they really are. Sometimes they just need the right support system to recognize it." He removed his phone from his pocket. "I'll call the chief right now. One of his officers will take the guy in for questioning." He tapped on the screen.

I sighed, feeling even worse about the situation that Slade was in. I prayed that she could get out. I realized she hadn't given me her phone number. I had no way of contacting her. Since Lily Fullbright's booth was closed for the rest of the festival, why was Slade still hanging around? If were her, I would stay as far away from here as I could.

"Shiloh!" Hazel's high voice rang throughout the Cherry Farm Market.

I stuck my head out of the booth and looked down the row. Hazel was running toward the booth. Her grandparents followed behind her at a much slower pace.

Chapter Twenty-Eight

✦

Y ikes." I pulled my head back into the booth to collect myself before the Killians descended.

"Yikes?" Milan asked. "What's *yikes*?"

"Hazel is here."

"You love her." He furrowed his brow in confusion.

"And her grandparents."

Understanding filled his eyes. "Ahhh."

Hazel ran around the back of the booth and gave me a hug. "I convinced Grandma and Grandpa to come to the festival. Isn't that great? I wanted to show them what I have been doing, so they would know that it was totally safe. You know how they worry." She spotted Milan, who was no longer sitting. "Oh hey." Her brow wrinkled. "Are you working here now?"

"Just helping out for a few hours," he said.

"I would think a county sheriff would have better things to do than sell pastries," Chief Randy said through the booth window.

Milan smiled. "It's nice to see you again, Chief."

I let out a breath. As much as he wanted to, Chief Randy

wasn't going to be able to rattle Milan with his snide comments. I wished I could say the same for myself.

I cleared my throat. "I'm glad you all decided to come to the festival. There's a lot to see. I believe there will be a concert tonight on the main stage. Some big-time country singer will be there."

"I don't like country music," Doreen said primly. Despite the humidity she wore a light pink sweater set and a pearl necklace with matching earrings. Her freshly dyed hair was perfectly in place.

"Well, the festival has something to offer everyone," I said. "I encourage you take a look around."

Behind me, I heard Milan chuckle.

"Hmmm," Doreen murmured. "We will see about that. This the first time I have been in years. I don't see anything of interest here to me." She looked at the cherry dangling over her head. "This booth is a bit extravagant. I can see why it cost what everyone said it did. I would not say that it was a good use of money."

I clamped my mouth shut.

"Grandma," Hazel said. "There's that soap that you liked at Jessa's Place." She picked up a bar and held it under her nose, then held it out to her grandmother.

Doreen took it from her hand. "How did it get here?"

"Shiloh made it," Hazel replied.

Doreen set the bar of soap down. "Maybe it smells differently to me in the diner. Anything is better than bacon grease." She took Hazel's hand. "Let's go see what else we can find."

Hazel waved at me as they walked away, leaving the police chief behind.

Chief Randy nodded at Milan. "I heard that you were helping Chuck with the murder investigation. I'm sorry to hear that a big-city cop can't handle a case on his own. With all the officers and resources he has?" Chief Randy scoffed. "You don't see me asking for help when someone gets killed in Cherry Glen."

"We are well aware of that, Chief," Milan said.

"I was hoping I would see Chuck here to be briefed on the case."

Milan bristled for the first time since the Killians arrived. "You think he owes you a briefing?"

"He came into my town and tried to arrest one of my citizens right under my nose."

"He wasn't there to make an arrest," Milan said. "He was there for questioning, and he told you in advance as a professional courtesy."

"He should have let me do the questioning. It's one of my people."

His people?

"You're not on the case."

"Neither are you," Chief Randy snapped back. His face grew increasingly red.

My mind scrambled for a way to break it up without upsetting Milan or the chief. Luckily, I was saved from doing anything because Milan's cell phone rang.

He looked at the screen. "I have to take this. It's one of my deputies."

"Yes, do your job, Sheriff," Chief Randy said.

Milan didn't even bother to reply and walked out of the booth.

My face felt as hot and red as the chief's looked. "Chief Randy, I would appreciate if you were a little nicer to Milan. He's my friend, and he's only here tonight to help because Chesney had schoolwork."

He leaned toward me. "I know very well he's your friend, and you're right, I should be nicer to him. I can't be scaring him off. I'd much rather you spend your time with him than with my son and granddaughter." With that parting shot, he walked away.

After the chief left, I was fuming. "Huckleberry, remind me to remove the Killians from the Christmas card list."

He snuffled at me.

"You're right. That would be too nice. I will instead send them an especially ugly card."

He barked his approval.

I tried to push the encounter out of my mind as I fell back into work at the booth. Out of the corner of my eye, I watched Milan pace back and forth while on the phone.

"I'd like one pound of your cherries," a young woman said to me.

"Sure thing!" I scooped the cherries into a plastic bag and weighed them on my scale before handing them over.

She gave me a five dollar bill in exchange for the bag.

"Enjoy!" I said.

She put the bag in her canvas bag. "This might sound like a weird question, but are you the lady that tried to help Professor Fullbright the other day?"

"You were at the cherry pit spitting competition?"

She nodded. "It was awful. I go to the university, and he's one of my favorite instructors. He's way nicer than most of the old professors there."

I felt a headache instantly form. She had better not tell me that she had been dating Dane too.

"Anyway, I read that he was killed."

My eyes went wide. As far as I knew, the information about Dane being murdered hadn't been released to the press, but then again, Penny Lee knew about it.

"And you're Shiloh, right? Shiloh Bellamy? In the paper, it was mentioned that you tried to save him."

"Where was this printed?"

"It's like a little community gossip circular thing."

I knew it.

"My friends and I read it because so many of the articles are so farfetched, they're hilarious. And it's free. But"—she bit her lower lip—"but this time, I wondered if it was true. There have been so many more police out at the festival this year. It makes me think that Professor Fullbright *was* killed."

"Do you have a reason to think he was in danger?"

She seemed to consider this. "He gets a lot of female attention on campus, if you know what I mean."

I did.

"I don't count myself in that number. He's so not my type. I like my guys more masculine, you know? Also, he's a teacher and old. Thinking of liking someone like that is just gross, you know?"

Dane Fullbright was forty if he was a day, but I made no comment on her "old" statement. Instead, I was immensely relieved I wasn't speaking to yet another of Dane's girlfriends.

"I read in the article that you were looking into the case and that you had solved a murder before."

The headache was getting worse.

"Anyway, if you are looking for someone who might have wanted him dead, I'd check out Slade Carra."

"Slade," I yelped. "Because she was dating him?"

"She wasn't dating him. She was stalking him." The young woman walked away, and I realized I hadn't even asked her name.

Chapter Twenty-Nine

M ilan walked back to the booth. "Chief Sterling's officers are onto Cayden. I spoke to the chief after getting off the call with my deputy."

"Is everything okay in your county?"

"Oh yeah, the deputy just wanted to tell me about the
twenty-pound walleye he caught." He smiled.

"If Chief Sterling's guys are looking for Cayden, they
should probably look for Slade too, because I have new
information," I said.

"You got new information while I was standing twenty
feet away?"

I shrugged. "What can I say? I'm good."

He snorted.

As quickly as I could, I told him about the student who
stopped by the booth and what she told me about Slade.

"Where is she?" Milan wanted to know.

I couldn't blame him. I wanted to know where she went
too. But I didn't think I would ever see her again.

"She left before I could even ask her name. I was just so

shocked by what she told me. Saying that Slade was stalking Dane Fullbright caught me off guard."

"Why did she tell you and not the police?"

I wrinkled my nose. "My guess is she didn't want to get involved with the police."

"But why you?"

"Apparently she read a Traverse City gossip column about the murder, and it mentioned my other experiences with murder investigations."

Milan placed a hand on his forehead like he was holding a headache at bay himself. "I knew about the community paper. I didn't tell you because I didn't want to upset you."

"Can I see it now?"

He sighed and pulled his phone out of his pocket again. He forwarded me a link to the *Sweet Cherry News*.

As I expected, the byline read "Penelope Lee Odders." Did she say all these untrue and terrible things about me because I didn't give her the full interview she had wanted on the first day of the festival? Or was it purely for sensationalism?

I read, "'In a strange turn of events, Shiloh Bellamy (thirty-nine) of Cherry Glen was on the scene of the cherry pit spitting competition. Ms. Bellamy has been involved in three murders, all within the last year. This journalist believes that would give anyone pause. As Mr. Fullbright began to struggle and beg for his life, Ms. Bellamy jumped into action and attempted to give him the Heimlich maneuver. However, he wasn't choking. We later learned that he had been poisoned.

Did Ms. Bellamy know that and attempt to perform life-saving measures to throw the investigation off track?

"'Soon after, Ms. Bellamy put on her detective hat for the fourth time and has been seen at the National Cherry Festival asking questions and making a general nuisance of herself.'"

I scanned the rest of the article, which covered Dane's wife and his apparent affair with Stacey. There was no mention of Slade.

"She didn't have to put my age in there," I grumbled.

Milan chuckled. "Out of everything outlandish in that article, you latch on to that detail."

I looked up at him. "I'm a bit sensitive about turning forty next year."

"You don't look a day over twenty-five. Next year, you won't look a day over twenty-six."

"You're very kind." I sighed. "As for the rest of the article, I just know that everyone in Cherry Glen is lapping this up. I'm certain Jessa's doing damage control for me at her diner."

"I expect so. She's a good friend to you."

I saved the article on my phone and shoved the phone into the back pocket of my jeans. "What I don't understand is Slade. I spoke with her for a long time today, and I really believed that she was in love with Dane and wanted to get out of her relationship with Cayden."

"Both of those things may be true," Milan said. "That doesn't mean Dane Fullbright reciprocated her feelings. We did contact the university and ask them if there were any inappropriate claims against Dane in relation to his students.

As reluctant as they were to tell us, they finally did say there have been no complaints in that regard."

"That doesn't prove anything," I said. "I can't see Slade telling a university official about her relationship with a professor."

"We will keep digging of course, but the romance might have been just in her head."

I moved the baskets of cherry samples around on the booth counter. When I was anxious, I had to do something with my hands. This conversation about Slade set me on edge. Not just because I'd believed her but because I had always thought I was a good judge of character. If everything Slade told me was a lie, I wasn't a good judge of character at all.

"I have to find Slade," I said. "I need to talk to her about this rumor about her stalking Dane. There has to be more to the story."

"I agree, but I want you to leave it up to the police."

I cocked my head. "Do you really think a young woman is going to be willing to talk to the police about a crush on her college professor? You wouldn't even know that the two of them were connected if it weren't for me."

He made a face.

"She trusts me, and I know I can get her to tell me the truth."

He rubbed his forehead a little more forcefully this time. "I tend to believe you, but this isn't my case. Chief Sterling will have to go along with it."

"Then ask him. I'm stuck at the booth until ten."

He sighed. "Let me make another call."

Milan walked back under the tree, and I attempted to concentrate on my business instead of the murder. It wasn't easy as every third person who came up to my booth mentioned Penny Lee's article and asked me if I solved the murder yet. I deflected their questions the best I could, and I was happy Milan was far enough away that he couldn't hear our conversations.

I sold a good number of cherries due to people's ghoulish curiosity, and I was more than happy to take their money, but I didn't feel good about it. I wanted customers to come to my booth because of the quality and reputation of my products and my farm, not because they might learn something about the murder.

If Kristy was still there, she would have told me to take the money no matter the buyers' reasons, so that's what I did.

Milan came back just as the fifth person in a row asked me, "Did Stacey do it?" My answer was always the same: "No."

Milan stepped in right as yet another person asked me about it. "Miss Bellamy is not at the liberty to speak about the case to anyone," he said.

"Who are you?" the man wanted to know.

"The sheriff." Milan flashed his sheriff's badge. I noted he took care to cover up the county name on the badge.

"Oh wow!" he said to me. "You're working with the sheriff on the case? You are really are part of the investigation! I'm super into true crime. Can I get my photo with you?"

"With me?" I squeaked.

He nodded vigorously.

"No," Milan said. "I suggest you take your cherries and leave."

"Wow! Run off by the cops. My friends aren't going to believe this," he said before moving on.

Milan shook his head. "True crime will be the death of me." He glanced at me sheepishly. "No offense." It was the genre I had made a living off of for over a decade.

"None taken. When I was filming it, I thought it would be the death of me too."

"It's almost eight. You done here, or do you want to stay to the bitter end?"

I looked around. "I think I'm done. Most of the farmers are packing up."

"Good, because we're going to find Slade Carra."

Chapter Thirty

M y first date, if I could even call it that, with Sheriff
Milan Penbrook wasn't like anything I expected that
it would be. In fact it wasn't a date at all, since it was to interview a murder suspect. As much compassion as I felt for her,
I had to start thinking of Slade as a suspect. Just as I couldn't
completely remove Stacey from the list, the same was true
for Slade.

What made me even more suspicious of Slade was
her home. I knit my brow together as we sat outside of
the large house with its immaculate lawn and trim hedges.
"She lives here?"

Milan looked at his phone. "Yes, this is the address the
chief gave me."

This wasn't the life that Slade described to me at all. She'd
said that she lived in an apartment with a bunch of roommates and could barely make her rent. This was not the
home of someone just scraping by. It was on the water, so
had to be well over a million dollars. Homes on the bay were
the most sought-after in Traverse City.

Even so, I told myself to reserve judgment. This was most

likely her parents' home, and just because Slade's parents had money, it didn't mean she did. Some parents cut their kids off after a certain age.

We walked up to the door, and Milan knocked. Huckleberry sat at our feet. It wasn't ideal to take the pug to our interview, but there was no one I knew in the city I could leave him with, and even in the evening, it was too hot to leave him in the car.

A pretty woman in her fifties opened the door. It was clear she hadn't been home long from the office. She still wore her high heels.

"Mrs. Susan Carra?" Milan asked.

"Ms. Carra," she replied.

"Please excuse me," he said.

She nodded. "What is this about?"

"We would like to speak to your daughter, Slade."

Susan pressed her lips together. "Her name is Saldona. I don't understand what it is about kids nowadays that gives them the right to rename themselves. I should at least get to name her after fifteen hours of labor."

At least I knew one thing Slade had told me was true: her real first name was Saldona. I was relieved to hear it. I wanted to believe Slade. I really did.

"Who are you two and what do you want with my daughter?" She removed her heels as she asked the question.

"I'm Sheriff Milan Penbrook, and this is Shiloh Bellamy, who is helping me with the investigation into the death of Professor Dane Fullbright. Does the name Dane Fullbright mean anything to you?"

She frowned. "Never heard it until this week when he died at the festival. It's big water cooler discussion in my office. There aren't many murders in Traverse City."

Milan nodded. "And we'd like to keep it that way, which is why we want to find out what happened to Mr. Fullbright as quickly as possible."

"I don't see how I can be of any help, and Saldona has never mentioned the name to me. I'm sure that she doesn't know him either."

"She is working for his wife."

She furrowed her brow. "She told me that she was working for an art gallery near the bay. I was happy that she was putting that expensive art degree I was paying for to some good use. It was the first summer she's been willing to work and not hole up in her room for three months and paint."

"How did Slade get the job?" I asked.

She looked at me, and I thought she wasn't going to answer. I can't say I blamed her. I didn't know that I would be willing to speak about my child to a stranger. In fact, I knew I wouldn't.

Susan cleared her throat. "She saw it on the job board in the art department and applied. I was so relieved. I have been trying to convince her to get a job for years." She looked down at Huckleberry. "Is that a police dog?"

"In training," Milan said. "We aren't sure he has what it takes."

"He's a pug," Susan said.

"We thought we'd go for unassuming with this one," Milan said with a straight face.

"No kidding," Susan replied.

"Ms. Carra, would it be all right if we came inside to speak to you more?" Milan asked.

She frowned. "I just got home from a twelve-hour work day. All I want to do is put on my pajamas and read with a glass of wine in my hand."

She was a woman after my own heart.

She sighed. "But you can come in. I have always had a soft spot for dogs, even failed police dogs. I don't have the time to care for now but plan to adopt one or two the moment I retire, whenever that is." She gave a short bitter laugh.

We stepped into the house, and she bent over to pet Huckleberry's head. He licked her hand. The little charmer got us in. He was definitely getting a teaspoon of peanut butter when we got home. It was one of his favorite treats. Also, I thought he might just have the chops to be a police dog after all.

The front door to Susan's home opened into a great room decorated in all shades of gray with floor-to-ceiling windows that looked out over the bay. Everything from the high corners to the baseboards along the walls was spotless. The ceiling had to be eighteen feet up, so that was no small feat.

"I'll call Saldona," she said and walked over to an intercom on the wall. "Saldona, please come to the living room."

There was no reply, but a moment later, the young woman appeared at the top of the open staircase. She spotted Milan, Huckleberry, and me standing by the front door. She hesitated, and for a moment, I thought she would bolt.

Her chest went up and down as if she took a great sigh, and then she came the rest of the way down the stairs.

"Saldona, this man is from the police. He says he needs to speak to you about your professor who died."

Slade's eyes were huge. "I already spoke to the police chief."

"I know that," Milan said soothingly. "But some new information has come to light that I need to ask you about. Shiloh is here to ease the conversation."

Her gaze slid in my direction, but Slade didn't look me in the eye. I wondered if some of the rapport I'd gained over tacos had been lost now that I was in her house, a home that was much different from the one she had described.

"Please, have a seat." Susan gestured to two white leather couches that faced each other in front of the massive fireplace.

Milan sat without a fuss, but I gingerly perched on the sofa. I was a farmer who had spent the entire day at the festival. There was no guarantee there wasn't a little bit of dirt on my pant legs. I took care to put as little of my body possible on the white leather cushion. A stiff wind would have easily blown me off. Thankfully, the large windows were closed.

Milan watched me out of the corner of his eye, and one side of his mouth tipped up into a smile as if he knew just what I was doing. Huckleberry lay on my feet. I took comfort in that.

"Saldona, have a seat too."

The young woman unceremoniously flopped on the couch across from Milan and me. She folded her hands on her lap and looked down as if she couldn't bring herself to make eye contact with anyone in the room.

"Can I get you something to drink?" Susan asked. "Water? Pop?"

"No, we are fine," Milan answered for the both of us. "We don't want to take up much of your time."

Susan nodded and looked as if she was about to sit down too. "If you are going to speak to my daughter, I want to be here."

"Ms. Carra," Milan said. "I completely understand why you feel that way, but Saldona is a legal adult. We would like to speak to her alone. She is more than welcome to tell you whatever she would like about our conversation after the fact."

Susan looked like she might want to argue, but in the end said, "Fine. I'll be in my office. I have some emails to catch up on. Saldona, make sure you see them out when they're finished."

Her daughter, who was still staring at her folded hands on her lap, gave a slight nod.

Susan shook her head as if she couldn't understand her daughter at all. Maybe she couldn't. Slade was a creative and sensitive soul, and it looked like Susan was far more practical and corporate. The two of them were bound to bump heads, but I could tell by the way Ms. Carra looked at Slade that she really loved her daughter.

Susan walked out of the room, and Milan waited a full minute after she left before he spoke. "Slade, we wanted to talk to you about Dane Fullbright."

"What about him?" she asked, still not looking up. "I told

the police chief and his officers everything that I knew. It's not much."

"We do appreciate you doing that, but what we would really like to get to the bottom of is your relationship with Dane."

She lifted her gaze up and looked at Milan. I noted that she had yet to look at me. "I already told Shiloh about it. Ask her."

"Slade," I began. "One of your classmates stopped by my booth this afternoon."

"Who?" Slade asked.

I widened my eyes at her sharp tone. She had come across as docile and even melancholy during our conversations. This more aggressive Slade took some getting used to.

"Her name isn't important," I said.

"I should know who is talking about me," Slade said.

"How did you know she spoke about you?" I asked.

"You wouldn't be here otherwise."

"So you're living here with your mom," I said. "That's not what you told me. You made it sound like you were desperate to find a job for the summer to pay your rent. You said you lived in an apartment."

"I was living with roommates during the semester on campus. I'm home for the summer."

"And the job with Lily Fullbright, is that true?"

Her head snapped up. "You saw me in her booth. She was the one who told you to find me."

"That's true, but Dane didn't get you that job with his wife, did he? Did he even know you were working for his wife?"

She pressed her lips together.

"Slade," Milan began. "We're trying to piece together Dane Fullbright's relationships so we can find out what happened to him. You told Shiloh and the police that you had a romantic relationship with him. Is that true?"

She sighed. "We could have if he hadn't been so distracted by Stacey. I hate her. She stole my chance with him."

I raised my eyebrows. The venom in her voice surprised me.

"He wasn't happy in his marriage. I wanted to help him get over it," Slade went on.

"Did he tell you he was having marital problems?" Milan asked.

She hung her head. "No, but his wife would come to campus and yell at him in front of his students. She said she wanted a divorce and that he was ruining her life."

This was a very different view of Lily Fullbright. I reminded myself to take everything Slade said as this point with a grain of salt. She had lied to me more than once already.

"How did you end up working for Lily?" Milan asked.

Slade cleared her throat. "Lily is a wonderful artist, and she came to the art department looking for an assistant. I applied and got the job."

"So Dane wasn't involved."

Slade wouldn't look at me. "No, but I thought if I was working with his wife, I would see him a lot this summer. I wanted him to know that he could lean on me. I wanted to help him any way I could."

It seemed like more and more like the mysterious college student who had stopped by my booth had been telling the truth, and Slade had been the one lying to me all this time. I felt like a fool. I thought of her ex-boyfriend. I had witnessed him pinch her arm. I saw the bruise. I believed her that he was unkind, maybe even abusive. But I knew I had to be more careful about coming to these sorts of conclusions.

"Did you ever tell Dane how you felt about him?" Milan asked.

Slade looked at him. "I did."

"And how did he respond?"

She shifted in her seat. "He said he appreciated my concern, and he planned to file for a divorce by the end of the summer. He said he was flattered, but he couldn't be involved with a student and he was already seeing someone else."

"Stacey?" I asked.

She nodded. "I didn't know that at the time I took the job, or I wouldn't have bothered."

"Did he say Stacey's name?" I asked.

She balled her fists at her sides. "I saw them kissing."

"When was this?" I asked.

"The day before he died," she said.

"And what did you do?" Milan asked.

"I told his wife that night. The next day, he was dead."

Chapter Thirty-One

Y ou seem to be implying that Lily might have had something to do with her husband's death," Milan said.

Slade picked at her nails. "If anyone would want him dead, it would be her." She paused. "Or me."

I arched my brow. It wasn't that common for a suspect to just come out and say they could be guilty.

"I think I have heard enough." Susan came into the room holding a glass of wine. "If the police wish to speak to her again, they can in the presence of our attorney."

Milan and I stood up. I got up so fast I knocked poor Huckleberry onto his back. He flailed about like an overturned turtle until I picked him up and tucked him under my arm. I guessed the police academy was out of the question for him after all.

"Ms. Carra, we were just asking Slade a few questions," Milan said.

"I heard your questions," she said. "And I can see what you're doing. You're trying to make my daughter look like a killer, and I won't have it. I won't. Now, I'll ask you to please leave before I throw you out."

Slade jumped up. "I would have never killed Dane. I loved him."

Her mother gasped. "He was your teacher."

"I don't care. I know we were supposed to be together. If we had more time, he would have seen that too." She took a breath. "He and Stacey would eventually break up, and I would be there to pick up the pieces. I was trying to help him."

It seemed like a very odd way of helping.

"Other than the timing of Dane's death, how do you know Lily was the killer?" Milan asked.

"By how was he killed. Who would know his allergies better than his wife? I didn't know."

She made a good point, and if Lily was furious with Stacey over the affair, stealing her medicine bottle to frame her would have been the perfect plan, but how would Lily know that Stacey had a three-month old bottle of penicillin in her medicine cabinet?

"Saldona, stop talking," Susan said. "I don't want you to say anything more."

"Lily killed Dane. I need to tell them the truth."

Susan turned to us. "Please leave."

I wanted to argue, but Milan put a hand on my arm. "Of course. Chief Sterling of the Traverse City Police Department will want to speak with Saldona again for an official statement."

"He can, in the presence of our attorney," Susan said, leaving no room for debate.

Milan nodded and tugged on my arm. We started for the door.

"Shiloh," Slade called after me.

I looked over my shoulder.

"I really do appreciate everything you tried to do for me."

I nodded in return.

Milan and I rode back to Open Space Park's small parking lot in silence. I had compassion for Slade, but I also couldn't believe how well she fooled me. My judgment was off. That wasn't a comfortable feeling.

"I'll drop you and Huckleberry off and then I'll see if Chief Sterling is available and tell him what we learned."

I opened my mouth.

"And no, before you ask, you can't come," he said, but his smile took the bite out of his words.

He parked his SUV and I unbuckled my seat belt. With my hand on the door handle, I asked, "Do you think Lily killed her husband?"

"I think Lily has a really good motive for murder. Slade is right; the timing is key. It was a quick turnaround. Slade told Lily the night before the festival what she saw, and in less than twenty-four hours, Dane was dead."

"But it wasn't a crime of passion. Whoever stole the pills from Stacey had been thinking about this murder for a long time."

"Right. Assuming that Stacey's pills were even used in the murder. That will be very difficult to prove."

"Does this mean Stacey is off the hook?"

He shook his head. "Not by a long shot. In fact, all three women are at the very top of my suspect list."

"Who else is on your list?" I asked as innocently as could be.

He gave me a side-eye.

"Cayden has to be there as the jealous boyfriend. I saw with my own eyes how he treated Slade. I don't think she was lying about that."

He sighed.

"You know what I'm thinking?"

"No, but I have a feeling you're going to tell me anyway."

"I think we are on the wrong track. If the murder wasn't so premeditated, I would like all of them, even Stacey, for the crime. But this *was* premeditated. All the suspects we have on our list right now are there because they were furious with Dane in the moment. They don't fit."

"If you're right, we are in a whole heap of trouble," he said. "Because we don't have any other suspects."

Chapter Thirty-Two

The next morning, I was happy to do my chores on my farm with Huckleberry snuffling along behind me and barking at inappropriate times. When I opened the front door of my little cabin, he ran out like he was ready to be a real farm dog. Then he saw a squirrel in a walnut tree, yelped, and hid behind my legs. Even so, I appreciated the enthusiasm to start the day.

Esmeralda wasn't nearly as excited to begin another day on the farm. I tried to coax her out of bed, but she refused to move. Instead she obsessively groomed her tail, paying special attention to her bald spot. If she wasn't back to her old bossy ways by the next week, I would take her to the vet for a checkup. As far as I could tell, the only part of her that was bruised from the incident was her ego. Since Esmeralda had a very large ego, it must have pained her quite a bit.

When Huckleberry and I were far enough away from the squirrel, I set him on the ground. "You can walk the rest of the way to the farmhouse. Remember you are a brave big boy. Keep repeating it over and over to yourself. It's called an affirmation."

He looked up at me as if he had never been so betrayed and then he whimpered.

"I can't carry you all day."

He cocked his square puggy head back and forth as if to ask, "You can't or you won't?"

I started walking, and after a great sigh, he followed me like I knew he would.

We reached the farmhouse, and I let Panda Bear and the ewes into their outdoor pen. Huckleberry barked at me and took two steps in the direction of the path that led to the orchard.

"Not today, buddy," I said. "I can't let the sheep in the orchard until I know how that snare got there."

His brown eyes nearly bugged out of his head.

After opening the henhouse and waiting for Diva and the rest of the chickens to march out, I went inside and collected the eggs and hurried through the rest of my chores. There was still a lot of the festival to go. It had been good exposure for the farm, and I would do it again next year, assuming they would take me back, but I was ready for it to be over. I realized too, I was done with the rush of the city. Being alone at my farm wasn't as bad as I'd thought.

Today, Chesney and Hazel would be back to help me out in the booth. In fact, they were opening the booth that morning so I could meet with my attorney, again, about my grandmother's stocks.

I ran back to the cabin to change and get ready for my meeting. I went to my closet and laughed. When I'd lived in LA, my closet had been filled with designer clothes and shoes. My closet in Michigan was a tad different. It took some time to find my one pair of black silk pants amidst the countless pairs of jeans and T-shirts I had.

They were a tad wrinkled.

Huckleberry smelled the cuffs.

"We'll just toss them in the dryer for a minute."

He covered his face with his paw as if to convey how far the mighty had fallen. There had been a time when all my laundry was sent out and came back to me pressed and on hangers. A lot had changed in the last year.

I threw the pants into the tiny dryer in the broom closet. The cabin wasn't that big and having my own laundry was a must when I moved in, so I bought the smallest stackable washer and dryer I could find. Thankfully, the closet shared a wall with the bathroom, so a plumber just tied into the plumbing there, and Quinn was handy enough to install a dryer vent going out the closet's exterior wall.

True, I couldn't wash more than two outfits at a time in the washing machine, but it came in handy when Huckleberry got skunked and I was the one who had to give him a bath. We'd had two unfortunate skunk encounters in the spring.

While the pants were being tossed around in the dryer, I got ready for my meeting by brushing my hair and putting on what little makeup I had. Tinted SPF goes a long way in my book. I grabbed my last remaining pair of high heels from the closet and dropped them in a canvas bag.

When I removed the pants from the dryer, they were slightly less wrinkled. There wasn't much else I could do about it. I finished getting dressed and slipped into my sneakers.

Esmeralda sat on my bed watching me.

"You ready to go outside, girl?"

She rolled onto her other side and faced the wall. The bald spot on her tail was definitely my fault as far as she was concerned. And maybe she was right. Whoever had put the trap there wanted to hurt me.

I told Esmeralda to get some sleep, and Huckleberry and I left the cabin.

My attorney had a small office above the general store in town. I parallel parked in front of the store. It wouldn't open for another hour, but I planned to stop in for a minute after my meeting to talk to Norman about selling my soaps like Jessa suggested.

I was in no rush to return to the festival. I think, like Hazel, I was officially burned out on everything cherry.

Before leaving the car, I changed from my sneakers to my heels. It had been so long since I wore shoes like those, my toes already felt pinched. Huckleberry looked at my shoes and barked at them. He didn't think they were worth the pain either.

There was a steel door on the side of the old building that opened into a set of stairs, which led up to the law office. Before going upstairs, I scooped up Huckleberry and tucked him under my arm. At the top of the stairs, I found myself in a hallway lined with office doors. The attorney's office wasn't the only business over the general store. There was also a surveyor, an accountant, and even a dentist.

Jamie Gate Esq.'s office was at the end the hallway. I went inside and greeted his wife, Cindy. She was also the office manager. They were an office of two, but I believed business had been good since they opened their practice a couple of years before. He was the first attorney to open offices in Cherry Glen, and they specialized in real estate and property law. With so many farmers in the county, land and property lines were something we worried about a lot. Thinking that brought my mind back to the snare.

"Shiloh!" Cindy said. "Good morning! Would you like a cookie?"

I must have gained five pounds since I started coming to Jamie's office, from the sheer number of cookies that Cindy foisted on me. She was a proud baker and a talented one too. I didn't want to offend her by refusing her offerings.

"I'll take one." I selected a sugar cookie from the tray.

"Take three."

What choice did I have?

"I'll let Jamie know you're here."

She picked up the phone, and I took my three cookies and a napkin to a waiting room chair. Huckleberry looked up at me with envy in his eyes. "Sorry, buddy, these aren't good for pups." I took a bite of one of the cookies, and it crumbled in my lap. Several pieces fell to the floor, and Huckleberry was on them like a flash of light. The only saving grace was there wasn't any chocolate in the cookies.

"Shiloh!" Jamie said, popping out of the door.

He startled me and I dropped more cookie pieces to the floor.

Huckleberry made short work of them.

I brushed cookie crumbs from the front of my shirt and

smeared frosting on my one pair of nice pants. Red-faced, I stood up.

"Thanks for cleaning up those crumbs, Huckleberry," Jamie said good-naturedly to the dog. He looked to me. "Ready to talk?"

I swallowed and followed him into his office. Jamie's office was like how I imagine all attorneys' offices looked in the 1920s. It was decorated with dark wallpaper, dark wood paneling, and a mahogany desk that took up a third of the space. Behind his desk was a wall of bookshelves lined with leather-bound law books that I doubted he even used. They were for show, and show they did. The collection was impressive.

I sat across from his desk in a leather club chair. The chair was low, and I always felt I was about to fall on the floor any time I sat on it. Huckleberry stood at attention at my side. My little pug was in tune with my emotions, and he felt my nervousness. I was grateful for his warm presence.

Jamie smiled at me. "I spoke with Stacey yesterday. She is just as eager to have this resolved as you are. But before we talk about that, let's recap. You found the stocks on the farm after your grandmother left you a note."

"I don't think she thought it would take me so long after her death to find the note. I left for California not long after she died, and my father closed up the cabin. He never went back inside after I left. It was like a time capsule."

He nodded. "Right. When did you find the note?"

"Last summer, shortly after I moved back to Michigan. I was cleaning out my grandmother's cabin to move in and found it."

"And when did you find the 'treasure,' as you call it?"

"The following January. The note she left me didn't say exactly where the treasure was. It was a sort of riddle. She loved riddles. She wasn't going to make it easy for me. Actually, I'm still in a bit of shock it was so valuable. I had thought it was some old family heirloom or something like that."

"Well, what she did was certainly unconventional, but from what you've told me, she wasn't a conventional lady."

That was an understatement. I shifted in my seat. I was dying to ask him how his meeting with Stacey had gone, but I knew that he would tell me in his time.

Huckleberry pressed his left ear into my hand.

"The goal for you, your father, and Stacey is to settle this without going to court."

I nodded. "That's what I want. I know deep down it's what my father wants too."

"I can imagine." Jamie nodded. "As you know, I met with Stacey yesterday. As of yet, she and her counsel have not filed anything against you. We expressed wanting to handle this without a filing as well."

I nodded.

"I tried to make her realize that you both could lose a large chunk of the overall value of the stocks because you will have to spend that on filings and attorney fees."

I rested my hand on Huckleberry's head for support.

"Stacey, as an heir to your grandmother, has every right to part of the money," he said.

"I know that, and I'm not denying her fair share, but my

father, as the last living child of my grandmother, believes he is entitled to it all to support our farm."

"I do wish Sully was willing to talk to me."

"He's not," I said. "He expects me to handle it. He really cares about Stacey. I'm trying to help him understand how this will impact her."

"He sounds like he is a stubborn man."

"You have no idea," I said.

"Stacey believes that she should get half of the value of the stocks because your father inherited the more profitable side of the farm than her father did."

"My grandparents decided how the farm would be divided. My father and I had nothing to do with it. I've given you a copy of my grandmother's will that clearly stated everything should be evenly divided. I would be fine with Stacey inheriting half of the money."

"I agree that it's the right thing to do because your uncle's will states, and I quote, 'All my earthly possessions present and future are bequeathed to my only child Stacey Bellamy.'"

This was news to me, but then again, I had never seen my uncle's will. I would have no reason to. "Stacey gave you his will?"

He nodded.

"It was almost like my uncle knew there was more money out there."

He shrugged. "It's possible, or he just wanted to be cautious if something more was discovered. Perhaps he had an inkling his mother was tucking money away all these years."

The only person who would know that for sure was my uncle, and he was dead.

"If your uncle was still alive, this would be a moot point. He would inherit half and that would be that. But as you can see, it gets a little sticky when we are talking about heirs of heirs. Your uncle died not long after your grandmother, correct?"

"It was three or four years later. I was in California at the time."

He nodded.

"Where do we go from here?" I asked.

"If you want this to go away quickly," he said, "you will have to convince your father to divide the money with Stacey. When that decision is made, we can cash in the stocks and begin the probate process. Even if he agrees tomorrow, it will be months before either party sees any money. If your father won't sign, it could be years."

"How much money is fifty percent of the stocks?"

"Until we sell them, we don't know for certain, but the financial adviser I spoke with estimated that if you began the process now, both your father and Stacey would receive six hundred thousand dollars."

I shivered and thought of everything I could do with that money for the farm. I could expand the orchard. The farm stand that I had been dreaming of could be installed, and I could hire more help. However, I could easily lose that much if Dad dug his heels in and fought with Stacey for years to come. How were we going to pay the legal fees? We didn't have extra cash sitting around. The farm could easily be driven deeper into debt because of his stubbornness.

"I have been practicing law for a long time, mostly in Detroit. Most of my cases were settled out of court. Everyone who made the difficult decision to settle and avoid the agony of being sued had the same expression on their face as you do now."

"I should convince Dad to agree."

"I'm not advising you either way at this point," he said. "With the incident that happened at the National Cherry Festival, Stacey isn't in a position to make a fuss about the stocks right now. Go home. Sleep on it. Wait until the National Cherry Festival is over. I know it's a major event for your farm. I don't want you making such a huge decision when you're distracted with so much else."

He was right. I was distracted with the farm, the National Cherry Festival, and the murder.

"All right," I agreed. "I'll discuss it with my father. It's his decision."

He nodded.

"Can I ask you for another bit of advice?"

He smiled. "Shoot."

"I think that someone is targeting the sheep on my farm."

"How so?" he asked.

I explained about finding the snare in the orchard.

"And you are sure it wasn't there before?"

"I'm certain it wasn't there over the weekend, and I found it on Monday. Actually, my cat found it."

His eyes widened. "Is your cat okay?"

"She wasn't hurt but is sorely offended."

Huckleberry whimpered. He loved Esmeralda dearly and hated to think of her in any pain.

"Are you thinking Stacey might have done this?" he asked.

"No. Honestly, that never crossed my mind."

"Is it possible?"

I swallowed. "I would hope my own cousin wouldn't want to hurt one of my animals or me."

"If you can prove that Stacey is behind the attack, then you would have a good case to get her to drop her objection to the inheritance."

I bit the inside of my lip. I didn't like the sound of this at all. If Stacey was behind sabotaging the farm, it would hurt my father as well as me.

"It would be helpful if you could find out. My suggestion is to put several trail cameras out there tonight," Jamie said. "It might be the best way keep an eye on things."

Cameras? Why hadn't I thought of it before? I came from a film background. Recording the events in the orchard should have been at the top of my list.

"How expensive is that?"

"The cameras aren't bad. We have them at our home. It's the monthly fee for the service that adds up. However, you can watch the cameras on your mobile device. It's worth the money."

Dollar signs danced in my head, but I knew he was right. Honestly, some sort of security system should have been on the top of my to-do list for the last year.

He wrote something on a piece of paper. "Here's the company I use. It's pricey." He shrugged. "It's a security system for your farm. You can write it off on your taxes. We can never be too careful these days."

I took the piece of paper and stood up. "Thank you. You've given me a lot to think about."

He smiled and walked me to the door.

When I was out in the waiting room, Cindy offered me three more cookies. This time I didn't hesitate.

Chapter Thirty-Three

When Huckleberry and I stepped out onto the street, my head was spinning. I wasn't in a great headspace to enter the general store and talk Norman into selling my soap. However, he didn't let me make that decision. The bear of a man, who could have been anywhere between forty-five and seventy, was outside of the store, sweeping dirt and leaves away from the front door.

He spotted me. "Shiloh Bellamy! Get over here. Jessa said there's something you want to show me."

I sighed. Jessa was well-intentioned, but at times, she forced my hand because otherwise she knew I would likely never get around to doing what I promised I would do.

Huckleberry and I walked over to him. "Hey, Norman."

"What do you have to show me?"

"I've been making soap."

"Soap? Jessa came over here and got all riled up over soap?"

I shrugged.

"Well, I should take a look at it or she'll come back and give me a hard time again. Bring them in." He leaned his broom against the wall and took Huckleberry's leash. "Huck and I will go get a treat while you do that."

Huckleberry's whole backend wiggled in delight at the mention of his favorite word, *treat*. The two of them went inside.

Leaving me with no other choice, I went to my truck to collect the box of cherry vanilla soaps I'd made.

Inside the general store, Huckleberry was living his best life, lying on a plush dog bed and gnawing on a piece of beef jerky. He didn't even look up when I entered the store. I didn't blame him. Snacks in bed were my favorite too.

"What do you have here?" Norman stood behind the old soda fountain counter. In the summer months, he sold ice cream and milkshakes in the afternoons and evenings. But after the conversation I'd just had with Jamie, a large strawberry milkshake would hit the spot a lot better than a cup of tea.

I set the box in front of him and opened it.

"These smell okay," Norman said.

"Really?" I raised my brow because in Norman-speak *okay* was equal to amazing. He wasn't an overly complimentary man.

"What are you looking to sell them for?"

"At the festival, I sell them for six dollars each."

"You could probably get more," he said. "The tourists that come in here love homemade Michigan things. A lot of the ladies browse while their husbands enjoy their milkshakes. I'd start at eight. We can always lower the price if they don't move. I'll take ten percent of every bar sold."

I pushed the box toward him. "You've got a deal." I shook my head. "That went way easier than expected."

"Well, I will confess that Jessa told me you were bringing in something and said I had better take them on consignment or she'd remove the Reuben sandwich I love from her menu."

"Wow." I reminded myself to thank Jessa later.

"You can imagine my relief that I do actually like your soaps. I can make both Jessa and myself happy, which is always my goal." He paused. "Did I see you come down from upstairs?" he asked.

I nodded. "I was meeting with Jamie."

"Over your grandmother's money?"

I sighed. It was impossible to keep a secret in the Glen.

"Stacey was there yesterday," he added.

I nodded. "Jamie told me. We're hoping we can come to some sort of compromise."

"Did he tell you Tanner Birchwood was with her?"

My heart stopped. "No."

I left the general store feeling good about selling my soaps on commission through Norman but also feeling awful about his revelation that Stacey had visited my attorney's office with Tanner. Why? I didn't know that the two of them were even friendly. I knew they had dated very briefly, but I thought for sure it was over when she admitted to her relationship with Dane Fullbright.

Did she take up with Tanner again when Dane died? Would Tanner kill Dane to get him out of the way? My head was spinning. Inside my truck, I leaned my head on the steering wheel. I needed to go back to the farm.

"You look like you could use a friend."

I looked up through my open window to find Quinn looking into the truck. Huckleberry jumped on my lap and leaned his forepaws on the door so he could get a head scratch from one of his favorite people.

Quinn was in his fireman uniform of a track pants and a department T-shirt. The thin garments were easy to pull a fireman's suit over if the need should arise.

"I was just resting my eyes, as my grandma would say."

He smiled. "I thought you would be at the festival by now."

"I'm heading that way," I said. "Did Hazel and Chesney get off okay?"

"Oh yeah, Chesney was right on time and even had breakfast from Jessa's to give Hazel in the car. You must have warned her how Hazel gets hangry." He chuckled.

"I think she already knew that from all the time they've spent together at my farm."

He nodded. "Are you staying for the fireworks after the festival tomorrow?"

"I wasn't planning on it." I scratched Huckleberry's back. "I don't know how Huckleberry will take all the noise. It would be awful if he ran off in the middle of the fireworks show."

"I understand." He cleared his throat. "If you do go, Hazel and I would like you to sit with us. Between the three of us, I think we can keep Huckleberry calm."

"You're not working tomorrow?"

He shook his head. "I worked Memorial Day, so I get this one off. To be honest, I got the better deal. The chance of fire is much higher on the Fourth." He rocked back on his heels. "Will you think about tomorrow?" He sounded hopeful.

"I will, but it's really up to Huckleberry."

The pug looked at me as if to ask why we kept saying his name over and over. I patted his flank.

Quinn scratched the pug between the ears. "I think in your case just about everything is up to Huckleberry."

He wasn't wrong.

"It's a good thing he likes me so much then, isn't it?" Quinn gave Huckleberry one more head scratch, waved, and walked down the street toward the station, leaving me to wonder what that all meant.

Chapter Thirty-Four

Something was bothering me about the case, so instead of going straight to the festival, I texted Chesney that I had to make one more stop, and I drove to my old university. After I finished school, I'd never returned to campus until I was there with Whit earlier in the week; I hadn't even gone to my graduation. Logan had been killed just a few weeks before, and I finished my classes and drove to California, planning to never look back.

Yet here I was, just like I had returned to the farm and returned to Jessa's Place. It seemed fitting that after all this time, I would come back here too.

Since it was summer, I didn't know how much luck I would have finding anyone in the theater and film department to talk to, but I felt like I had to try.

When I was a student, the dramatic arts building had been brand new. It was a glass and steel structure that was meant to remind people that acting and production excellence wasn't just on the two coasts; it could happen in the Midwest as well.

I stepped into the building and a rush of memories

washed over me. The building still smelled the same, a mix of set paint and old cloth. I passed the theater where my movies used to be shown and walked toward the faculty offices. The glass door that led into the office area was ajar.

"I think it's time he got the respect he deserved," a high-pitched woman's voice said. "He gave everything to this university and was pushed aside by jealous man. I'll write an article about it if I have to."

An article. I recognized that voice. It was Penny Lee Odders. It sounded like she was here on assignment, but that surprised me. Wouldn't the bigger story be at the festival?

"I feel terrible about how everything went for Theodore, but it wasn't my decision."

"You would have spoken up! Rest assured I will include that in my article."

There was the thunk of a door hitting the wall, and Penny Lee appeared in the hallway. She pulled up short when she saw me standing there. "What are you doing here?"

I blinked. "Since I'm in town for the festival, I thought I would come visit my old school. What are you doing here?"

"My job. Writing articles." She narrowed her eyes. "I have my eye on you. I know you're up to something, and I will get to the bottom of it."

Before I could respond, a door opened and an man with white hair stepped into the hallway. "Shiloh Bellamy, as I live and breathe, is that you?"

He grinned from ear to ear. He wore pair of wire-rimmed glasses on his nose and another hung from his neck on a chain. He always had two pairs of glasses like that because he needed them for distance and for close-up, but he could never get used to bifocals.

"Professor Chan!" I said. "I didn't know you were still teaching here."

He laughed. "I'll never leave."

Penny Lee glared at us both. "Remember what I said, John."

"I could not forget it," Professor Chan said in reply.

Penny Lee stomped out of the office.

I watched her go. "Yikes. What was that about?"

He shook his head. "I'm glad you caught me. I was just about to leave. Come back to my office, and let's catch up."

I followed the professor into his office and let out a breath. To my delight, the room was just as soothing as I remembered it. Professor Chan was a true minimalist. There were no plaques on his walls or even blinds on his windows. The only items on his glass desk were his laptop, phone, and a sand garden I remember fiddling with when I was a student and had to come to the professor to help me out of a jam. He was always willing to listen.

"I heard that you were back in Michigan," he began.

"I'm running the family farm now," I said.

He chuckled. "You're still a TV producer too. We would love to have you as an adjunct at the college if you ever want to."

I raised my eyebrows. Teaching television production wasn't something I had ever thought about, but I was certainly qualified to do it. "I'll think about it," I said.

"Good. So are you here to just visit campus, or something else?"

He always seemed to know when something more was going on.

"I wanted to talk to you about Dane Fullbright."

He made a face and leaned back in his chair.

"I was there when he died." I paused. "Because I have a booth at the National Cherry Festival," I explained. "I tried to save him."

He nodded for me to go on.

"My cousin was in a relationship with him."

"Stacey. Yes, I know. I advised her against it, but she did not listen."

"How did you know about it?"

He pressed his lips together. "I overheard a conversation. These office walls are thin." He left it at that.

"Did you tell Stacey he was married?"

He shook his head. "I assumed she knew."

"She didn't."

He made a face. "At the time, I thought I was overstepping, but now, I wish I had said more. If I had, perhaps they would have parted ways long before the play began, and Dane would still be alive."

"I want to find out what happened, and the best way to do that is learn all that I can about Dane."

He steepled his hands together. "And how can I help you with that?"

"Was anyone upset with Dane here at the university?"

"There were plenty of people upset with Dane and for all sorts of good reasons," Professor Chan said.

"Can you give me an example?"

He nodded. "I can give you one that is at the top of my mind. I know you weren't a theater major, but do you remember drama professor Dr. Theo Cassen?"

"Oh yeah. A lot of his students acted in my productions, and he always came to the practices to give them notes. He was a nice man." I frowned. "But he was very elderly even when I was s student."

"He was. He held on to his position as long as he could. He would have stayed longer if he'd been able." His face fell. "Theo's in a facility for dementia now."

"I'm sorry to hear that."

He nodded. "After he retired, he went downhill very quickly. Even when he was teaching, he was showing signs of confusion and forgetfulness, but he was managing it. Dane joined the faculty at just about the time Theo began to struggle."

"Let me guess: he didn't like Dr. Cassen," I said.

"He didn't, and he very much wanted Theo out of the way. Dane felt like Theo was holding the department back. It took Dane two years, but he was relentless and he convinced the university to force Theo into retirement. Dane said that his quick decline after retirement was proof Theo was unfit to teach, but it was my belief that working slowed the progression of the disease." His face fell. "I know Theo couldn't teach forever. No one can, but I do wish Dane and the university had given him just a little more time."

"I'm so sorry."

He nodded. "His son is a student here, and I try to do whatever I can to help Theo's son. It's a promise that I made to Theo, even though by the time I made it, he no longer understood me."

"He understood you," I assured him. "As for Dr. Cassen's son, do you mean Eliot, who is in the play?"

"That's right. He's Ferdinand. I hear he is wonderful in the role. He might have even been wonderful at Prospero, but Dane wanted that part for himself. That's what Dane was like. Selfish. He didn't care who he hurt to make it to the top." He cleared his throat and his face flushed. "I'm sorry. I shouldn't speak so."

"It's okay," I said. Even so, I was surprised at the uncharacteristic venom in his voice.

Chapter Thirty-Five

I had a lot to think about while Huckleberry and I drove the short distance between the university and Open Space Park.

Since I was arriving so much later than I'd planned to, I expected to circle endlessly looking for a parking spot, but as luck would have it, someone was leaving just as I pulled in. I slid into the spot and said to Huckleberry, "Maybe things are turning around for us."

He cocked his head back and forth but didn't look convinced. Huckleberry was a glass-half-empty kind of pug.

My parking space was closer to the beach than the Cherry Farm Market, but I was happy to have it.

Huckleberry and I hopped out of the cab, and I opened the tailgate. I lifted yet another crate of baked goods I had stayed up baking from the back. We had just stepped on the grass when someone shouted, "Come one, come all. The highly anticipated cherry pit spitting competition is back!"

I almost dropped the heavy crate.

I had Huckleberry's leash looped around my wrist, and he whimpered at my feet. I was pretty certain after our busy morning, he was ready to curl up in his dog bed in the booth, but it wasn't like I could pass up this chance to snoop.

"It won't take long, Huck, I promise."

He blew air out of his wrinkled mouth, sending slobber flying through the air. He acted like he'd heard that before. The truth was he had.

I carried the crate and led Huckleberry to the edge of the crowd. Even though it was a weekday afternoon, the crowd was much larger than the crowd that had been standing around when Dane was killed. It made me think that most of the people there wanted to see if something else tragic would happen.

I spotted the man who had made the announcement about the return of the cherry spitting competition. He wore a red, white, and blue top hat, star-patterned suspenders, and had a bullhorn in his head. He was doing his best to dispel the stigma of the cherry pit spitting competition being dangerous.

He held the bullhorn to his mouth. "As the younger ladies haven't had a chance to compete due to complications, we will begin today's spitting with the thirty-and-under women! Ladies, get your cherries ready!" Four women stood next to the emcee. "We are so glad that you are here and willing to take part in this traditional event."

To my shock one of those women was Slade Carra. She held a cherry in her hand and stood with the other women, politely waiting for her cue to spit.

"We will begin today's competition with Slade Carra. Some of you remember Slade from the International Cherry

Pit Spitting Contest in Eau Claire. She is the reigning spit-ting champion in the youth category in that contest. No one has come close to her distance of forty-eight feet. She hasn't spat in years but has decided to come out of retirement for this very special day. We are grateful to you, Slade. Are you ready?"

Slade gave the slightest of nods.

So she had been telling the truth about growing up spit-ting cherry pits? Had she and her mother moved to that big house on the bay recently? I was so confused when it came to Slade. I wanted to believe what she said, but at the same time, she'd told so many lies up to this point. How could I possibly tell fact from fiction?

Slade popped the cherry in her mouth, chewed up the fruit, and gave the emcee the thumbs-up sign that she was ready to spit.

I shook my head. Of all the weird games and sports I had seen in my life, this had to be the oddest.

"Here we go!" the emcee shouted into his bullhorn. "Whenever you're ready, Slade!"

Slade stepped back, then lunged forward hard on her right foot. As her foot hit the ground, the cherry pit flew from her mouth. It landed dozens of feet away.

A man dressed head to toe in cherry red went out on the sand to measure the distance. He even had a hat with a black cherry stem coming out from the top of it. I didn't remember this during the first cherry pit spitting compe-tition. I had been too distracted by Dane, but I thought I would have remembered that hat. It made me believe that the festival committee was pulling out all the stops to make the crowd forget about the unfortunate events from the last competition.

The cherry man called out, "Forty and half feet."

"Oh my!" The emcee called. "That's not close to her youth record, but it is going to be hard to beat. Slade's is going to be the number to beat in the women's competition to be sure!"

Slade blushed and stepped back to let the next female competitor take her place.

I scanned the crowd. Chief Sterling was among the spectators, and I felt a little better about the competition with him being there. I also saw two other Traverse City police officers nearby. They were all keeping a close eye on things.

I sidled up to the chief.

He glanced at me and then returned his attention to the competition. "You know, I have seen people do this hundreds of times in my life. I'm from Traverse City, born and raised, but I have to tell you, I have never watched this contest as intently as I have today."

"Do you expect something to happen?"

"Not particularly." He removed his sunglasses and tucked them into the breast pocket of his uniform. "We have no reason to. It's as clear as day that Dane Fullbright was the target last time and most likely killed by someone he knew."

I thought the same. "Even so, is it wise to leave the cherries out in those little paper baskets?"

"No worries there," he said. "The committee changed it so contestants have to bring their own cherries with them now. It's the best way to ensure that nothing unsightly is done to the cherry prior to the competition."

Unsightly? Like poisoning? I wondered.

"That's probably something they should always do," I said.

"I think so too," he agreed.

While we had been talking, the second contestant had spat her cherry pit, but it only flew a disappointing forty feet. Slade remained in the lead.

"I'm surprised to see Slade participating," I said.

Slade was on the other side of the rope that kept the spectators from getting too close to the competition. She was searching the crowd for someone. When her eyes landed on me, she gave me a look that surely would have sent me straight to my grave if looks could kill. It seemed that I was no longer the nice lady who listened to her problems and bought her tacos.

"I was surprised too," the chief admitted.

"Is Cayden here then?" I asked, looking around.

"I haven't seen him, but I'm not surprised. He's in a lot of trouble over the way he treated Slade and likely doesn't want to be around her or the police."

My brow went up. "Did Slade agree to press charges?"

He frowned. "No, but her mother made a statement of how she witnessed Cayden mistreat her daughter. It's not enough to make an arrest on, unfortunately."

"And Cayden's involvement in the murder?" I asked.

"We haven't determined that yet." He answered this last question with finality to let me know very clearly that my game of Twenty Questions had come to an end.

He turned to me. "How about I ask you a question?"

I blinked. "About the murder? I've already told you everything I know about it."

He folded his arms. "It's not about the murder. It's about your intentions with Milan."

"My intentions?" I squeaked.

"He cares about you. It's as clear as day to me, and he's said as much. Don't break his heart. If you aren't sure he's the one for you, don't start anything. He's been hurt before, and I don't want to see that happen to him again."

"I'm glad Milan has a friend like you, Chief." I paused. "And I promise, I won't hurt him."

He nodded and moved to the other side of the beach.

Chapter Thirty-Six

"Gee whiz, Shiloh, where have you been?" Chesney asked as Huckleberry and I entered the booth a little while later.

I set the crate, which felt like I had been carrying it for years, on one of the folding chairs. "I'm sorry. I just got caught up in—"

"Solving a murder," Chesney said. "We know." Her chuckle took the bite out of her words.

"How's the day been?" I asked.

"Amazing!" Hazel spoke up.

Chesney grinned. "She's right. We are closed to selling out of your baked goods, so I'm glad you brought more. They were a big hit in the morning. I spoke to the coffee truck and we worked out a deal that if someone bought three of our pastries, they get a coffee from the truck for free. It's cost us very little. The regular coffees are two dollars each and increased our sales considerably." She wrinkled her nose. "I hope it is okay that I did that without checking with you first."

"Of course it's okay. It's a great idea!" I said.

She grinned.

"Now, why don't you two girls go and enjoy the festival? I've trapped you here for too long."

"Really?" Hazel asked.

"Now, you are really making me feel bad, like I have kept you captive here."

"It's not captive," Hazel said. "Trust me. It's way better than being stuck in my grandmother's house when her friends are playing bridge. And for the record, that game makes no sense."

I laughed. I had never been able to understand bridge either.

After Chesney and Hazel left, Huckleberry and I settled into the booth. The next hour or so went by with great sales—Chesney's three pastries for free coffee idea was a real hit—and chatting with friendly customers. I almost felt like a real farm owner again and not a half-baked sleuth.

That feeling didn't last long when a very drawn Lily Fullbright came to my booth. "Do you have a moment to talk?" she asked.

I had just finished up with my last customer and it was close to dinnertime, so many of the visitors were making their way to the food trucks or into town to one of the restaurants.

"Sure," I said, "why don't you come back behind the booth?"

She walked around the side of the booth and slid into one of the two folding chairs. Huckleberry sensed her sadness and promptly lay on her feet. Lily didn't appear to mind.

She looked down at the pug. "Is it odd to mourn a man that I was in the process of divorcing?"

I didn't know what I had expected her to say, but it wasn't that.

"I don't think it's odd. You were married to him a long time."

"Over fifteen years," Lily said. "I wanted him out of my life, but I didn't want him dead. And I know people think I might have done it, but I didn't kill him."

Even though I couldn't prove what she said was true, I believed her. As the thought crossed my mind, I could hear Milan saying in my head not to jump to conclusions this way or that way.

"And now I find out that my assistant was infatuated with him."

I raised my brow. I hadn't been the one to tell her that. I decided to play dumb. "What do you mean?"

"The police came to my house and asked me about Slade. They said she had a motive to kill my husband because she had feelings for him." She shook her head in disgust. "Dane was many things, and I know that he cheated on me more than once. Stacey Bellamy wasn't the first."

This news didn't come as a surprise.

"But one thing I knew for sure: he would not have an inappropriate relationship with one of his students. That is where he drew the line. I honestly don't think he knew how Slade felt about him."

"What happened when you learned about Slade's feelings for your husband?"

"I called her and fired her over the phone. I was going to let her go anyway, and why would I want my husband's killer on my payroll?"

Huckleberry snuffled in agreement, and I had to admit it was a fair question.

"What makes you so sure that Slade killed your husband?"

"Well, because of the note I found in his study. I gave it to the police." She wrinkled her brow. "I thought you would know about that. I've seen you going around the festival with that county sheriff, and I read the article about the other murders you have solved."

I grimaced. That article by Penny Lee would be the death of me yet.

"I should admit that I'm not a police officer or officially on the case. I have been looking into it—"

"Because you tried to save Dane's life," she finished for me. "Yes, I know your motives are pure."

I shifted uncomfortably in my seat. My motives were pure...kind of. I did want to know who killed Dane because he died at my feet, but I also wanted to clear my cousin's name in the hopes it would encourage her, and my father for that matter, to come to come kind of agreement about my grandmother's money. I'd be lying if I said that my motives were purely altruistic.

"What did the note say?" I cleared my throat. "Umm, the chief hasn't shared it with me yet."

"It was warning him that her ex-boyfriend was coming to town for the festival, and he planned to 'mess Dane up.'"

My eyes went wide. Was this the smoking gun that

proved Cayden, Slade's volatile ex-boyfriend, was the one who killed Dane Fullbright?

Shouts and commotion rose from across the park. It was coming from the direction from where the aviation club had been meeting.

"Can you stay here with my dog?" I asked Lily.

She blinked at me. "Your dog?"

"Yes, the pug lying on your feet. You don't have to do anything in the booth, just tell anyone who stops by that I will be back soon."

"Oh-kay?" she stammered, still clearly confused by my excitement.

I ran from the booth toward where the aviation club had parked the old Wildcat. I wasn't the only one. It seemed that half the people at the festival were running or walking in the same direction to see what all the commotion was. Michiganders weren't ones to walk away from a fight. We tended to move toward it and then reminisce about it with a detailed play-by-play for years to come.

"I will not tell you where my son is!" Sam bellowed as he stood in front of the trailer door. "He's done nothing wrong, and I don't appreciate what you are implying by flashing that warrant in my face. This is private property, and you have no right to go inside without my permission."

Sam was standing toe-to-toe with Chief Sterling. It seemed that the note Lily shared with the police caused them to close in on Cayden. I wondered if Chief Sterling was already planning to make this arrest when I spoke with him by the cherry pit spitting competition a few hours before.

"I have every right," Chief Sterling said mildly. "As you said, I am waving a warrant in your face, and it clearly says I can search your home and this trailer."

Sam held out his wrists to the chief as if he were asking him to arrest him. "You'll have to take me in before you can go in there."

The chief's shoulders went up and down in a great sigh. "We've served the warrant. If you neglect to recognize it, that doesn't matter at this point. Collins, can you please search the trailer?"

A young police officer moved around Sam and stepped up to the door. He placed his hand on the door handle. Just as he did, Cayden busted out of the trailer, knocking Officer Collins off his feet. Then Cayden made a run for it, straight to the dock and off the end. At least six police officers ran after him and jumped into the water. They grabbed him, pulled him out of the water, and handcuffed him on the beach.

"What did he think he was going to do? Swim to Canada?" one spectator asked as he sipped a beer from a large plastic cup.

"Not the smartest killer I've ever seen," his friend agreed.

"You've seen a lot of killers?" the first man asked.

"I watch TV, okay?"

I had to agree with the second man. Cayden wasn't the smartest killer I had ever seen either, and I had seen more than my fair share in real life.

Chapter Thirty-Seven

Lily and Huckleberry were peacefully sitting in my booth when I returned to it a few minutes later. Lily stood up. "What's going on? So many people ran by. I was scared to even peek out of the booth and see what the commotion was. Then two police officers walked back the other way. They were soaking wet."

"They arrested Cayden, Slade's ex-boyfriend." I paused. "For Dane's murder."

She covered her mouth with her hand. After a long moment, she said, "So it's over. Now that Dane's killer has been caught, I can get on with the business of putting my life back together."

I nodded.

She walked over to me and took both of my hands in hers. Despite appearing so put together, I noticed she had paint under her fingernails. She was an artist after all, but it made her seem more human to me. She wasn't perfect, and she had endured a lot during her marriage with Dane. There are always two sides to any relationship, but I was firmly on her side on this one.

"Thank you so much! I feel like I can breathe again." She let out a big breath as if to prove that was true.

"There is no reason to thank me," I said. "Chief Sterling and his officers solved that case."

"I will thank them too, but I know that you played a part." She let go of my hands. "I should head home. There is so much I have to do, but right now, I just want a glass of wine and long nap."

"Sometimes rest is the best way to recover," I agreed. "Wine isn't bad either."

Lily stepped out of the booth, and I watched her walk away.

An hour later, Hazel ran back to the booth with a pink and yellow cotton candy cloud on a stick that was twice the size of her head.

"Are you going to eat all that?" I asked.

"Not in one sitting," she replied.

"Please don't tell you grandmother that I was the one who bought it for you."

Chesney stepped behind the booth with an equally large cotton candy cloud. Hers was blue and white. "I was the one who got it. I love the stuff."

"It doesn't make you sick?" I asked.

She pulled off a large piece. "Sick. No way. It's just sugar." Chesney popped the piece in her mouth.

Ahh, to be in my twenties again.

"Anything exciting happen while we were gone?" Chesney asked, pulling another piece of cotton candy from her cloud.

"Yes, actually." I went on to tell them both about Cayden's arrest.

"What?" Chesney asked. "That's great! It means you don't have to be running around Traverse City looking for a killer any longer. We can just go back to the cherry business."

"Right," I said, but some thought I couldn't reach was still in the back of my mind.

Chesney narrowed her eyes. "You're done with the case, right?"

"Yes, right," I said perhaps a little too quickly. "Chief Sterling solved it."

She cocked her head. "Are you disappointed that *you* weren't the one to crack the case?"

"Don't be silly." I reached for her cotton candy and pulled off a piece no larger than my thumb. I put it in my mouth and could feel my teeth begin to decay on contact.

At first it was difficult to put thoughts of Dane, Lily, Slade, and Cayden behind me, but the business of the festival soon took care of that. I sent Chesney and Hazel home at five and spent the remainder of the evening selling pastries and soaps to tourists and locals alike.

When I finally loaded up my pickup for the night, I was exhausted. It seemed that Huckleberry was too because he passed out on the passenger seat as soon as he sat down. Oh to be a dog and not have to drive.

The farmhouse was dark when we rolled down my drive-way. It was after eleven at night now, and Dad would have gone to bed hours ago. Between his part in *The Tempest* and the long hours I was putting in at the festival, I had yet to find the time to talk to him about Stacey and the stocks my grandmother left behind. I promised myself I would make the time tomorrow morning before I left for the festival, even though it was going to be an uncomfortable conversation. My dad was not a fan of heart-to-hearts.

I was almost too tired to walk to the cabin and considered sleeping in my childhood room in the farmhouse. However, knowing how angry that would make Esmeralda motivated me to get out of the truck.

Before I headed down the path, I coaxed the sheep into the barn and was happy to see that Diva had already put herself and all her chicken minions into the henhouse. All I had to do was latch the door after them.

The security company that my attorney, Jamie, suggested I use for the farm couldn't come out for another two weeks. In the meantime, I had two trail cameras rush delivered to the farm while I was at the National Cherry Festival, and I put them up on either side of the orchard before heading to the cabin for the night. I wished that I had been able to put them up sooner to watch the orchard on the app on my phone throughout the day. I still didn't know who or why someone put a snare in my cherry orchard.

As I walked down the path to my cabin with Huckleberry trundling along on my heels, I opened the app again.

I watched the real-time video. There wasn't anything out of the ordinary. Perhaps I could put the sheep back into the orchard the next day.

I was just about to close the app when the figure of a man walked into my screen.

I froze midstep, and Huckleberry, who was determined to make it to the cabin ASAP so he could go back to sleep, ran into the back of my legs.

"Oh no," I whispered.

What should I do? Should I go to the orchard and see who the trespasser was all by myself? I supposed I wasn't completely alone. Huckleberry was with me, but he wasn't going to be able to hold his own in a fight.

On the screen, I watched the figure move through the orchard. As much as I wanted to rush into the orchard and ask the person what they thought they were doing there, I knew it was a terrible idea.

I didn't want to wake my father. He was unsteady on his feet, and knowing him, he would come out of the farmhouse with one of his Civil War–era pistols and shoot himself or me. First and foremost, I didn't want anyone to be shot, not even the person in my orchard.

I couldn't call Quinn; he just started another shift at the firehouse. I more or less knew his work schedule because I watched Hazel so often for him. And I was reluctant to call Chief Randy. He wouldn't take me seriously. I tapped on the screen and called the man that I realized I had come to rely on the most in the last six months. In my heart, I knew that meant something I wasn't ready to admit even to myself.

Chapter Thirty-Eight

Sheriff Milan Penbrook was out of his pickup even before the tires fully settled on the gravel driveway. "Are you all right?"

Huckleberry and I were perched on some hay bales outside of the barn with Esmeralda. The cat had come looking for us when we were late showing up at the cabin. She must have used the cat door in the back door of the cabin to come looking for us.

If I didn't have someone lurking around my orchard, it would have been the perfect night. The air was warm and there was a light fresh breeze. I could smell the rain that was promised by the end of the week.

I stood up. "I'm fine. Nervous, but fine. I don't like the idea of someone trespassing on my farm. I have been sitting here second-guessing myself and wondering if I should just stomp over there and flush the culprit out."

He raised his brow. "Flush the culprit out? Like a duck?"

"Just like," I said.

His mild attempt at a joke put me more at ease. I had been on edge since calling him.

"I'm glad you didn't go to the orchard. We don't know who is there, and that person could be very dangerous. Thankfully, I was nearby. I do wish you had told me about the snare sooner. Can I see your app?"

I handed him the phone. He squinted at the screen.

"They're not there anymore," I said. "They left, or at least it looks like they did."

"I'll go check it out."

"I'm coming with you."

He sighed. "Fine, but you need to leave the cat and dog behind."

Huckleberry looked up at me with tired eyes. He wasn't interested in going anywhere but bed.

I pointed at the hay bale. "Stay."

The little pug promptly fell to his side and went to sleep.

"Rough day?" the chief asked.

"The roughest for Huck," I said.

Esmeralda hissed at me, but she curled up next to her pug brother. With the animals settled, Milan and I headed to the orchard.

The sky was clear, and there was more than enough moonlight to see the way to the cherry orchard. As the low cherry trees came into view, he held a finger to his mouth. I nodded in understanding.

The gate to the electric fence was open as I had left it. Nothing seemed to be amiss. Then I saw something move in the trees. A form crossed between two of the rows and was hunched over.

Milan shot through the gate. "Stop. County Sheriff!" Milan cried and took off after the person.

I followed closely behind, but Milan's legs were longer, so by the time I reached him he already had Tanner Birchwood pinned to the ground.

"Tanner! What are you doing in my orchard in the middle of the night?"

Milan had Tanner's cheeks pressed into the grass. The organic farmer struggled to get out of Milan's grasp.

I touched Milan's shoulder. "It's okay. It's my neighbor."

Milan let go of Tanner and stood up. Tanner rolled over onto this back. "I think you broke something."

Milan glared at him and adjusted his glasses, which had been bumped askew by his tackle move. "Stand up."

Tanner stood and shuffled his feet. In the moonlight, I could see dirt on the front of his polo shirt and a leaf stuck to his cheek.

I took a step toward him. "Are you the one who put a rabbit snare in my orchard? Was it some kind of sick joke? Esmeralda lost half of her tail fur. She or Huckleberry or one of my sheep could have been seriously hurt."

Tanner knocked the leaf from his cheek and stepped backward, stumbling over a tree root in the process. He righted himself before he fell. "It wasn't me!"

"Then what are you doing here?" I asked.

"I was walking around my property," he said in an offended voice.

"At midnight?" I asked.

"I have a lot on my mind. If you want to know the truth, farming is a lot harder than it looks."

He was saying this like it was news to me.

"It's not advancing as quickly or as well as I would like it to. I'm not making any money." He brushed dirt from his shirt, but it didn't help; it just pressed the dirt deeper into the fabric.

I almost laughed. What farmer made money? The profits that were made were always put back into the farm. There was no excess. However, Tanner might not have known that before moving here to Michigan and buying half of my family's land. He came from a business background in Chicago where making money was the name of the game. A year in Michigan not making a cent must have been a very rude awakening to him.

"I'm thinking of selling my farm and going back to the city. I had the idea of being an organic farmer, and I certainly made lots of improvements to the property. However, I can't spend all my money on land with no return."

"Okay," Milan said. "Say we believe you on that. That still doesn't answer why you were on Shiloh's side of the property line."

Tanner pressed his lip together. "I thought I saw someone in the trees and came over to check it out. When I got here, the person ran off."

"You're lying. I would have seen you. I have cameras set up, and I did see someone, but if you 'came over to check it out,' I would have seen two people not just one!" I scowled.

"What did the person look like? Were they male or female?" Milan asked.

Tanner turned to him. "It was a man. I don't know his exact age. He was young. White."

"Hair color?" Milan asked.

Tanner shook his head. "He was wearing a hat, and I only saw him for a split second. I stepped on a twig. The sound alerted him, and he took off."

Milan didn't say anything and seemed to be mulling this over.

While Milan was deep in thought, I asked, "What were you doing with Stacey in my attorney's office this week?"

He blinked at me. "How do you know about that?"

"Cherry Glen is a small town, Tanner. Someone saw the two of you."

He frowned. "Stacey and I are friends. She told me how you wanted to steal her money, and due to my extensive business background, she came to me for advice. She wanted me to be there when she heard the attorney out since I know more about such things."

"I'm not trying to keep Stacey from the money. I want her to have half just like she wants. It's not up to me. It's up to my father." I couldn't keep the frustration from my voice.

Milan placed a hand on my shoulder. The warmth of his skin burned through my T-shirt. I bit my tongue from saying more.

"Well," Tanner said. "You should tell your cousin that, because she believes it's coming from you."

How well I knew that.

"Can I go now?" Tanner didn't even try to keep the whining out of his voice.

"Yes," Milan said. "But don't come over here again. If you see something in Shiloh's orchard, call the police."

"Gladly." With that, Tanner stomped away.

Milan and I watched him go, and I didn't take a full breath until he disappeared from sight.

I turned to Milan. "It can't be Cayden who Tanner saw. He was arrested."

He nodded. "It may be unrelated to the events at the National Cherry Festival."

"It may," I said, but I wasn't convinced.

Milan and I checked the orchard for any signs of more snares or other traps that might injure one of my animals. We didn't find anything. Even so, Panda Bear and the ewes would be in their yard by the barn for at least another day.

After checking the grounds, we walked back to the farmhouse and barn.

I stood by Milan's truck. "Thanks for coming."

"I'm not leaving yet," he said. "I'm walking you, Huckleberry, and Esmeralda back to your cabin."

"It's already one in the morning. I can't ask you to do that."

"You're not. I'm telling you that's what I'm going to do."

I saw there was no point in arguing with him, and I was too tired to try. We collected the cat and dog. Milan carried Huckleberry, who fell back asleep in his arms. Esmeralda walked behind us with her half-bald tail held high.

We were halfway to the cabin when I spoke, "I don't know if this is the right time, Sheriff, but you asked me a question once upon a time."

He eyed me. "What question was that?" The right corner of his mouth turned up in a small smile.

I knew he remembered the question, but he wanted me to say it. "You asked me to dinner. I never gave you an answer."

"No, you did not."

My cabin came into view. Esmeralda made a dash for the door. Huckleberry wriggled in Milan's arms until he put the pug down on the ground. He galloped after his feline sister.

We reached the door. I unlocked it and let the animals inside. Both bolted for the bedroom. I laughed. "They are going straight to bed."

Milan chuckled too, and then his tone turned serious. "Did you have answer to that question now?"

I looked up into his dark eyes that sparkled in the reflection of my porch light. "I do. The answer is yes. I very much want to go to dinner with you."

His face broke into a grin. "That was worth the wait." He leaned forward and kissed me on my doorstep. "Happy Independence Day, Shiloh Bellamy." He turned and walked down the long road back to his truck.

For me, I didn't need to see the fireworks to know they were there.

Chapter Thirty-Nine

The next afternoon in our booth at the Cherry Farm Market, Chesney eyed me. "Shiloh, what's up with you?"

It had been a very busy day. I thought the weekend at the National Cherry Festival was crowded, but that couldn't even compare to the Fourth of July.

"Up with me? What do you mean?"

"You have been smiling all day."

I wrinkled my brow. "Don't I usually smile?"

"Yes, but not with that giddy look in your eye. Spill!"

"There's nothing to spill."

"Please." She snorted and then her face changed. "Ohmigosh, you agreed to go out with Sheriff Penbrook!"

"Ches," I hissed and looked around to see if there was anyone I knew nearby.

She lowered her volume. "That's it, isn't it? I'm so happy."

"You are?" I asked.

"Yes! You have been waffling back and forth between the sheriff and Quinn for months. I'm so glad you finally made the right choice."

"The right choice?" I asked.

"Sure. Quinn Killian is a nice man, but he has too much baggage and history with you. But Milan..." She sighed and placed her hands over her heart.

"I worry about Hazel," I admitted.

"Hazel will be fine. She cares about you because you're her friend, not because of your relationship with her dad."

I prayed that Chesney was right.

We didn't have time to talk about it more as the traffic at the booth picked up again. There was no doubt in my mind that the Fourth of July was going to be our most profitable day yet.

Darkness settled over the bay, and I set the last crate on my wagon to transport my wares back to my pickup and go home.

Chesney wiped her bandanna over her brow. "Three more days of this. I'll be happy going back to the farm. This has been a little people-y for me."

I chuckled. "Me too. It's been a long week. I can't thank you enough for all the extra hours you put in."

"I wouldn't miss it. The festival is a huge event for the farm, and I've learned a lot about how other farms operate. It's been invaluable to my graduate work."

"Why don't you go enjoy the fireworks, and Huckleberry and I will take this last load to my truck and head home."

"You're not staying for the fireworks?" she asked.

"I don't think Huckleberry would enjoy it."

She leaned over and patted the pug. "Probably not." She straightened up. "You don't need help getting this into the truck?"

I shook my head. "Now go, so you can get a good spot before they start."

"Okay!" She took off her apron and tucked it into the wagon. She waved at me. "See you tomorrow, Shi."

I waved back. I really didn't know how I could run the farm without Chesney. The money from grandmother's stocks would be enough to keep her on full-time. I had to talk to my father. I didn't have the opportunity to talk to him like I had wanted to that morning because I overslept after my late night adventure in the orchard with Tanner and Milan. Thinking of last night made me remember Milan's kiss, and I couldn't help but smile. Chesney was right. I was giddy.

"Come on, Huckleberry. Let's go home." I had Huckleberry's leash in one hand and the wagon handle in the other and pulled the wagon around the booth.

I was just thinking about texting Quinn that I was heading home when Hazel came running at me. "Shiloh! Her father followed behind her at a much slower pace."

I stopped. "You guys headed to the fireworks?"

"Yes," she said. "You and Huckleberry should come."

I shook my head. "I don't think it's a good idea. Fireworks and dogs don't mix."

"I'll hold on to him," she insisted.

I smiled. "I know you would, but Huckleberry is just a big chicken, and when I say *chicken*, I don't mean Diva. She's one tough bird."

Hazel's face fell. "I get it."

Quinn caught up with us. "Did you talk her into it?" he asked his daughter.

Hazel shook her head. "No. Huckleberry is a chicken."

Huckleberry snuffled at my feet as if he took issue with that statement.

"Can we help you load your truck at least?" Quinn asked.

I felt my cheeks grow hot. Could he tell by looking at me that I had agreed to a date with Milan? Chesney had been able to tell. Could Quinn?

There was a big boom, and the first firework exploded over the bay in a bright display of yellow and red. Huckleberry hid behind my legs and buried his face in his paws. I had been right in thinking that the little pug wasn't up to fireworks.

"No, I got it. You guys go down by the water so you can see the show better. Chesney is down there somewhere. I'm sure she got the best spot. Text her and find out where she's at. She's likely with her sister."

There was another boom and the fireworks began in earnest. Huckleberry pulled with all his might on his leash. It was time to make our exit. All the while, Hazel was pulling on her father's hand, tugging him toward the bay.

"I don't want to miss it," she cried.

"All right," Quinn said good-naturedly and smiled at me. "Maybe the three of us and Huckleberry can do something together another time that doesn't involve explosions."

My stomach turned. I wasn't the type of woman to be involved with two men at the same time. "I don't know if that's a good idea."

Quinn's face fell. "Why is that?"

"Dad!" Hazel called.

"Go have fun," I said.

Quinn left but not before giving me one last questioning look.

Even though I wasn't down the water, I could see the fireworks clearly on the short walk to the parking lot. Before I loaded the truck bed, I put Huckleberry in the cabin with the windows rolled down. Still terrified from the noise, he flattened himself on the floorboards of the passenger side.

"Oh, Huck," I said. "I'll be as fast as I can."

I was a good ways away from the water, but the noise was deafening between the fireworks, the brass band accompanying the show, and the excited shouts of the crowd.

I opened the tailgate and slide the crates inside. I folded the wagon and slid it into the truck bed between the crates. I had just closed the tailgate when someone came up behind me and covered my mouth and painfully pinned me against the back of the truck. I couldn't move my arms. I couldn't breathe.

I knew it was a man and someone close to my own height. I kicked back, trying to connect with any soft tissue I could.

The man's hot breath was on my neck. "I wouldn't do that if I were you. You don't want that dog of yours hurt."

I froze.

He chuckled. "Thought so. Now, I've tried to be patient with you, but you've forced me to do this. I thought your cat's bald tail would have been warning enough. You're lucky that's all that happened to her. Consider this your last warning to leave the death of Dane Fullbright alone. You understand?"

I couldn't answer because his hand still covered my mouth. I gagged. His skin smelled like barbeque. I would never eat barbeque sauce again.

"That's all," he said. "Do not turn around until I'm gone." He loosened his grip, and I thought for a moment I would get away until he grabbed the back of my ponytail and banged my forehead on the side of the truck. I saw stars.

The pain was instant, and I slid to the ground. I wasn't unconscious though. I had a much thicker skull that my assailant thought I did. I tried to focus on everything around me. The pavement was dirty and grainy. Next to my tire there was a discarded pop can that someone had carelessly dropped.

Without turning my head, I looked the other way. A pair of gray sneakers stared me in the face. I blinked and tried to focus on every detail of the sneakers. They had blue laces. I only saw the front of them, so I couldn't see the name of the manufacturer. They weren't terribly expensive from what I could tell. All these thoughts went through my head. It could have been over in a matter of hours or seconds. I had no sense of time. I just knew that I had to remember those shoes as if my life depended on it. It very well might.

I was too dazed to move, and I didn't try. My instinct told me to play dead until he left.

The right sneaker stepped on my hand, and I willed myself not to react to pain that radiated through my fingers and hand and up into my arm. As if he were satisfied that

I was unconscious or even dead, the sneakers turned and ran away.

I lay there for a long moment before I dared to stir. My assailant was gone I thought, but I wasn't taking any chances by moving too early. Finally, I fumbled in my shorts pocket for my phone, but the fingers of my hand that had been stepped on were stiff. I couldn't seem to wrap my fingers around it.

I stopped and took a break. All the while overhead, the fireworks continued to light up the sky. No one would hear me if I screamed.

I must have passed out for a minute or two because when I awoke, Huckleberry was licking my nose.

I touched my forehead and felt a bump right in the middle of it. I would have an impressive bruise. The spot was tender.

Huckleberry licked the spot on my forehead, and it was strangely comforting. I wanted to ask him how he got out of the truck. Huckleberry wasn't much of a jumper. He must have really wanted to reach me if he had been willing to jump out of the truck window. Not being the most agile dog in the world, I hoped that he hadn't hurt himself when he landed on the pavement.

"Huckleberry?" I asked, but I wasn't sure the words even came out. My tongue was stuck to the roof of my mouth.

Huckleberry stood next to me and howled.

I heard running footsteps. "Miss, miss, are you okay?"

I groaned. I thought I was saying words, but they weren't coming out right.

"Oh, she's bleeding. We need to call 911."

"Oh gross. I hate blood," the second voice said.

Bleeding. I felt my forehead again. I didn't know I was bleeding. Then I saw the cut on the back of my hand. I didn't know if it from falling or being stepped on. It wasn't much blood, not much more than a bad scratch. Diva in one of her moods had done much worse to me in the past.

I stared at the shoes in my line of sight. The sneakers this time were bright white with red laces. They weren't the sneakers that had attacked me. I lifted my head.

"Are you okay?" someone above me asked.

"I'm okay," I said, but again, I wasn't certain the words were coming out of my mouth. My tongue didn't feel like it was moving.

Someone kneeled next to me. I lay my head back down, and Huckleberry growled at anyone who dared step close to me.

"Huck, can I see her?" a familiar voice asked, but I didn't have the strength to open my eyes and see who it was.

I vaguely remember being lifted onto a stretcher and put in the back of an ambulance. While riding in the ambulance, I thought my head would burst as I was jostled back and forth. I was grateful when the movement stopped.

My vision was beginning to clear, and I watched as two EMTs I didn't know lifted my stretcher out of the ambulance and rolled me into the hospital.

The scents of the hospital instantly hit me. It was a nauseating mix of antiseptic, soup, and aggressive air fresheners that did nothing mask the other smells.

"She's going to need a CT scan at the very least," someone above me said.

"You think concussion?"

"The way she is going in and out, it would have to be."

I just wanted to sleep.

Chapter Forty

Sleep was something the doctors and nurses in the hospital did not let me do. The CT scan confirmed I had a concussion, but from what I gathered from their whispers above me, it wasn't nearly as bad as it could have been. "If she takes it easy for a few weeks, she should be fine," one of the doctors said.

Throughout the rest of the night, I was constantly poked and prodded to keep me awake. After what seemed like hours, they stopped poking me and let me sleep.

When I woke up again, I gingerly touched the raised bruise on my forehead. I winced. Even the slightest bit of pressure was like being stabbed.

A tall nurse in scrubs stood next to my bed. "Oh good, you're awake. You have visitors outside; can I let them in?"

"Where's my dog?"

She chuckled. "They told me that was the first thing you'd ask. I was told to tell you he's with Hazel."

"Oh good," I said.

"Now, can I let your guests in?" she asked in her too cheerful voice.

"Okay," I said.

She left the room, and a second later Sheriff Milan
Penbrook walked into the room. He was followed by Chief
Sterling. Dark circles hung under Milan's eyes. He hadn't
gotten much sleep either.

"Miss Bellamy," the chief said. "How are you feeling?"

"Like someone hit my head against a truck," I said.

He nodded. "I heard you had quite the Independence
Day."

"I guess I did."

Milan hung back, letting the chief take the lead. It was
Chief Sterling's jurisdiction.

"What do you remember?" the chief asked.

"I was leaving the festival just as the fireworks began.
Huckleberry, my dog, is afraid of them. I didn't want to stay
and torment him. I put him in the truck and loaded the back
to go home. I had just finished when someone came up from
behind me and pinned my arms against the truck and covered my mouth his hand."

"You believe it was a man?"

"I'm certain it was a man."

"Did he say anything to you?"

I shivered. "He said something like *leave Dane Fullbright's
death alone* and that he had been warning me to stay out of it.
He said my cat's bare tail should have been enough."

"Your cat's tail?" Chief Sterling asked, clearly confused.

Milan filled him on the cherry orchard, the snare, and
Esmeralda.

"What happened after his warning?" the chief asked.

"He hit my forehead on the side of the truck."

Behind the police chief, Milan had his hands balled up at his sides. His whole body was rigid.

The chief made notes in his phone. "Can you describe him? What did he look like?"

I shook my head and instantly regretted it as pain washed through me.

"Are you all right? Should we call the nurse?" Milan asked.

"I'm fine," I said. "Just a little headache. It's to be expected, I would think."

No one laughed at my attempt at a joke.

"To answer your question, I can't describe him. All I saw were his shoes. They were sneakers. They weren't expensive looking and were gray with blue laces."

"Do you know the brand of shoe?"

"No." I stopped myself from shaking my head just in time. "I didn't see the side of the shoe, just the front. I didn't notice any logo or anything like that."

The chief nodded. "Do you have anything else to add?"

"I can't think of anything else. When it happened it felt like forever, but it probably was only a minute or two."

The chief stepped back. "I'll go file this report at the station. I'm hoping one of my officers was able to recover video footage of the parking lot. Hopefully we can see a face or something to add to the description of the person who attacked you," the chief said.

I thanked him.

Chief Sterling tucked his phone into the breast pocket of his uniform. "I do have one more question for you. Are you still poking into the murder of Dane Fullbright?"

I licked my lips. They were terribly dry. In fact, my whole mouth was dry, just like it had been when I had been when I was lying on the blacktop in the parking lot.

"I've been asking questions," I admitted. "But I haven't done a thing since Cayden was arrested. Stacey Bellamy is my only cousin. I wanted to protect her and clear her name."

He frowned. "You're not going to be able to protect anyone if you're dead," he said. "I hope that you will remember that." He walked out of the room.

I was left alone with Milan. Neither one of us spoke. Since the silence was killing me, I said, "How was your Fourth?"

He took a deep breath. "'How was your Fourth?' That's the first thing that you can say to me?"

"Sure," I said. "You already know how mine went."

He scowled.

My jokes weren't landing right. I blamed it on the concussion. Maybe it was impacting my delivery.

"What did you do yesterday that led up to this attack?" Milan asked.

"What do you mean?"

"Who did you talk to? Who did you upset? Who might want to have you removed?"

I wanted to make another joke, but I thought better of it; Milan did not look like he was in a jovial mood. I had never seen him like this before, and I had been in a lot of other dangerous spots—like falling through lake ice last winter while being shot at. That was more dangerous than one whack to the head.

"Yesterday was busy at the booth. I left it only to go to

the bathroom and grab items from my truck. That's it. Both Chesney and I were busy all day. I couldn't have gotten away from the booth if I wanted to."

"So you didn't wander off from the booth and ask questions?"

I gingerly touched the bump on my forehead. "There wasn't time for that. I thought opening day on Saturday was busy, but it was nothing like the Fourth. Three times as many people were there. A lot of them were staking out the best spots for the fireworks as early as lunchtime."

"Then why were you attacked?"

"I don't know."

"This is my fault. I shouldn't have involved you in any of this. The only person I have to blame is myself."

"You can't control what I do. I would have been involved with your approval or not. You shouldn't blame yourself."

The door opened and the nurse came back inside. "Ms. Bellamy, if you feel ready to go home, I'm here to discharge you."

"I'm more than ready." I sat up and suppressed a wince. I didn't want to give the nurse or Milan any reason to keep me in the hospital. I hated hospitals. They were all I remembered of my mother, who died when I was very young, and they reminded me of when both Logan and my grandmother died. I would do just about anything to escape.

"Do you have a ride home?" the nurse asked. "You shouldn't drive for at least three days and should follow up with your family doctor."

Before I could answer, Milan said, "I'm driving her home."

There was no room for debate.

"Are you her husband?"

"He's a friend," I said quickly. "And I'm fine with him taking me home."

The nurse looked from Milan to me and back again. "Okay then." She held a clipboard out to me. "Please sign in the all the places that are highlighted."

I signed the forms and handed the clipboard back to her. All of my movements felt like I was making them underwater, but I wasn't going to tell anyone that.

"I'll be right back with a wheelchair," she said.

"A wheelchair? Is that really necessary? I can walk."

The nurse leveled a look at me. "It is the goal of the hospital to get you out of this building in one piece. If I can assure that by moving you through the building in a wheelchair, so be it." She left the room, presumably in search of that wheelchair.

While she was gone, Milan said, "You're not going to drop this, are you?"

"Would you if you were attacked? It had to have been the killer who hit me. Who else would want me to stop looking into Dane's death? That can only mean the police arrested the wrong person, and Cayden is innocent."

He sighed. "I thought that's what you would say."

Chapter Forty-One

Milan wheeled me out to his departmental SUV and helped me out of the wheelchair and into the passenger seat. Once I was settled and buckled in the seat, he returned the wheelchair and got in himself. "Next stop, Bellamy Farm."

"Can we make a detour?" I asked.

He glanced over at me. "You're kidding, right? You do know you were in the hospital for the last fifteen hours with a concussion?"

"I do know that. I have the bump on my forehead to prove it." I tentatively touched the spot in the middle of my forehead. "Is the bruising bad?"

He started the car. "It's not great. You will probably get a black eye, if not two."

"Great."

"Where do you want to stop, and just because I'm asking doesn't mean that I'm agreeing to it."

"Can we stop by my booth at the festival? I want to check on Chesney. She's been alone at the booth a lot this week, and here I am again leaving her in a lurch today."

"It's not a lurch. It's not your fault. You were attacked."

"Please. I would feel a lot better if I could see with my own eyes everything is handled. Our success at the festival is really important for the farm."

He groaned. "Fine, but that's all we're doing. We stay five minutes and then I take you home."

I smiled. "Deal." I paused. "You know, you're really cute when you are annoyed."

Finally, it was his turn to blush.

Traverse City may have the word *city* in its name, but it really was a small town, and it took us all of five minutes to drive from the hospital to Open Space Park.

Milan and I walked from the parking lot to the booth. He had his hand on my arm as if he was worried I might topple over. Toppling over was a very real possibility to for me. I hoped this dizziness would pass soon.

There was a line of customers in front of the booth, and it did my heart good to see it. Huckleberry's head popped out from around the booth, and when he saw me, he leaned his head back and howled for all he was worth. It was almost as if he were calling on his long-lost doggie ancestors to celebrate with him that his best friend was back.

I pulled my arm away from Milan's gentle grasp and rushed over to my little pug. He raced toward me and jumped into my arms, which felt a lot like getting hit in the chest with a sack of potatoes. I buried my nose in his neck, not caring that he needed a bath and smelled like dog.

"Shiloh!" Hazel called and ran out of the booth. A moment later Chesney and her sister were with her.

"What are you doing here?" Chesney wanted to know. "Aren't you supposed to be home resting?"

"That's what I told her," Milan said. "She doesn't listen to anyone."

Hazel looked at my face. "Wow, you really got hit." She reached her hand toward the bump on my forehead. "Can I touch it?"

"No," I said and took a step back. I scratched Huckleberry under my chin. "Looks like you all have everything well in hand."

Chesney arched her brow. "Was there any doubt that we would?"

I shook my head. "Not a bit."

"How did you get away from the guy that attacked you?" Hazel asked. "Did you give him an uppercut?" She mimicked the punch with her fist.

"No, I didn't. He just left, and Huckleberry called for help."

"Huckleberry called for help?"

"Yep, he has a powerful howl. He saved my life. Otherwise I might have been lying there waiting for someone to find me a lot longer."

Hazel gave me a hug. "I'm so glad you're okay. That was way scary. When Dad told me that they had to take you in the ambulance, I was really worried."

"You scared me too," Chesney added. "Kristy has been texting me every ten minutes for an update. I'm glad I finally have something to tell her."

I winced. I knew I would be getting an earful from Kristy when I saw her. She made me promise I wouldn't get hurt, and I hadn't lived up to my side of the promise.

My heart warmed at the thought of all these people who cared about me so much. When I came back to Michigan, I thought it was going to be so difficult slip back into my old life. It had been difficult, and in the end I hadn't been able to do it. But I had made a new life here with new friends who really cared about me and wanted me to be okay. I might not have a big family, but the friendships I did have more than made up for it.

Hazel waved. "Dad! Shiloh is back."

I watched as Quinn walked through the crowd. "They said they would tell me when it was time to pick you up from the hospital," he said when he reached us.

"I was there and told the nurse I'd take her home."

Quinn pressed his lips together.

Milan looked down at his phone.

"Something wrong?" I asked Milan.

"There has been a boating accident on Torch Lake."

"Oh no. Is anyone hurt?" I asked.

"Not seriously, but I should go out there and assess the scene. Are you ready to go? I can run you home and then drive out to Torch Lake."

"I can find another ride home," I said. "You would waste too much time if you drove me all the way to Cherry Glen and then made your way back to Torch Lake."

By the look on his face, he knew what I said was true even if he didn't like it.

"I can take her home," Quinn said.

Milan's frown deepened as if he really didn't like that idea.

"That's the solution," I said. "I'll just catch a ride from

Quinn. That makes more sense anyway. He's my neighbor. You would have to go far out of your way."

"I don't mind that," the sheriff said a little churlishly.

"I appreciate you wanting to look out for me, I really do, but you have to go," I said. "Your citizens need you."

"All right," he finally agreed.

Quinn stepped forward. "I can take care of Shiloh. Don't worry about her. I know how to get Shiloh home. I have been to her farm thousands of times since we were kids. We have a history," he added, as if purposely rubbing salt in the wound.

Chapter Forty-Two

W hen do you want to leave?" Quinn asked after the sheriff was gone.

"If you had asked Sheriff Penbrook that question, he would have said that I need to leave right away," I said.

"I didn't ask him. I asked you."

"She can't go anywhere," Stacey said as she walked up to us. She was in full hair and makeup for a matinee performance of *The Tempest*. Although she was wearing a T-shirt and denim shorts. I supposed it was too hot to stand around and await her cue in a long dress.

"You have to watch your father in the play," Stacey said.

I grimaced. The idea of sitting through a two-hour play in a hard folding chair did not appeal to me after spending much of the day already in a hospital bed. "I saw it the other day."

"I saw you from the stage, and you left. You didn't even see half of the first act."

I sighed. What I wanted to say to her was I left because I was following a lead to clear her name, but I didn't even bother.

"What happened to your face?" she asked, apparently looking directly at me for the first time.

"The killer attacked Shiloh," Hazel said, as if that was something to be excited about.

"I thought they already arrested the killer. It was that Cayden guy," Stacey said.

"The police thought that too," I said.

"Did you see him?" Stacey asked. "Did they arrest him?"

"No. All I know it was a man and what his tennis shoes looked like."

"In any case, I should be off the hook. That's all that I care about. Nice work, cousin." She started to walk away. "I expect you to be at the play."

After Stacey left, Quinn asked, "What do you want to do? The play starts in an hour."

I had a throbbing headache, but I knew if I didn't go to the play, Stacey would remind my father of the fact that I missed his lead performance for the rest of his life. Even more than the headache, I couldn't deal with that level of guilt.

"I'll go to the play. In fact, we should all go. Chesney, you can close the booth up early."

"I don't think that is a bad idea. We're almost out of everything anyway. We really made a killing this week." She winced. "Poor choice of words. Sorry."

"Sounds good to me," Quinn said. "I can't see Milan disagreeing with that when we are all with you."

I knew very well that Milan could and would disagree with that idea, but I wasn't going to say that.

For the last hour that we were open, Chesney and I sold

everything that was left in the booth. Packing the truck took no time at all; there was very little to pack up. My head throbbed while we worked, but I did my best to follow my doctor's orders by not bending over too much, and Quinn and Chesney wouldn't let me do any of the heavy lifting.

We had everything tucked away in my pickup by curtain time.

Quinn and Hazel and had gone ahead of us to save us seats. Chesney looped her arm through mine as we walked through the Cherry Farm Market for the final time. "I'm proud of you, Shiloh. This market has been a real success."

"Except for the murder bit."

"Yeah, that was sort of a low point," she admitted.

My father wasn't a big man, but his presence filled the stage. He had definitely missed his calling as a stage actor, and I finally realized where Stacey got her talent for the art.

Next to me, Hazel's face glowed as she watched the actors. If Quinn wasn't careful, he might have someone with the Hollywood bug on his hands too.

It was Paisley though, playing Ariel the sprite, who was the true standout. My father did an amazing job, but Paisley was a star. I hoped that she did find her big break someday, because she deserved it.

As much as I enjoyed the play, my head spun and I had trouble focusing. Prospero was a major part and was in countless scenes, but when there was finally a time my father was offstage, I leaned over to Chesney and whispered, "I need to get something to drink. My head is bothering me."

"Do you want me to go with you?" she whispered back.

I shook my head. That was a mistake.

I slipped out of the row and felt Quinn watching me as I went. I didn't make eye contact with him. I didn't want him to see how much pain I was actually in.

I walked behind the seating and to the left of the stage. The college's trailer was there, and the door was slightly open. From where I stood, I could feel the cool air from the air-conditioning unit inside.

That was what I needed. I had to cool down and then my head would stop throbbing. If anyone came in to kick me out, I would just explain I was Stacey's cousin and hope they would leave me alone.

The trailer was empty and the air was set to sixty degrees. It felt heavenly. Bottles of water stood on the counter. I took one and chugged it down. I would pay Stacey for it later.

Even after drinking the water, I still didn't feel well, so I lay down in the middle of the trailer on the floor. When I had been in LA, I used to get migraines from the stress of my job, and it wasn't uncommon for my assistant to find me lying on my stomach in the middle of my office floor just like this. It didn't matter how many times I did it, it always made her jump. She said I looked like a dead body.

I rested my right cheek on my hands. From where I lay, I could see the bench seat along the wall. Underneath it was a bunch of discarded papers, food wrappers, a bottle of foundation, and a pair of shoes. But they weren't just any shoes; they were gray sneakers with blue laces.

I reached under the seat and pulled them out. I knew those were the shoes I had seen last night when I was attacked. I sat up with the shoes in my hands.

The trailer door banged open. "I see you found my shoes."

Eliot, who was still in his costume for the role of Prince Ferdinand, grabbed me by the arm, pulling me to my feet. I knew by feel he was the man who attacked me. How he could play such an innocent and kind prince onstage was a mystery to me. Maybe he was the very best actor in the bunch.

"Eliot, there are hundreds of people outside of this trailer. If I scream, they will hear me. I suggest you just leave and run away while you can."

The door opened again, and Penny Lee stepped inside. "I told you she was in here, son."

"Son? Penny Lee is your mom?" I gasped.

Eliot laughed. "My stepmother, actually, but the two of us have one thing in common: how much we care about my father, who Dane Fullbright ruined. As far as stepmothers go, she's not bad."

It was all starting to make sense to me now. When I visited campus, I thought Penny Lee was there working on an article, but she was there because of her husband. Hadn't she said something about it "not being fair"? Was she referring to Dr. Cassen being pushed out?

Eliot still had ahold of my arm.

I gripped his shoes as if my life depended on it. And it very well might have. They were my evidence that Eliot was the one who attacked me. "Listen, both of you should get out of here. The police are going to catch on. If you hurt me, you will just make it worse for yourselves."

"You have a lot of faith in the police. They already arrested that flight geek Cayden. When I saw that framing Stacey wasn't working, and how interested you were Slade's drama, I thought he was a perfect fit. What is better than a jealous boyfriend for a killer? It's like a play that wrote itself."

"Then what are you going to do?" I asked.

"We're going to walk you to a boat and take a little trip out into the lake. Do you consider yourself a good swimmer?"

"I'm not getting into a boat with either one of you."

Penny Lee removed a gun from her purse. "Yes, you are."

I flung one of Eliot's shoes at Penny Lee. My aim wasn't good enough to knock the gun out of her hand, but it startled her and caused her to shoot a hole in the ceiling of the trailer. Someone outside must have heard the shot.

I wasn't going to let Eliot hurt me again; I hit him in the face with the other shoe. He loosened his grip enough so I could get away. I charged Penny Lee, even though she was still holding the gun, and pushed her aside.

As I went out the door, she fired off a shot. Had she hit me?

There was a crowd outside, clearly drawn by all the noise, and I ran right into Milan's chest.

"You came back," I said.

"As soon as I could get away," he said. "I will always come back for you."

I looked up at him. "Good, because I wasn't getting on that boat."

His brow creased. "What are you talking about?"

Attracted by the commotion, three police officers, running from different directions around the park, surrounded the trailer, and Eliot and Penny Lee came out with their hands up.

Epilogue

Six weeks later, Chesney ran into the farmhouse. I was working on paperwork on the kitchen table with Huckleberry sleeping on my feet. My goal was to finish everything before Milan picked me up to take me to the movies that night. Since my run-in with Penny Lee and her stepson, Eliot, I had been making the most of my time getting to know Milan. It was safe to say we were very much still in the honeymoon period of our relationship and very happy.

The same could not be said for Penny Lee Odders or Eliot Cassen. Eliot, who as an actor had access to Stacey's theater, stole her bottle of penicillin and poisoned Dane Fullbright's cherry right before the cherry pit spitting competition began. He awaited trial in prison. The last I heard, his attorney requested he be released on house arrest until the trial.

Penny was out on bail to await trial, charged with being an accessory to murder and attempted murder.

"Shi!" Chesney shouted as the screen door slammed closed after her.

I looked up. "What's wrong? Are the sheep okay?"

"Yeah, they're fine. Tanner Birchwood's Organic Acres is up for sale. You could buy it all back. You have the money now."

My laptop sat in the middle of the table and was open to the farm account. I stared at the number on the screen. It was all the money sitting in the bank. It would be enough to pay all my debts and even start a small roadside market at the farm. I could sell my baked goods and soaps every day as travelers made their way to Traverse City.

"You have to buy it." Chesney's glasses slipped to the tip of her nose, and she pushed them back up again.

Did I?

I could buy back all of my family's land with the money and remain in debt and gamble on being able to be successful enough to make up the difference. It was a classic case of security against risk. I wished my grandmother was there to tell me what she would do.

Grandma Bellamy was a risk-taker in her way. I wouldn't have all this money from her stocks if she hadn't been. But she was a practical woman at heart. All successful farmers were practical.

Chesney leaned across the small kitchen table. "What are you going to do?"

I looked at her. "Can you call the Realtor who is selling Tanner's farm? I'd like to meet to her."

Chesney grinned from ear to ear.

SHILOH'S
Quick Farm Tips

T here are so many ways to make homemade soap. The most common way is using lye, which is what I use for the homemade soaps I sell at Bellamy Farm. However, lye—and chemicals like it—can be tricky to use. You need proper safety equipment and ventilation. For the novice, I suggest that you skip that step and purchase a premade soap base at your local craft store. From there, you can make your soap any color and fragrance you would like, and it's a lot less work. Below is my recipe for cherry vanilla soap using a soap base.

TOOLS

- A two-quart microwave-safe glass measuring cup
- Microwave
- Metal whisk
- Any old pots or pans that are ready to be retired from food prep
- Silicone soap molds, any shape and size
- Toothpicks

INGREDIENTS

- One pound of soap base, cut into one-inch cubes
- ¼ tablespoon of vanilla essential oil
- ¼ tablespoon of cherry essential oil
- Pink soap colorant one to two drop

DIRECTIONS

Melt soap base in the microwave-safe measuring cup in your microwave until liquid. Start with one minute at a time until it is the consistency of liquid soap.

Add two drops of vanilla essential oil and two drops of cherry essential oil into the liquid soap and whisk.

Pour soap into the molds.

Add one to two drops of pink colorant to each mold, and swirl the color with a toothpick.

Let dry for at least twenty-four hours.

Remove from the molds and enjoy!

Acknowledgments

Special thanks to all my readers who have enjoyed reading about Shiloh Bellamy's adventures in Michigan's cherry country.

Thanks too to my amazing agent, Nicole Resciniti, and my wonderful editor, Anna Michels. Also at Sourcebooks, I would like to thank Emily Engwall, who has worked tirelessly to promote the series.

Also thank you to my reader Kim Bell for taking the time to read the manuscript.

Love and thanks to my wonderful husband, David Seymour, who is there every step of the way.

Finally, thank you to my Lord in heaven for allowing me to share my stories with the world.

About the Author

Amanda Flower is a *USA Today* bestselling and Agatha Award–winning author of over fifty mystery novels. Her novels have received starred reviews from *Library Journal*, *Publishers Weekly*, and *Romantic Times*, and she has been featured in *USA Today*, *First for Women*, and *Woman's World*. In addition to being a writer, she was a librarian for fifteen years. Today, Flower and her husband own a farm and recording studio, and they live in northeast Ohio with their adorable cats.